AMY THE ASTRONAUT
AND THE FLIGHT FOR FREEDOM

I0671375

AMY THE ASTRONAUT AND THE FLIGHT FOR FREEDOM

A novel by

Steven Donahue

Hydra
Publications

Hydra Publications
337 Clifty Drive
Madison, IN 47250

www.hydrapublications.com

Chapter One

Amy Sutter tightened her grip on the yoke as she stared at the monitor on the console. Sixteen oval-shaped, purple objects dotted the screen. She took a deep breath, targeted one of the alien ships and fired her first missile. The enemy craft exploded and created a fireball that destroyed the ship beside it. Amy smiled and wiped some sweat from her forehead. The other ships began firing missiles at her as she turned the *Liberty Bell* to the right and dove hard toward the surface of the planet below. A proximity alarm sounded behind her as the missiles flew over the top of her ship. Amy then pulled back hard on the yoke and lined up her next shot.

She waited until the enemy fleet got closer before she fired the laser cannons mounted on the outside of her 150-foot long spacecraft. She obliterated two more vessels before the *Liberty Bell* took a direct hit of laser-fire on the portside wing. The shielding held but the concussion of the blow caused Amy to smack her head against the console. Thankful she was wearing a helmet, Amy shook off the momentary dizziness and tried to line up another shot. Before she could, three more laser blasts wiped out her cannons. Two more blasts caused another alarm to blare. Amy looked at the console and saw that her life support systems were failing. However, her engines were still online. She sent out a distress call as the enemy ships started to surround her. She then steered the ship away from the fleet and initiated the Sprint Drive system. The *Liberty Bell* bolted through a gap in the enemy's formation and the crafts disappeared from the ship's radar as they fell far behind the spaceship.

Amy let out a sigh and quickly searched the digital maps for a suitable planet to land on. Before she could find one, the *Liberty Bell* began to violently shake. The temperature inside the cabin shot up. Before she should shut down the Sprint Drive, Amy heard a loud explosion behind her. Then all of her instruments stopped working and the cabin grew dark.

The exasperated pilot unbuckled her safety belt and flipped a switch on a side panel. The door over her head opened and the twelve-year-old girl climbed out of the simulator and down a ladder to the concrete floor. She took off her helmet and looked at her reflection in a small window on the simulator. She brushed back a lock of her dark brown hair and saw a welt forming over her right eye. Amy shook her head and smiled at her clumsiness. "Serves you right for sneaking in there," said a voice behind her. Amy turned around and saw Lt. Yale Brown marching toward her. The officer had a clipboard in her hand and a relaxed look on her face.

Amy shrugged. "I got four of them this time," she said. "Then the Sprint Drive exploded as I was getting away." She handed the helmet to the lieutenant and walked with her toward the equipment storage room. Around them other pilots were training for various missions, while security officers stood guard at the building's four entrances. Amy glanced at the busy soldiers and noticed their tense expressions.

"You can't trust that engine," said Yale. "They haven't perfected it yet." At 5'10", the twenty-eight-year old woman towered over her young friend. Yale's frame was lean and strong as a result of her military training and her short blonde hair fit neatly under her green cap. She wore a camouflage shirt and matching pants, standard issue for Union soldiers, and no makeup. Her light green eyes had a tendency to change colors in differently lighted rooms.

They reached the door to the storage room and Yale unlocked it by running a blue key card with a magnetic strip along a black keypad. Amy followed the lieutenant into the room and watched Yale tuck the helmet on a shelf next to other flight gear. Then she turned to face Amy. "Should I even bother asking how you got into the machine?" she asked. She put her hands on her hips and smiled.

Amy reached into her pocket and pulled out another blue key card with a magnetic strip. She waved it in front of Yale's face. "Just got to have the right tools," she said. Yale glared at her and yanked the card out of the girl's hand. The lieutenant stuffed the card in her shirt pocket and pointed to storage room door. "I'm going, I'm going," said Amy. The girl tiptoed past her friend and watched the lieutenant lock the door.

Yale chastised the guards on duty for letting Amy slip past them, before she handed another officer the clipboard. Then she escorted the girl out of the facility and they walked side-by-side toward the adolescent's living quarters. The crisp morning air was a delightful change from the normally arid atmosphere on Paldor, a small hot planet just outside the Milky Way. The Sutter family resided in building 400, in one of the more elegant homes in the 23 square-mile Pioneer Settlement.

A fighter jet flew overhead. Amy squinted at the tail markings for Earth's Union Defense Fleet. She thought about their ongoing war against the Crownaxians, an alien species that no surviving human has ever seen. The highly intelligent warriors attacked a human settlement on the planet Blaros. More than 3 million people were killed in the attack and eight years later the human death toll had skyrocketed past 29 million, with no end in sight.

Amy knew that Earth's overpopulation and dwindling natural resources forced mankind to seek shelter elsewhere among the stars. However, the Crownaxians refused to negotiate a peaceful resolution to the conflict, which had forced the Union to institute martial law on all human colonies. The five major settlements on Paldor all fall under the jurisdiction of Gen. William Knox, a 55-year-old career officer. Amy had heard rumors that the general had become overly cautious, sending out only defensive patrols, and that some of his subordinates had lost faith in him.

Yale and Amy walked into Amy's home and found Clayton Sutter sitting at the dining room table. The diplomat was typing on a laptop computer. His chestnut brown hair was prematurely receding toward the top of his skull and his fierce brown eyes stared intently at the screen in front of him. Amy said a quick hello to her father and tried to duck into her bedroom, but her mother spotted her in the hallway.

Pam Sutter's hazel eyes widened as she put her hand on her daughter's chin. "What happened to you, young lady?" she asked, shifting her gaze from Amy to Yale, who was still standing behind the girl.

The lieutenant spoke first. "I'm afraid she bumped her head while running a program in the flight simulator," said Yale. She tightened her fists as she glanced at Clayton. Amy watched her dad rise and walk toward her. He put his hand on his daughter's shoulder and looked at the bruise. "I promise this won't happen again," said Yale.

Clayton shrugged and turned toward his wife. "It doesn't look too bad to me," he said. Amy let out a sigh of relief. Then she saw him turn and glare at her. "But you shouldn't have been in that simulator," he said. His face reddened. "What were you thinking?" He moved his face close to hers. "This base is not your playground. You cannot go wherever you want any time you want to. There are a lot of dangerous places that you need to stay away from. I want you to promise me that you will follow the rules from now on," he said.

Amy nodded, having heard this before, and forced herself not to blink. "I will, Daddy. I promise," she said. She opened her arms and wrapped them around him. He hugged her back and gave her a quick kiss on the cheek. Then he let go and sat back down at the table. Pam crossed her arms over her chest. Amy knew what she was waiting for. "I'm sorry," said the young girl. "It won't happen again."

Pam looked at her watch and sighed. The auburn-haired woman was a few inches shorter than Yale, but Amy found her far more intimidating. She was a meticulous and ambitious physician with a strong need for order and discipline. Pam tended to be less affectionate than her husband, at least toward her daughter, who frequently felt uneasy around her.

The doctor glared at Yale. "I hope this breach of security is not commonplace, lieutenant," she snarled. "I'd had to think what a spy for the Crownaxians could do if given the chance."

The lieutenant cleared her throat. "I assure you it is not," she replied. "And those responsible will be punished." She glanced at Amy, who offered a sympathetic shrug.

"I have to go to work," said Pam. Then she addressed her daughter. "There's an ice pack in the freezer. Put it on your bruise for twenty minutes, then take it off for twenty, then put it back on for twenty more," she said to Amy, without looking at her. "It will help keep the swelling down." Amy watched her grab her physician's bag and move toward the door. Pam stopped by her husband and kissed him on his forehead. He looked up at her and smiled. "I should be home by six," she said.

He kissed her goodbye, and then continued typing. Yale held the door open for Pam, and then followed the woman out. Amy noticed the pained look on Yale's face and she wondered if her friend would get into trouble for her stunt. After the door closed, Amy went into her bedroom and quietly shut the door behind her.

She flopped down on the bed and quickly forgot her mother's medical advice. Instead she stared up at the stars and planets painted on the bedroom ceiling. She silently counted each star and gave each one a name, something she always did when she was trying to calm her nerves. Then she thought about the Union Academy again. It would be two more years before she would be old enough to apply. Not that she thought she could get in. Amy knew that her math grades weren't high enough and that her language skills needed to improve. Still, she hoped that she could follow in her parents' footsteps and graduate from the academy someday. Then she would study for her pilot's license and try to get a job on a real spacecraft.

After dozing off and dreaming about the academy, Amy awoke to the sound of someone knocking on her door. She sat up and told the visitor to come in. Amy brightened when she saw Madison walk through the doorway. The 6'6" robot closed the door behind it and walked to the middle of the room. A briefcase dangled from the robot's left hand. The sleek, dark green metallic machine was modeled on the human form. "I'm sorry I'm late," it said. "Suzy Porter asked me to stop by and replace the Science data file she lost over the weekend." Amy smiled at the familiar brass sound of her friend's voice. Madison rested the briefcase on the desk that sat four feet away from the top of Amy's bed. The robot took out a mini-comp and turned it on.

Madison was the first fully automated, sentient being to successfully emerge from the laboratory of a Union science group headed by biologist Stanley Greenland. Unfortunately for the group, they were not unable to duplicate that success with later models, nor were they ever able to explain why the androgynous Madison worked and those that followed didn't. Amy believed that it was because Madison had a soul, an opinion not shared by anyone else.

Originally conceived as a supersoldier for the Union Defense Fleet, Madison was reassigned to Paldor after several Union Council members lost faith in Greenland's work. The constant setbacks became too disheartening for the biologist, who then decided to retire after the Council cut off his funding. With no teachers living in the Pioneer Settlement, Madison was reprogrammed to tutor the students of various ages who resided with their parents in the small hamlet. Since none of the other kids were Amy's age, Madison taught her privately. Amy felt honored to be among the robot's pupils but she still wished that she could attend a regular school on Earth. Her father's numerous assignments kept them moving from place to place and the Sutter family hadn't been back to Earth in nearly four years.

"We are going to start with Algebra today," said Madison. The robot pulled a chair away from Amy's desk, placed it against the wall and sat down in it. Another chair was pressed against the desk.

Amy plopped down in the empty chair and rolled her eyes. "Algebra is so boring," she said. "Can't we start with something else?" She picked up a pencil and started doodling on a small pad of paper. Without thinking, she began to sketch the outline of a spacecraft. Although she had never seen the real *Liberty Bell*, Amy could imagine what it looked like from having been in the simulator. When she finally realized what she was doing, she filled in the details of her sketch from what she thought the outside would look like.

"Please turn on your tutor-comp and go to page 43 of the math section," said the robot. "We have a lot to cover this morning. Your last test score was very disappointing." Amy frowned and put aside the sketch. She picked up her tutor-comp and sighed as she searched for the page. "Look at the first problem and tell me how to begin."

Amy did as she was told and the duo spent the next hour deciphering the mysteries of Algebra. Then they moved on to History, Science, English and Social Studies. After the lessons ended, Madison packed up its teaching materials, while Amy sat on the bed and stared at the stars on her ceiling. "Why did this stupid war have to start?" she asked, looking over at the robot.

Madison zipped up the briefcase and sat down on the bed beside her. "You know all about that," it said, shaking its head. Amy shrugged. "I don't have anything new to tell you. Blaros was attacked and the Union fought back. It certainly is a terrible thing, this war."

"Have you ever seen a Crownaxian?" asked Amy. The robot

shook its head no. Amy leaned against the wall. "I know, I know, no one has ever actually seen one. But I hear that they want to take over every planet in the universe. And nobody can do anything to stop them."

"Where did you hear that?" asked Madison.

Amy crossed her arms over her chest. "From some of the other kids. They say the Crows are mindless killing machines, just bred for war. And they'll eat anything, even each other." Amy grimaced. "That's so gross. I hope I never have to see one of them. If I did, I think I would just die." The words slipped out before she realized the gravity of them. "Oh, I don't mean like the people at Blaros. I know that was tragic and all. But I'd be terrified to come up against a Crow unless I had a laser gun in my hand."

Madison stood up and grabbed the briefcase. "I wonder what their children say about humans," it said. The robot extended a hand and helped Amy stand up. The cold, metal surface of the robot's hand made her shiver. She quickly let go and led the instructor to the door. Amy exited first and Madison followed her through the living room to the front door. Clayton walked over from the kitchen and thanked Madison before the robot left.

Amy and her father spent the rest of the afternoon together. They ate lunch, cleaned up the apartment, and played two games of chess before Pam came home from work. The doctor watched her husband prepare dinner while she talked about her busy shift at the hospital. Amy sat in the living room and played a video game until dinner was ready. The scent of lasagna drew her to the dining room table.

The Sutters had just started eating when Clayton's beeper sounded. The diplomat read the text message and excitedly rose from his seat. "It's Gen. Knox," he said, pushing his chair in. "He's calling my staff in for a meeting at his office. I'm sorry, but I have to go."

Amy watched her mother nod as Clayton moved toward the master bedroom. He closed the door and Amy continued to eat. After a few bites, she noticed that her mother was sitting very still with her fingers wrapped tightly around her fork. The girl took a sip of milk and studied the tense expression on Pam's face. "What's wrong, Mom?" she asked.

Pam looked at her and sighed. "Oh, nothing. I guess I'm just annoyed that he has to go." She laid her fork on her plate, and then pushed the plate away from her. "We're both so busy. We get so little time together." An eerie silence then filled the room as the woman stood and drifted over to the living room couch. She picked a magazine up from the end table and flipped through the pages as she sat down. Amy shrugged and kept eating.

Clayton hustled out of his room a few minutes later. He was wearing a dark blue suit and a red tie. Amy watched him pack up his laptop computer and dart toward the front door. "I'll be home as soon as I can," he said, not looking back toward his family. The door closed behind him and the eerie silence returned. Amy quietly finished eating, and then brought her plate, utensils and glass into the kitchen. She rinsed them off and carefully placed them in the dishwasher.

She entered the living room and asked her mother if she was done with her dinner. Pam glanced at her daughter with a sad smile on her face and said yes. Amy nodded and cleared off her mother's dinnerware. She dumped the food into the garbage disposal before rinsing off the items and putting them in the dishwasher. The girl wanted to watch TV on the big set in the living room but she didn't want to bother her mother, so instead she sauntered into her room and closed the door. The youngster relaxed on her bed with a tattered paperback copy of *Little Women*.

A few hours later, Amy finished taking a shower and walked down the hallway toward her bedroom in her bathrobe when she heard the front door open. She glanced over and saw her father enter. She said a quick hello to him then went into her room to get dressed. With her door slightly open, she listened to her parents' conversation, hoping for some news about her father's meeting. Clayton excitedly told his wife about his conference with the general. "The council approved my plan this afternoon," he said. "And the Crownaxians agreed to meet with us. We take off in two weeks."

Eager to hear more, Amy came out of her room in her pajamas and sat on the couch. The diplomat smiled at his daughter before he continued. "We're going in the *Harmony*," he said, sitting across from his wife at the dinner table. "We'd go sooner but my staff and I need to brush up on our emergency training. Just to be safe." He reached over and placed his hand on Pam's. "This is what I've always wanted. A chance to make a real difference." Amy saw his right foot tapping against the floor and noticed his shortness of his breath. "After all these months, our work here is finally paying off."

"How many ships will be escorting you?" asked Pam. Amy could hear the apprehension in her mother's voice.

Clayton looked down at the table for a moment, then back up at his wife. "There won't be any escorts," he said. Pam gasped and Amy saw her close her fingers over Clayton's hand. "It's the only way the Crownaxians would agree to meet with us," said Clayton. "Any military presence would jeopardize the whole mission. Besides, we're bringing the triboleserene they asked for. They won't try anything with a substance that valuable on board."

Amy rose and walked over to her father. She stood by his chair and put her right arm over his shoulders. "I don't know, Dad. It sounds really dangerous," she said. He gave her a comforting smile. "What if something goes wrong?" she asked.

"Yes, Clay, what if something goes wrong?" asked Pam. She pressed her lips together and pushed a lock of hair away from her face. "Do you really trust the Crows after all they've done to us? Why do you have to put yourself in such a dangerous situation?"

"Someone has to take the first step toward peace," he replied. "We've all suffered enough, seen enough misery, enough death. Both human and Crownaxian." He leaned over and gave Amy a gentle kiss on the cheek. "This is important, honey," he said to her. "The fighting has to stop."

"I know Daddy. I'm just scared," she said. She hugged him tightly and pressed her head against his shoulder.

"It's ok to be afraid," he said. "I'm afraid too. I'm sure everyone on this mission is. But we can't pass up this opportunity. We may never get this chance again." He then tousled her hair and she playfully put up her hands to ward him off. She giggled for a moment, before stepping away from him. Amy appreciated his enthusiasm and she tried to put on a brave face.

Pam didn't say much the rest of the night. Amy knew better than to try to get her to talk, so she stayed out of her way and did her best not to make too much noise. Her father appeared to be doing the same thing. Clayton went back to work on his computer, while Amy hung out in her room. She played a few video games on her computer until it was time for her to go to bed.

Clayton knocked on her door just before 10 PM. "Lights out," he said, walking up behind her. Amy was playing "Space Pirates," a game he bought for her on her last birthday. "New high score," he said, looking over her shoulder. "Very impressive." She nodded and saved the game before turning off the computer.

Amy took a deep breath and turned toward her father. "I'm really glad they're letting you do this," she said. "They couldn't have picked a better person for the job." She stepped forward and hugged him.

Clayton kissed the top of her head, and then let her step back. "Thank you honey," he said. "I wouldn't do this if it weren't important, and I'm glad that you understand that. Besides, it won't be that bad. My staff and I should only be gone for a few weeks. And maybe I'll find a little souvenir to bring back for you."

Amy smiled. "A Morleanne space rock would be cool," she said. "It shouldn't be hard to find one. They're all over this part of space." She climbed onto her bed and pulled the covers up to her chin.

"I'll see what I can do," said Clayton. He turned off the light and closed the door behind him. Amy heard him move toward his bedroom and she was glad that he was finally quitting for the night. She lay back in her bed and closed her eyes.

A half-hour passed and she was still awake. She couldn't stop thinking about her dad's mission, so she sat up and wrapped her arms around her knees. Her bedcovers had fallen to the floor and her tiny body was shivering, so she leaned over the bed and pulled the blankets into her lap. She cloaked herself up in them, and then spoke in a soft voice. "God, it's me, Amy Sutter," she said. "I know I don't talk to you that much but I have a problem. Well, you already know what it is."

She looked around in the darkness and felt a little foolish for speaking out loud. "Can you please watch over him? We love him so much and I don't know what we'd without him." She paused to fold her hands. "Please. Let him come home safely," she said. She then lay back down and closed her eyes, hoping that He heard her prayer.

Chapter Two

The tension in the Sutter household grew steadily over the next two weeks. Pam frequently snapped at Amy and Clayton for even the most minor infraction. Amy compensated by trying not to make any noise when her mother was home and she noticed that her father was doing the same thing. To make matters worse, Clayton's work hours increased, forcing the Sutters to request a home attendant from the military's social services unit to look after Amy during the day. The request was granted and Amy fell under the watchful eye of Mrs. Penelope Cranberry, a 58-year-old woman with silver hair and chestnut-brown eyes.

The training finally ended and Amy was glad that she would be able to spend a few days with her dad before he left. Pam requested a short leave from work and the Sutters took an impromptu vacation without Cranberry at the nearby Whitman settlement. They stayed in a civilian hotel that had a game room, a tennis court and an outside swimming pool. For nearly three days they forgot about work, school, and the war as the trio enjoyed all the hotel's amenities.

Paldor's sun was particularly bright on the morning of their last day. For once, Amy was actually glad it was hot so she and her parents could hang around the pool. The Sutters were relaxing in lounge chairs when Amy saw a man in a tan shirt and blue shorts stroll over to her father. The man was short, with fiery-red hair and yellowish teeth. A pair of glasses with thick lens pressed against his pointy nose. Clayton rose from his chair and extended his right hand to the man. He heartily shook Clayton's hand and told the diplomat how happy he was to see him.

"Honey, this is David Zigler," Clayton said to Pam. She smiled politely but didn't shake his hand. "Ziggy is joining my staff on this mission," he said. Clayton then introduced his daughter and Zigler nodded toward her before the men sat down together. Clayton flagged down a passing porter and asked the young lady to bring Zigler a drink.

The men chatted about their academy days while they enjoyed their drinks and the beautiful sunshine. Then they started talking about their mission. Hearing this, Pam got up from her chair and grabbed her towel. She marched toward their room without saying a word. Amy and her father exchanged a knowing glance. Clayton waited until Pam was out of earshot before he explained her behavior to Zigler. The man nodded and told Clayton that he was having the same problem with his wife. Amy listened to their conversation and marveled at how calm both men sounded. Then she noticed her father's right hand shaking as it rested on his knee and she realized that both diplomats were putting on brave faces of their own.

Clayton invited Zigler to join his family for lunch, but the diplomat politely declined, saying that he would see Clayton the next afternoon. Amy and her dad caught up with Pam in their room, where she was taking a nap. Amy changed her clothes in the bathroom and her parents dressed by the beds. Again, Pam said very little as the family ate dinner in the hotel restaurant. Amy tried to lighten the mood by talking about her schoolwork, but she got the impression that her mother wasn't listening to her. Pam just pushed her food around her plate and stared out a nearby window.

The Sutters then packed their bags and checked out of the hotel. Clayton put a music CD in the car stereo to kill the unbearable silence during the ride back to their settlement. Amy hugged her pillow and leaned back against her seat with her eyes closed. The soft music relaxed her and she was soon fast asleep. She dreamt about the academy again. She was about to graduate when her father woke her to tell her they were home.

Pam's mood was no better the next morning and Amy decided not to say anything at all to her mother. Instead, she stayed close to her father as he ate his breakfast and looked over some paperwork. At 8:30 he hugged his wife and daughter and hurried out the door. Mrs. Cranberry arrived a few minutes later with a bag of fresh bagels that she shared with the Sutters. Pam finally smiled when she smelled the food. She even hung around long enough to enjoy one of them, smothering it with cream cheese.

Madison showed up on time that morning. The robot began the day's lessons with a lecture on Earth history but Amy had even more trouble than usual paying attention. When they moved on to Science, Amy forced herself to concentrate. She kept her eyes locked on her tutor-comp and folded her hands so she wouldn't doodle on her notepad. Her determination paid off as she began to fully grasp the material her teacher was presenting. Before she knew it, her lessons were over and the rest of the day was hers to enjoy.

Amy played cards with Mrs. Cranberry and listened to the woman recite her personal history. The woman talked about her childhood, which she spent on a farm in Iowa. Then she discussed her later years, traveling the stars with her husband Philip. Mrs. Cranberry's voice cracked when she described the circumstances of his death. They were living on Blaros when the Crownaxians attacked the planet. Her husband was killed by a laser blast as he fought alongside the soldiers defending the settlement. Hearing that caused Amy to tear up and she developed a deeper respect for the lady.

There was a knock on the front door shortly after Pam came home from work that night. The doctor was still in her room, so Mrs. Cranberry looked through the peephole and then answered the door. Amy stood behind the caretaker and she saw Yale in the hallway with a smile on her face. "Yale, what are you doing here?" asked Amy. She grabbed her friend's hand and guided her into the apartment. Mrs. Cranberry closed the door.

The lieutenant sat on the couch and Amy plopped down next to her. "I came to talk to your mom," said Yale. "Is she home yet?" The young lady was wearing her formal uniform and her hair was pulled tightly back in a bun.

"Yeah, she's getting changed," said Amy, who nodded toward her parents' room. "Why are you all dressed up?"

"That's what I wanted to talk to her about." Before she could continue, they heard the bedroom door open and they turned to see Pam walking toward the living room. She was wearing a tan sweater and a pair of faded blue jeans. Yale politely stood up to greet her.

"Wanted to talk to who about?" asked Pam. She sat down in a chair and motioned for Yale to sit as well. Pam had removed her makeup and Amy thought that she looked very tired.

Yale cleared her throat. "I just found out that the Council has planned a surprise sendoff party for the diplomats," she said. "I wanted to let you know, since it's kind of short notice." She rolled her eyes and smiled.

"A party? That sounds wonderful," said Pam. "When is it?"

"Tonight," said Yale. She then peeked at her watch. "In about 90 minutes. In the recreation center's ballroom." She smiled again.

"Whoa, that sounds like fun," said Amy. She turned toward her mother. "Can I go mom? I promise I'll behave."

Her mother was about to reply when Yale cut her off. "Sorry, kiddo," she said to Amy. "This is for adults only." She sympathetically rubbed the disappointed girl's right shoulder, and then she looked at Mrs. Cranberry.

"I can stick around if you need me to, Mrs. Sutter," said Mrs. Cranberry. "I don't have any plans for the evening." The older woman stepped over to the couch and sat beside Amy. "I could use the company."

Pam slowly nodded and Amy saw that she wasn't happy about this sudden engagement. The doctor stood up and stretched her arms over her head. "I guess I need to shower," said Pam. "Thank you for staying," she said to Mrs. Cranberry. Then she looked at Yale. "You said a surprise party. How are we expected to get them to the party?"

Yale stood up and brushed a wrinkle out of her pants. "That's all been arranged," she said. "In about an hour, the general will page them to his office and then he'll take them over himself."

"Oh, ok," said Pam. "I guess we'll just meet them there." She then leaned toward her daughter. "Don't give Mrs. Cranberry a hard time now dear," she said. "She's doing us a favor." Before Amy could respond, Pam turned and walked back to her bedroom.

Yale started toward the exit and Amy got up to show her out. The lieutenant said goodbye to the caretaker as the officer opened the door. Amy sulked as she stood close to her friend. "I'll tell you what," said Yale as she stood in the doorway. "The *Harmony* is undergoing one of its last inspections tonight. If I can slip out of the party for a little while, maybe I can take you down to the launch bay to watch the crewmen get the ship ready."

A smile shot across Amy's face. "Really? That would be so

cool."

The lieutenant then looked back at Mrs. Cranberry. "If that's ok with you, Mrs. Cranberry," she said. The older woman nodded. "Great. Then I'll try to get back here around 8:30," she said to Amy. "See you later."

Amy said goodbye and skipped over toward Mrs. Cranberry. "Wow, I've never seen a real ship up close before," she said, excitedly. "That beats a party anytime." The girl hopped on one foot, then the other. "I wonder if it's bigger than the *Liberty Bell*." Mrs. Cranberry shrugged and Amy noticed the lack of interest in her expression. "What are we having for dinner?"

The woman opened the refrigerator door and scanned the contents. Amy heard the shower start in the bathroom. Mrs. Cranberry found a package of fresh hamburger meat and put it on the counter. "When your mother gets out of the shower, we'll ask her if she wants cheeseburgers for dinner," she said. Amy nodded. Mrs. Cranberry then took a deck of playing cards out of a cabinet drawer. "How about a game of Rummy till then?"

They played five hands before Pam came back out wearing a dark blue dress, black shoes and a white pearl necklace. "How do I look?" she asked, spinning around like a runway model.

"Like a million dollars," said Mrs. Cranberry, picking up a row of cards from the table. She then put down a set of three eights and added a nine to another pile before discarding a five. Amy tallied up that score in her head and grimaced, knowing that the five did her no good.

"Thank you, Mrs. Cranberry," said Pam. "What do you think, dear?" she asked Amy, peeking at the girl's hand. Amy repeated Mrs. Cranberry's compliment, then focused on her cards again. Pam smiled and adjusted her necklace.

"Would you like cheeseburgers for dinner?" asked the attendant.

"Nothing for me," replied Pam. "I'll eat during the party." She breezed back to the bathroom and closed the door. The card players were still competing when she reemerged a few minutes later with makeup on. "We'll try not to be too late," said Pam, on her way out of the apartment.

The hamburgers sizzled in a deep frying pan as Mrs. Cranberry stood in front of the stove with a spatula in her hand. The aroma of the cooked meat filled the kitchen. Amy leaned against a counter and dangled a green yo-yo over the floor. She snapped her wrist to pull the toy back into her hand, and then let it roll out until the string tightened. She watched Mrs. Cranberry flip the burgers and put cheese slices on them. Amy rubbed her grumbling stomach and hoped the food would be ready soon.

The cordless telephone rang as Amy pulled two plates out of a cabinet. The girl put the plates down, grabbed the phone from the cradle mounted on the wall and leaned back against the counter. "Hello," she said, playing with the yo-yo again.

"Hi Amy, its Yale," said the voice on the other end. "It doesn't look like I'm going to be able to get away from the party anytime soon."

Amy frowned. "It's ok, I understand," she replied. She put the yo-yo down on the counter and pulled the string off of her finger. The string left a slight indentation on the girl's delicate skin. She rubbed her thump over the crease and tried to smooth it out.

"But I'm here with Madison," said Yale. "The robot can take you instead, if it's ok with Mrs. Cranberry."

Amy's face brightened. "Hold on." She turned toward her sitter and relayed Yale's message. Mrs. Cranberry nodded and said it was ok. "Yeah, she said I can go," Amy told Yale. "When will Madison be here?"

"I'm sending Madison now," replied Yale. "It should be there soon. Listen, I'm sorry I can't go. I want to but the general is set to make a big speech and wouldn't be good for my career to miss it."

"That's cool, we'll do something else another time," said Amy. She saw Mrs. Cranberry turn off the stove. "I gotta go. Dinner is ready. Bye." She put the phone back on the cradle and then she handed her sitter the plates. The woman put the plates down and opened a package of rolls. She then slid the burgers onto the rolls and put them on the plates.

They brought their food out to the dining room table where a pitcher of iced tea rested between two glasses. Mrs. Cranberry filled the glasses before sitting down across from Amy. The eaters were halfway through their first burgers when the doorbell rang. Amy sprang up from her seat and rushed to the door. Mrs. Cranberry told her to wait and the woman hustled past Amy, keeping her at arm's length. She looked through the peephole and turned back toward Amy. "It's Madison," said the sitter, opening the door. The dark green robot greeted them both, and then followed them back to the table. "Would you like something to eat?" asked the woman, as she turned toward the kitchen.

"No thank you, ma'am," said the robot as it sat down next to Amy. "I don't consume food. I run on electric power generated by four batteries located in my mid-section." The robot pointed to a spot below its chest. "I recharge them once a week and replace them twice a year."

Mrs. Cranberry sat back in her seat with an uncomfortable smile. "I'm sorry," she replied. "I don't know much about robotics. In fact, you're the first android I've ever seen."

"You'll never see another one like Madison," said Amy.

"Why is that dear?" asked the woman. Amy had her mouth full, so the robot answered. Madison briefly recapped its history and described its primary functions. The sitter looked impressed. "How long will you continue to function?" she asked.

"I don't know," said the robot, folding its hands and resting them on the table. "My creator could not duplicate the aging process and since all of my parts are replaceable, I imagine that I could go on indefinitely."

"You mean you could live forever?" asked Amy, wiping her mouth with a napkin. She finished the rest of her drink and set the glass down.

Madison looked down at the table for a moment before answering. "Yes, Amy, I suppose you could say that." The robot picked up her glass and refilled it with iced tea. Then it looked at the sitter. "Would you like some more, Mrs. Cranberry?" it asked. She nodded and Madison refilled her glass as well. Then the robot looked over at Amy, who was just beginning her second burger. "What does that taste like?" it asked.

Amy shrugged, wondering how to describe the taste to something that doesn't eat. "It's spicy, I guess." She saw the sitter raise her eyebrows. "But not in a bad way. I like how you mix peppers into the meat. And the hot mustard is my favorite. It gives it some extra kick." Mrs. Cranberry smiled.

Madison nodded. "I wish I had been built with taste buds. I would like to know what that's like. But I guess that wasn't a priority." Amy noticed the sadness in her friend's voice and she wondered how the scientists could have overlooked such a basic function. The robot touched the pitcher of iced tea that had a thin layer of condensation on it.

"It's really no big deal," said Amy. "And at least you're spared the taste of spinach and broccoli." She finished her burger a few minutes later and drank the rest of her tea. "I'm ready when you are," she said to Madison.

The robot stood as Amy shot out of her chair and put her glass and dish into the kitchen sink. The girl then put on a light jacket and hugged Mrs. Cranberry, thanking her for dinner. "We'll be back by 9:30," said Madison. Then the robot led Amy out the front door and across the settlement to the aircraft hangar as a chilly wind blew at their backs.

The *Harmony* was docked in Hangar 10. The white, triangular-shaped craft glowed under the warm, fluorescent lights. Amy let out a whistle as she examined the ship. "That thing is enormous," she said, leaning on a smooth railing.

Madison nodded. "The ship is 350-feet long, 122-feet high, and 130-feet wide with three decks," it said. "It houses a regular compliment of 25 crew members." Two guards stood at either end of the ship as Amy and Madison watched the maintenance crews make the final adjustments to the craft. Yale had provided Madison with written permission to visit the hangar as long as Amy and the robot remained at least 100-feet away from the *Harmony*. However, Amy still caught a few unsettling glances from some of the soldiers as they worked.

The guests had monitored the preparations for a half-hour when Amy saw Yale enter the hangar. The lieutenant spoke to the maintenance supervisor before making her way over to Amy and Madison. "Keeping your distance, I see," said the officer. Amy nodded. Yale turned toward the ship. "So what do you think of her?" she asked.

"She's tremendous," said Amy, widening her eyes. She took a step forward and looked at the craft from end to end. She had to squint to see the front of the spacecraft. "Is she bigger than the *Liberty Bell*?" she asked.

Yale smiled. "Much bigger. And faster too."

Amy gave her a puzzled look. "Faster? I thought the *Liberty Bell* had the Sprint Drive engine? Does the *Harmony* have it too?"

The lieutenant moved closer to the girl and lowered her voice. Madison inched forward to hear. "No, it doesn't. But you know that the Sprint Drive doesn't really work yet, so this ship is faster because it has a bigger standard engine," said Yale. She then gave Amy a stern look that told the girl that they shouldn't be discussing this sensitive military information. Yale's face softened as she looked at her watch. "You should take her home now, Madison. It's getting late."

Amy sighed then followed her mechanical friend out of the building and across the dark settlement to her home. The temperature dropped even more and Amy folded her arms across her chest and lowered her head to keep the wind off of her face. Madison put an arm around her to keep her warm but the robot's cold metal skin only made it worse.

Mrs. Cranberry was knitting on the couch when they entered the apartment. "Did you have a good time?" she asked, rising to greet them.

"The best," said Amy, still shivering. "Are my folks still out?"

"Yes, I haven't heard from them yet," said Mrs. Cranberry. Then she noticed Amy's shaking body. "Oh, dear, you look nearly frozen," said the sitter. She went to a hall closet and took out a blanket. She wrapped it around the child and sat her on the couch. "I'll make you some hot chocolate," she said, heading toward the kitchen. "Do you want marshmallows?" she called back.

"Yeah, that'd be great," said Amy. Then she turned toward Madison. "You want to watch TV?" she asked, picking up the remote. She turned the set on and flipped to a cartoon channel.

The robot leaned over the couch and gazed at the television screen. "It's amazing how clear the signal from Earth is," it said. "How many channels do you receive?"

Amy shrugged. "About 600, I guess," she said. She grabbed a

pillow and stuffed it into her lap. "This one is my favorite. They show cartoons from the 20th century. This one is called *Tom and Jerry*." She wrapped her arms around the pillow and leaned back against the couch. "Tom's my favorite. He never gets the mouse but that doesn't stop him from trying."

Madison nodded and stepped away from the couch. "I should be going," it said. "I have some lessons to plan." The robot turned and moved toward the door. Amy rushed over to Madison, wrapping her arms around her friend and nearly knocking the robot off its feet.

"Do you have to?" asked Amy. The robot nodded again. "Ah, c'mon, stick around a little longer. Besides, tomorrow is Saturday and you don't have any classes on Saturdays." She tugged at its right arm. "Please, it's a lot more fun with someone to watch with," she said. "And there aren't many kids on this stupid planet."

Mrs. Cranberry came in from the kitchen with two cups of hot chocolate. "I'll watch with you, dear," she said, placing the cups on the coffee table in front of the couch.

Amy looked over at the sitter and tried to mask her disappointment. "Ok," she said, in an artificially high voice. Then she turned back to Madison. "Promise me you'll stop by tomorrow," she said.

"I promise," said Madison. "I'll come over in the morning and I'll go with you to the launch site. It should be very exciting." The robot pried its hands loose from Amy's grip. "Goodnight Mrs. Cranberry," it said, looking over toward the sitter. Then the robot brought its gaze back to Amy. It gently placed a hand on her right shoulder. "Goodnight Amy," it said.

"Goodnight." She watched her friend leave and she sat down on the couch after the door closed. Then she sipped her hot chocolate. The steam rose up from the surface and warmed her face. "This is really good," she said, carefully sitting back. "Thank you for making it."

"You're welcome," said Mrs. Cranberry, sipping her own drink. They watched four episodes of the cartoon series before Amy got up to go to the bathroom. On her way back, she asked her sitter if she could play on her computer for a little while. Mrs. Cranberry said yes, and then started flipping through the channels for something else to watch. Amy went into her room, closed the door and turned on her computer.

Amy was scrolling through a document a half-hour later when she heard a knock on her bedroom door. Before she could answer, her father stepped into the room. Startled, Amy spun around and tried to cover her computer screen with her right arm. "Daddy, you scared me," she said, leaning in front of the monitor.

"Sorry," he said, moving closer to her. "I just wanted to tell you what happened tonight." He had an enormous smile on his face and his eyes shined. Then he lowered his eyebrows. "What are you doing?" he asked.

"Nothing. Why?" asked Amy, still sitting at the odd angle.

"Well, you look like you're about to fall over." He took another step forward and gently straightened her posture. Then his eyes caught the computer screen. "What is this?" he asked, with an angry tone. Amy kept quiet as he looked at the blueprint for the *Harmony* that was displayed on the monitor. "How did you get this?"

Amy shrugged. "It really wasn't that hard," she said. "I just tapped into the Union's database and surfed around until I found the file. Then it was just a matter of getting past the firewall." She leaned back in her chair and smiled at how easily she succeeded.

"Amy! You can't just go around hacking into confidential files," he shouted. "What's wrong with you? First the simulator and now this. I thought you said that you were going to stop getting into trouble." He turned away from her and threw his hands up over his head. "I don't know what to do with you." He turned back toward her. "Why do you do these things?"

The young girl felt her throat close up as her eyes filled with tears. She knew that hacking into the database was a bad idea, but she couldn't help herself. She gradually began to sob. "I'm sorry, Daddy," she said. "I was curious. I wanted to know more about the ship. I didn't mean to make you mad."

"Make me mad? That's the least of your concerns. Do you know what would happen if you got caught? The amount of trouble you would be in?" He paused for a moment and regained his composure. "Do you know what would happen to me if you got caught? They'd kick me off the mission."

Out of the corner of her eye, Amy saw her mother enter. The woman approached them and stood beside her husband. "What's going on?" she asked, as Amy kept quiet.

Clayton took a deep breath, and then pointed to the computer screen. "Our daughter has been doing some hacking," he said. Pam's eyes widened as she looked at the screen. Clayton then cut off the net connection and turned off the computer. "It's time for you to go to bed," he said, picking up her computer. "You're grounded from using this thing for two weeks," he announced. "And no television either."

Clayton silently turned and walked out of the room with the computer under his right arm. Pam shook her head at her daughter, and then followed her husband. Amy crawled into bed, pulled the covers over her face and cried. She clenched her hands into tight fists as her entire body shook. She was angry at herself for doing something so stupid.

Chapter Three

The next morning was chaotic in the Sutter home. Despite getting up earlier than planned, Clayton dashed around the apartment, hunting for things to bring aboard the ship and making last minute adjustments to his paperwork. Amy wanted to apologize again but she just stayed out of his way and tried not to get into trouble. Pam and Mrs. Cranberry tried to help Clayton with his final preparations but he kept telling them to leave the tasks to him. Finally, the diplomat grabbed his briefcase and duffel bag and walked with his family to the hangar.

The Sutters entered the building through the north gate that had four guards posted on either side of the entrance. The guards checked Clayton's security tags before permitting them to enter. They walked into a green reception room where Gen. Knox and his aides were waiting for them. The general shook Clayton's hand and smiled. "Good morning Mr. Ambassador," said the general. "Did you get a good night's sleep?"

Clayton shook his head. "Yes sir, I did." Then he turned toward his family. "This is my wife, Pam and our daughter, Amy," he said. The general greeted them with handshakes as well. Clayton looked around for a moment before he spoke again. "Am I the first to arrive this morning?" he asked.

The general nodded. "Yes, you're early as usual," he said. "But we should get started just the same." The general turned and spoke to a nearby guard. "Private, take the ambassador's belongings to the ship. And be careful with that briefcase. It's got very important papers in it." The private nodded and Clayton handed him his gear. The general paused for a moment to let the soldier depart, and then he inched closer to the diplomat. "Clayton, now would be a good time to say your good-byes," he said.

Clayton nodded and the general moved off to give the Sutters some privacy. Clayton wrapped his arms around his wife and hugged her tightly. "I won't be gone long, dear," he said. Amy took a step back and pretended not to listen. "I love you very much." He kissed her and hugged her again.

She stepped back and looked at him. "I'm very proud of you," she said. "And I'm sorry I wasn't more supportive." He started to say something but she cut him off. "No, really, I could have complained a lot less, I know. But I just love you so much. If anything were to happen to you . . ." He cut her off with a kiss as Amy tried not to cry. Instead, the girl circled away from them for a moment before returning to her spot. "Do me one favor," said Pam. "Come home safely. That's all I ask."

Amy watched her parents embrace again while other groups of people entered behind them. She caught pieces of their conversations and realized that they were the families of the other diplomats. They were saying their farewells. There was a lot of hugging and kissing and even some crying. Amy's eyes darted around the room until she saw a familiar face. Mr. Zigler was saying goodbye to his wife, a tall, thin woman with long locks of blond hair that ran to the middle of her back. She was also crying.

A hand landed on her shoulder and Amy turned to see her father looking at her with a slight smile on his face. "Goodbye honey," he said, pulling her close to him. He kissed the top of her head before letting her go. Then he stared into her eyes. "I'll make you a deal," he said. "You be good for your mother while I'm gone and I'll bring you that Morleanne space rock you asked for." He tousled her hair. "Deal?"

Amy nodded. "Deal," she said. Then she watched her father turn and walk through a door that led to another room in the hangar. Pam put her arm around her daughter and guided the girl out of the green reception room. They followed the signs to the observation room and found an elevator to ride up in. They squeezed into the packed car and Amy held her breath as the car moved upward. It stopped with a slight jolt at the tenth floor.

The crowd spilled into the observation room and moved toward the seats that ran in rows facing the launch pad. The Sutters found two seats that were three rows back from the glass. They sat down and observed the crewmen who were inspecting the *Harmony*. Amy then looked up at a clock on the wall and realized that there was at least another hour to go before liftoff. "Can I please have my book?" she asked her mother.

Pam reached into her backpack and handed Amy a worn paperback copy of Hemingway's *For Whom The Bell Tolls*. The novel was a gift from Amy's grandmother and although she had already finished it, she loved it so much that she started reading it again. Out of the corner of her eye, she saw Pam open a medical journal and start reading it. Amy cleared her throat and dove into her book, trying hard to ignore the sounds of the conversations going on around her.

Amy was on the twentieth page of the book when she felt a tap on her shoulder. She turned around and saw Yale standing behind her. "Hi Amy, how are you?" asked the lieutenant. Amy smiled and said she was fine. Yale sat down in the empty chair next to the girl and noticed what Amy was reading. "That's a pretty heavy book you got there," she said. Then she looked over at Pam. "Good morning, Mrs. Sutter. How are you?"

"I'm fine, thanks," she said, leaning forward to see the officer. "It looks like a good day for a launch. No clouds in the sky."

"None at all," said Yale. She put her arm on the back of the empty seat in front of her. "You must be very proud of your husband, Mrs. Sutter. This mission could be the turning point in our relationship with the Crownaxians, and Mr. Sutter's efforts to get it off the ground are quite remarkable." Pam nodded and Yale then turned to Amy. "Your dad is a brave man. Not many people supported this plan."

Amy noticed the looks they were getting from the people sitting around them. "Well, they were wrong," said Amy, quite loudly. "All of them." She glared at a lady sitting in the front row when the woman turned around with a disapproving look on her face. "This will work."

"Oh, I'm sure it will," said Yale, standing up. "Well, I need to get back down there and check on a few things." She leaned over and shook Pam's hand. "Nice seeing you again, Mrs. Sutter," she said. Pam returned the compliment. Yale put her hand on Amy's right shoulder. "I'll see you later Amy." The lieutenant turned and walked back to the elevator. Amy watched her step into the car before the doors closed.

A short time later, a voice came over the loudspeaker mounted high above the spectators' heads in the front wall. "Attention guests.

The countdown for launch will begin in four minutes." A rumble of excited voices filled the room. Everyone looked out the window as the *Harmony* was moved to the launch pad. Workers eased the ship into position as the astronauts walked toward the craft. The spectators applauded at the sight of the crew, who turned and waved at the crowd. Amy saw her father and Mr. Zigler among the group, which included two other men and three other women. They were wearing the Union's green and white spacesuits and their attire included red patches on the sleeves to indicate their diplomatic status.

As the applause died down, Amy leaned toward her mother. "I don't see any pilots with them," she said. "Whose gonna do the flying?"

"Mr. Zigler is the pilot," said Pam. "He served in the military before becoming a diplomat." She pointed toward the tallest woman in the crew. "Ms. Elsben is the copilot. She served too."

Yale and four security officers led the crew to the spaceship. The security team stopped at the foot of the entrance and saluted the diplomats. Amy watched the crew enter the craft. The door slid closed and the security team marched back to the hangar. The voice returned over the loudspeaker. "Liftoff will commence in one minute." The room quieted as everyone kept their eyes on the ship. An automated voice counted down the final thirty seconds. The ship levitated thirty feet above the ground and shot forward. Amy held her mother's hand and said a silent prayer as the spectators stood to see the ship dart toward the atmosphere.

Three days later Madison was giving Amy a science lesson in the living room while Mrs. Cranberry prepared dinner in the kitchen. The topic was Chemistry and Amy was having trouble with the formulas. "Why do I need to know this?" she yelled. She crossed her arms over her chest and pouted. "I'm never going to use it."

"It's important to be a well-rounded student," said Madison. Amy rolled her eyes. "Besides, it's a big part of the academy entrance exam."

Amy sighed. "I know. But it doesn't make sense for anyone to memorize all this when you can just look it up on your computer." She slid her right hand over the tutor-comp screen until she found where they stopped. She took a deep breath and tried to figure out the answer.

A moment later, she looked up in frustration. "I'm not getting it."

Before Madison could answer, they heard a knock on the front door. Mrs. Cranberry came out of the kitchen with an apron around her waist and opened the door. "Yale," she said, holding the door open. "What a surprise. Come in, come in. Can I get you anything?"

The lieutenant shook her head, then glanced over at Amy. The officer had a tense look on her face. "Hi Amy," she said, softly. "Is your mother home? I need to talk to you both about something."

"She's taking a nap," said Mrs. Cranberry, shutting the door. "But I can wake her if it's important."

Yale nodded. "Yes. Please wake her." The soldier clasped her hands together behind her back as the sitter walked over to Pam's door. "Maybe you should go," she said to Madison.

The robot stood and began to gather up the teaching materials. "Wait, what's going on?" asked Amy. Yale started to speak then she stopped. Amy stepped closer to her. "What is it? And why do you want Madison to leave?" She grabbed Yale's hands and pulled them apart. "Talk to me!" she shouted. Out of the corner of her eye she saw the robot walking away. "No Madison. I want you to stay." The robot looked at her, then Yale, who just nodded.

They all turned around as they heard Pam walking in with the sitter. Pam yawned and raised her hands over her head. "What's going on out here?" she asked. She glared at Yale. "You have something to tell us?"

The officer pointed to the couch. "Maybe we should all sit down," she said. Pam shrugged then sat down on the couch. Amy sat beside her while Madison and Mrs. Cranberry remained on their feet. Yale took a deep breath and spoke slowly. "We received a distress call from the *Harmony* twenty-five minutes ago." Both Amy and her mother gasped. "They reported that they were under attack by the Crownaxians."

"Under attack? I thought this was a peaceful mission." said Amy, clutching her mother's hand. Her eyes filled with tears and her bottom lip quivered. "What happened?" she asked.

Yale pressed her lips together. "They said that they met the science ship at the rendezvous coordinates when two destroyers suddenly emerged from a nearby nebula and fired on them without provocation." The officer shook her head. "The *Harmony* has a limited arsenal. They fired back but there wasn't much they could do to defend themselves. I'm so sorry."

Pam rose and pushed her face a few inches away from Yale's. "How many ships were dispatched to help them?" she asked.

Yale took a step back and put her hands on Pam's shoulders. Again she spoke slowly, as if the words were too painful to utter. "Mrs. Sutter, the general ordered that no ships depart the base."

"What? Why?" asked Pam.

"He said that it was too risky to send any more that deep into Crow space," said Yale. Pam's face turned white and she looked like she might faint. Amy shot up and put her hands on her mother's back to steady her. "The Crows were probably just interested in the triboleserene. I'm sure the crew got away in the escape pods. That's part of their training."

Amy and Yale then eased Pam back onto the couch as Mrs. Cranberry dashed into the kitchen before returning with a glass of water. The sitter held the glass to Pam's lips as the woman slowly drank the liquid. Amy then looked back at Yale. "Won't the military do anything?" she asked.

The lieutenant shook her head. "Not unless the general gets a direct order from the Council." She took another deep breath. "I shouldn't even tell you this but two of the general's officers sent a secret request to the Council asking them to override the general's orders. We haven't heard back from them yet but I'll let you know when we do." she said. She then turned toward Pam. "Mrs. Sutter, if there's anything I can do to help, just ask."

Pam glared at her again. "Yes, take me to the general," she said. "Let him tell me to my face why he's going to let my husband die." She rose again, this time more steadily. "Take me right now."

Yale nodded. "I'll take you," she said. "But I don't know if he'll see you or how much good it will do if he does. But I'll help you try." She put an arm around Pam's shoulders and guided her out of the apartment. Amy and Madison followed behind them as they walked across the compound to the command center. Despite the heat of the sultry night, the girl's hands shook as she pictured her father fighting off the alien attack. She wondered if she would ever see him again.

The group was met at the front gate by four armed guards who grudgingly followed Yale's order to let them enter. The command center was buzzing with activity. The 150-foot square room was lined with computer terminals, each manned by uniformed soldiers. Gen. Knox was talking to a middle-aged colonel while a weary-eyed sergeant stood behind them. Amy glared at the general and held back the urge to scream at him. Yale told Pam to wait at one of the desks before the officer turned and marched over to Gen. Knox. Amy and Madison stood behind Pam after she slid into a chair.

Despite the noise, Amy could hear what was happening. "General," said Yale, offering a salute. "Mrs. Sutter would like a moment of your time." She took a step back and turned toward the group. The general nodded without saying a word, then he walked over to Pam. Yale followed behind him with a doubtful look on her face, while the sergeant stayed put.

"Mrs. Sutter," said the general, offering his hand. She rose and politely shook it. "I'm sorry for what happened," he said. "But you must understand that I can't risk any more of my men."

Pam took a deep breath. "Gen. Knox, that's my husband you've stranded out there," she said. "And the other crew members, they all have families too. We put our faith in the Union and in you to protect them. How can you just abandon them like that?" She started to cry. Amy moved closer to her and put her right arm around her mother.

The general glanced at Yale, and then he looked back at Pam. "If I thought I could get them back safely, I would send an entire squadron out to rescue them. But all that would do is risk the lives of even more soldiers with even more family members," he said. "And with all due respect, Mrs. Sutter, everyone on the *Harmony* knew the risks when they agreed to take on this mission, including your husband." He paused and his voice softened. "I'm very fond of Clayton, Mrs. Sutter, and all of his shipmates. It took lots of courage for them to do what they did and I admire them for it. But that doesn't change the fact that, right now, there's nothing I can do for them. I'm very sorry." He turned around and walked back over to the sergeant.

Yale put a hand on Pam's shoulder. "I wish there were something more I could do. If you need anything, anything at all, just ask. I'll do whatever I can to help you." She removed her hand and wiped tears from her eyes.

"Just take me home," said Pam. Yale nodded and led the group out of the command center. They exited the building and Yale escorted the Sutters home. When they got there, Pam silently went into her room and shut the door. Mrs. Cranberry invited Yale to stay for dinner, but the officer declined.

Madison was about to leave with her when Amy asked the robot to stay. Madison looked toward Yale, who told the robot that it was ok. After Yale left, Amy asked Madison to join her in her room. The young girl closed the door behind them and quietly turned on her computer. Madison leaned over the girl's shoulder as Amy began surfing the computer net.

Amy used her hacking skills to get inside the Union database again. "What exactly are you doing?" asked Madison, as top-secret information poured onto the computer screen. She didn't answer. Amy refused to accept the general's decision. If no one else was going to attempt a rescue, she would do it herself, as irrational as that might be.

The young girl scanned the data before her. "You know that this is going to get you into trouble, right?" said Madison. "As a Union member, I have to report you for this breach of security." The robot tried to shut off the computer but Amy grabbed its hand.

"No, wait," she said, pushing the metallic hand away. "I'm almost there." She continued typing and clicking her way through the mass of data files until she stopped at one marked L.Bell. "This is it," she said, opening the file. She navigated her way through smaller files until she found the one marked B.Prints. She clicked on it and the blueprints for the *Liberty Bell* opened before her eyes. "This is what I need."

"Why do you need this information?" asked Madison.

Amy ignored the question and started printing out the documents. Her laser printer spit out the pages while Amy examined the data on the screen. "I know the ship was designed for a crew of five people but I bet with a little reprogramming, you could get by with just two," she said.

The robot suddenly took a step back and put its hands by its side. "Please tell me you are not thinking what I think you're thinking," it said. Amy looked at the robot's face without blinking. "Oh, no. You can't be serious. Tell me you're not serious." Madison sat on the bed and folded its arms.

"Madison, my dad is out there and he needs help. And so do the other crew members." She stood in front of the robot with her hands on her hips. "No one else is going to do anything to help them. It's up to us." She could see that she wasn't getting through to her friend. "I can't just let him die."

"And what are we supposed to do? Steal the ship and fly off to Crownaxia to save him?" asked Madison. Amy tilted her head to one side. "Even if we could, we have no idea where he is or even if he's still alive." Amy's eyes glistened as she bit her bottom lip and turned away from Madison. "I'm sorry, I don't want to upset you but this is crazy. All of our intelligence shows that their homeworld is heavily fortified. That's why we've never tried a direct assault. A solo rescue mission would only wind up getting us killed. I can't let that happen to you."

"You are programmed with free will," said Amy, still not looking at her friend. "You can do anything you want."

"I don't want to do this," said the robot. "I don't want to see you die."

Amy snapped her head back around and glared at the robot. "It's worth a try!" she shouted. "And it's better than just sitting here wondering." She took a breath to calm down. "Besides, we have detailed maps of Crownaxian space. It wouldn't be that hard to get there." She realized how ridiculous that sounded. "Ok, it would be hard, but not impossible. And it's so crazy that Crows would never expect it."

"And what would we do if and when we got there?" asked Madison. "We couldn't just stop and ask for directions. We'd be captured the moment anyone saw us. Assuming we could even get off Paldor."

A mischievous smile crept across the girl's face. "I know a way we can get the ship into space but we'll need to break a bunch of rules to do it." She put her hand up to shush the robot as it started to object. "Madison, there are some things more important that following the rules. And look at it this way, we wouldn't have to do it if Gen. Knox would just send out some search parties. So, in a sense, it's his fault we're doing this."

"Your logic is extremely flawed," said Madison. The robot rose to its feet. "However, if you insist in following this reckless course of action, I have no choice but to go with you."

Amy's face brightened. "Really?" The robot nodded. "Oh thank you, Madison, thank you," she said, hugging her metallic friend. Then she sat back down in front of her computer. She closed the blueprint file and began hunting for another folder. Madison moved closer to see what she was doing. "I saw the file for the stellar maps in this section," she said, clicking the mouse. A new document opened up. "There they are." She clicked the mouse again and the printer spit out more pages.

Suddenly, a small red window flashed onto her screen. "Oh no!" she said. "I've been detected." Amy quickly shut down all the windows on her screen and severed the net connection. Her computer moaned to a stop as she shut it off. She took a breath and looked over at Madison. "I don't think they traced me," she said. "But that was close."

Madison leaned over and picked up the papers on the printer tray. The robot sifted through the documents and nodded. "I think you got all of the maps," it said. Then it looked at her. "Are you sure you got out in time?"

She shrugged. "Pretty sure." Madison handed her the documents. "It doesn't matter anyway," she said. "By tomorrow at this time, we'll already be gone." She looked up at her friend and smiled. "I know I'm asking a lot from you and I appreciate what you're going to do. And I realize that it's a long shot and that I'm asking you to risk your life for me." She took a contemplative breath. "So, thanks. And if, rather, when we make it back, I'll take all the heat for this."

Madison nodded. "Don't worry about that. Just tell me you have some kind of plan for rescuing the diplomats." Amy quietly smiled again and saw that her lack of response only added to her friend's trepidation.

Amy tried to act naturally the next day as she planned their escape. She knew she needed to come up with a diversion to draw the guards away from the hangar that housed the *Liberty Bell*. She made several short trips to the building and was careful to spend only a few minutes observing all the activity around the structure. Amy mentally noted how long each guard shift was and how long it took them to change personnel. She even peeked through a window and saw that the ship was the only one in the hangar, which explained why there were only two sets of two guards on duty at one time. When Amy passed the large wooden supply shed 10 yards south of the hangar, she noted the small combination lock that secured the door.

Nighttime finally came and Amy crawled out of her bed and kept the light off. She changed out of her pajamas and into a pair of black pants and a black T-shirt. Then she slipped on her hiking boots, grabbed a backpack and quietly opened her bedroom door. Mrs. Cranberry had been gone for hours and Amy figured that her mother must be asleep by then. However, a thin ray of light emanated from the bottom of her parents' bedroom door, so Amy eased her way along the carpeted floor to the front door. Softly opening it, she stepped into the hallway and carefully shut the door. Then she quickly took the back steps to the first floor and stepped out into the surprisingly cold night.

Amy found Madison waiting for her by a patch of trees near the medical building. She greeted the robot in a quiet voice. "Thanks for going through with this," she said. Madison nodded. Then Amy turned toward the supply shed. "C'mon, let's go." The duo prowled across the compound, mindfully dodging the searchlights that routinely swept across the base. They dropped behind a thicket of bushes when two patrol guards came dangerously close to them. Wiping themselves off, they kept going.

When they got to the shed, Amy pointed to the lock without saying a word. Madison nodded and snapped the lock off with its superior strength. Amy opened the door and surveyed the contents in the dim light. She saw boxes of uniforms, paper, food trays, utensils and other semi-essential products. As she had hoped, there were no weapons in the shed or anything that could explode. Taking a breath, she dug the book of matches out of her pocket and struck one of the tiny sticks. It flared up and she touched the rest of the book before tossing the torch on top of a box of paper. She and Madison then sprinted toward the nearby woods and waited for the fireworks to begin. In a matter of minutes, the entire shed was engulfed in flames.

Alarms blared in the cold night air as the soldiers guarding the hangar ran toward the shed with fire extinguishers. Yale and several other soldiers with firefighting equipment soon joined them. In the midst of the confusion, Amy and Madison slipped unnoticed into the hangar. Amy gasped as she got her first good look at the *Liberty Bell*. It was far more majestic than she had imagined. The sleek ship was painted blue and had red and white stripes running the length of it. An odd humming sound emanated from it. Amy reached out to touch the hull when she was suddenly knocked backwards by an invisible force field that protected the craft. She landed hard on the wooden floor and her backpack slid off her shoulder.

Madison quickly ran over to her. "Are you injured?" asked the robot. It slowly helped her to her feet and she shook her head no. The robot handed her the bag, led her to a chair and eased her into the seat. "Rest a moment," it said. "I'll take care of the force field." Amy nodded and watched Madison hustle over to a computer terminal that sat on a desk against one wall. The robot turned on the computer and swiftly typed in commands on the keyboard. Amy listened to the commotion outside and wondered how long it would be before someone came in to check on the ship. After a few minutes, the humming sound from the ship ceased and Madison touched the hull with its right hand. Nothing happened. Amy hopped to her feet as the robot opened the door on the port side of the ship.

The duo boarded the craft and hurried to the bridge. The layout of the bridge matched the simulator program that Amy hadn't quite mastered. They began the prelaunch sequence together before Madison exited to find the terminal that operated the hangar doors. Amy watched the robot locate the terminal and set a timer to open the doors in two minutes. Madison ran back aboard and sat in the co-pilot's chair. While the engines warmed up, Amy opened a supply locker door and found a helmet and flight suit. "Turn around for a minute," she said to Madison. The robot did and Amy quickly put on the suit, which was a little too big for her. She put on the helmet and saw that the engines were ready.

Red lights inside the hangar flashed as an alarm screeched. Amy took a deep breath then grabbed hold of the yoke. She stepped on the accelerator and steered the ship through the doors and out into the darkness. As the ship sped up, she saw the Union soldiers aiming their weapons at the craft. "Turn on the shields!" she yelled. The robot typed in a command on the keyboard in front of it just before the soldiers opened fire. The laser blasts ricocheted off the shields and landed harmlessly on the ground.

Amy flipped the switch for the thrusters and the ship began to lift off of the ground. She saw some soldiers hurrying toward the smaller, fighter ships. "C'mon, C'mon," she said, tapping the console in front of her. Amy then caught of glimpse of Yale's angry face as the *Liberty Bell* rose higher and she felt some regret for having to do this to her friend.

The *Liberty Bell* roared through the night sky toward the planet's atmosphere. Six small Union fighter crafts pursued the ship, firing their laser cannons. Amy held tightly onto the yoke as the shields took a pounding. She steered the ship into a controlled roll to avoid as many laser blasts as she could. She read the shield gauge and realized that the rear deflectors wouldn't stand too many more direct hits. Taking a chance, she fired the reverse thrusters and the ship came to a jarring halt, sending Madison crashing into the console in front of the robot. "Sorry," said Amy, shrugging.

The other ships flew past them and the *Liberty Bell* fell in behind them. "Target their weapons systems," ordered Amy. Madison nodded, and then fired laser shots at the ships, hitting two of them. The damage was minimal but enough to send them back to the planet. However, the four remaining crafts turned around and began firing again. Amy banked hard to her left and tried to fly under the laserfire. The side shields absorbed three hits but Amy was able to put some distance between her and the others.

Amy scanned the radar screen and found something interesting. "There's a nebula about 120,000 miles ahead," she reported. "We're going in." She steered toward the space cloud as the other four ships continued to follow her. She pushed on the accelerator and the ship began to shake as the engines strained to keep up. Within seconds they reached the edge of the nebula. Their pursuers fired a few last shots that never reached the ship.

Once inside the nebula, Amy steered the *Liberty Bell* toward the thickest patch of the cloud. Radiation from the nebula scrambled her radar screen. "They're as blind as we are in here," she said. "Let's hope we don't bump into them." A half-hour passed before the *Liberty*

Bell's inertia caused the ship to drift out of the nebula. Amy checked the radar and saw no signs of the other ships. She plotted a course toward the Crownaxian homeworld and hit the accelerator. Then she took a deep breath and looked at her friend. "Here we go," she said. "God help us."

Chapter Four

Lt. Yale Brown stood at attention as Gen. William Knox paced silently behind her. The sound of the general's footsteps echoed through his spacious office. A large oak desk sat a few feet away from one wall and a black leather chair was pressed up against it. The desk was covered with piles of folders, an in-bin filled with papers, and three pictures of the man's family. From where she stood, Yale could see the photo of the general's deceased wife, a frail woman who was killed during the attack on Blaros. Suddenly the general stopped and glared at Yale. "Tell me how the Hell a 12-year-old girl steals the Union's most top secret developmental weapon right out from under our noses!" he yelled. "How does this happen?"

"It's completely unacceptable sir," replied Yale, without moving. "I take full responsibility as it happened on my watch. Whatever punishment you deem appropriate, sir, I'll take without objection." She continued to stare ahead and she wondered just what that punishment would be."

The general sighed. "At ease, lieutenant," he said, in a softer tone. The young woman relaxed and turned to face him. Out of the corner of her eye she could see Pam seated in a chair by the office door with two armed guards on either side of her. "I don't want to punish you Yale," he said. "You're too good of an officer to lose over this. But it was your security staff that let this happen so I'm going to let you clean it up." He walked over to his leather chair and sat down in it. Yale turned again to face him. "Find that ship and bring it back," he said. "I don't care how you do it."

"Yes, sir," she replied, saluting him.

The general returned the gesture then dismissed her. Before she could reach the door he called her name again. She stopped and stood at attention again. "Yale, you know what will happen to both of us if you fail?" he asked. She nodded. "Both of our careers are on the line lieutenant." The general looked away from her and opened a folder on his desk. Yale took that as her cue to leave. As she spun back around, she glanced at Pam's face.

The woman looked terrified. Her face was pale and dark lines surrounded her red eyes. Pam had her daughter's copy of *For Whom the Bell Tolls* in her hands. The guards were part of a special military police squad that answered only to the general. One of them glared at Yale as she stood there. She saw the guard's hand tighten around his laser rifle as he pressed his lips together. The officer wanted to reach out and comfort the worried mother but instead she hustled out of the general's office.

Yale stopped at a water cooler that sat against a wall outside Knox's office. She pulled one of the disposable cups from the dispenser above the cooler and filled it with the water. She drank slowly, watching the general out of the corner of her eye. Yale saw him begin his interrogation of Pam and the officer tried to listen over the sound of the commotion around her. But the noise from the busy soldiers drowned out the general's voice. Yale glanced over at Knox and saw his angry face as his head intermittently bobbed forward. However, she stood there too long and one of the guards noticed her, and he walked over and closed the door. She shook her head, and then stormed out of the building.

The fire at the supply shed was out. Yale saw four soldiers digging through the rubble for clues. The men lined several scorched and soaked boxes along the outside of the shed. The stench of burnt plastic and paper filled the air. Yale coughed into her hands as she approached the site. She stopped next to a rotund sergeant. "How bad is it, sergeant?" she asked.

The man shrugged. Soot covered his face and hands. "We lost a lot of uniforms and mess hall supplies but not much more than that." He looked at her and smiled. "Fortunately there were no injuries."

"That's good to hear," replied Yale. "I want a full report in a half hour. I'll be in my quarters." She saluted him and moved off as he did the same. Yale then walked through the compound to the hangar on the far south end of the base. Two guards stood at attention by the front door. They saluted her as she passed them and entered the hangar.

The starcraft *Justice* and several other ships the same size sat in the middle of the immense room. A lone soldier was seated behind a desk along the far wall doing paperwork as Yale strutted over to him There was a computer and a telephone on the desk. The man rose to his feet when he spotted her. "At ease, soldier," said Yale, standing in front of him. He relaxed and sat back down. "How long would it take to get the *Justice* ready for a week-long trip?" she asked.

The soldier raised his eyebrows. "Begging your pardon ma'am but the *Justice* isn't really suited for that type of mission."

"And why not?" she asked.

"Well, she's just a fighter craft, mainly used for quick-strike missions. What you want is a shuttle. If you go to Hangar 18 you can get one there that would be all ready to go for you," said the soldier.

Yale shook her head. "I don't want a shuttle. They're too slow. I need a fast, maneuverable ship that can also travel into deep space. How long would it take a maintenance crew to retrofit the *Justice* to do that?" She put her hands on her hips and looked over her shoulder at the ship she wanted.

The soldier looked puzzled. He clumsily opened a folder on his desk and rifled through some papers. "Ah, let me see," he mumbled. He pulled out the duty roster sheet and ran his fingers over a column of names. "Yeah, ok. I can get three technicians to do that for you right away ma'am."

"Great, how long will it take them?" She looked down at the sheet and tried to read the names but the soldier's hand was in the way. Then she peered up at his nervous face. Sweat formed on his glowing forehead.

"At least an hour, maybe more," he said, in a creaky voice.

Yale sighed. "Fine. Get it done and send someone to my quarters when it's finished." She turned around and marched back toward the exit. As she passed the *Justice*, she couldn't help touching the smooth underside of the ship's right wing. The cold surface was oddly reassuring.

The lieutenant entered her sparse quarters after typing in her security code on the lock. She let the door swing shut behind her. The tiny living space only afforded her with enough room for a bed, a single chair, a desk and two bureaus. Yale pulled her duffel bag out from under her bed, put it on top of her mattress and unzipped it. Then she removed clothing from the drawers of her larger bureau and packed them neatly in the bag. Next she went into her bathroom and brought out her toothbrush, a tube of toothpaste and several other items that she put on top of her clothing. She zipped the bag shut and left it on the bed.

She then turned on the computer on her desk and began to compose a letter to send to her parents on Earth. Her folks lived in a modest home in their New Jersey neighborhood that was just a few miles outside of Camden. Her Irish father was a computer programmer, while her German mother worked at a bank in the city. As Yale tried to think of what to tell them, she stared at a photo of her family that was nestled in the corner of the desk. She smiled as her eyes moved from her parents to her two younger sisters.

Yale never heard her father say that he regretted not having a son, but she always suspected that he did. He always encouraged Yale to be her own person but that didn't stop him from introducing her to the fine art of athletics. In school, she was always one of the fastest kids in her class and she could throw a baseball harder than most of the boys. She pitched on her school's softball team and played guard on the basketball squad. However, she never quite got the thrill from sports that her father did.

Yale started to type. She told her parents that she was embarking on a new mission that would take her away from Paldor for a while. She noted that she couldn't get into specifics but she just wanted to tell them that she might not be able to write to them for some time. Although she asked the soldier to prep the *Justice* for a weeklong mission, she knew that it could take longer and she didn't want her parents to worry about her.

She recalled the more mundane details of her week as she typed the letter on her computer: the dry roast beef she had for dinner the night before; the incessant heat that drove temperatures over 110 degrees; the grumblings of her men who had been stationed here for far too long; and the mind-numbing paperwork that she was required to file each week. Then she told them how much she missed them all and how she hoped to get some shore leave soon so she could visit them on Earth. Yale reread the letter three times before sending it to her father's email address.

A short time later, she heard a knock on the door. She stood up and told the visitor to enter. The sergeant who had been fighting the fire walked in carrying a hand-held computer. The man stopped a few feet away from Yale and saluted her. The soot was gone from his face and he was wearing a new, clean uniform. "Sir, the report you wanted is ready." She saluted him back and took the mini-comp from him. Yale scanned the data that appeared on the tiny screen. Then she inserted the mechanism into the computer on her desk and downloaded the information.

"You were right, sergeant, this could have been a lot worse," she said, handing the small computer back to him. "See that the general's office gets a copy of this report. Dismissed." He turned without saying another word and left the lieutenant's quarters. Yale sat back down at her desk and composed a letter to give to Lt. Luke Jefferson, the officer who would have to cover her duties while she was gone. She kept it brief, knowing that Jefferson needed little instruction regarding his new responsibilities.

An hour passed before Yale heard another knock on her door. This time a doughy technician with bad teeth entered and saluted her. Then he spoke with a slight lisp. "The *Justice* is ready. You have a 10-day supply of food, water and fuel, and the latest star charts have been downloaded into the main computer." He took a breath and wiped his sweaty face.

"Good," said Yale, leading him to the door. "I'll be ready to take off in about 15 minutes. Have the ship moved to the launch pad." The soldier nodded then headed back to the hangar. Yale turned off her computer, grabbed her duffel bag and typed in her security code as she locked the door.

Yale marched over toward Gen. Knox's office. The guards at the front of the building let her pass and she weaved her way through the crowd of soldiers that cluttered the hallway. She knocked on the general's door then entered when she heard his gruff voice. Yale stood at attention in front of his desk after she put her bag down on the dusty floor. The general looked up at her for a moment before he spoke. "Are you ready to ship out?" he asked.

"Ready, sir," she replied. He leaned forward in his chair and nodded as he tapped a pen against the top of the desk. The green light radiating from his computer screen reflected off of his nervous face. "With the general's permission, I'll take off immediately," said Yale.

"At ease," said Knox. Yale relaxed. "Who's going with you?"

"No one, sir," she replied. Knox raised his eyebrows. "I think it's too dangerous to risk anyone else on this mission. Besides, it's my mess to clean up and I want it done right," said Yale.

The general nodded again. "I guess I'd say the same thing if I were in your shoes. What's your plan?"

"It stands to reason that Amy Sutter will head for the Crownaxian homeworld to find out where the diplomats are," said Yale. "But I doubt she'll take the most direct route, knowing that we are coming after her." The officer reached into her bag and took out a mini-comp. She turned it on, scrolled through some files, and then handed the device to Knox after she found what she was searching for. "I've plotted a course that I think she'll take. It's not too far off a straight line and there are plenty of places for her to hide along the route. I'll also send out long-range sensor probes."

The general studied the plan then handed the device back to Yale. She turned it off and put it back in her bag. "It's a long shot but it could work," said Knox. "What will you do when you find her?"

Yale sighed. "I'll try to reason with her. If that doesn't work, I'll make her come back. By force if necessary." She glanced at her feet for a moment, and then looked back up at Knox. "I don't think it will come to that. Madison is with her. I don't know how she got the robot to agree to do this but I think I can reason with at least one of them. But if I can't . . ." her voice trailed off.

The general stood up. "We need that ship back. But more importantly, the Crownaxians cannot be allowed to capture it. They're way ahead of us technologically but we know that they don't have anything like the Sprint Drive engine. We're very close to perfecting it and if they get their hands on it before we do, we'll have lost the only advantage we have in this war." He took a deep breath and slowly let it out. "It's not easy for me to say this. I like the Sutters. They're a good family and an asset to the Union. But if it comes down to it, you must be prepared to destroy that ship."

Yale's eyes moistened. "I understand general," she said. "I

won't let you down again." They exchanged salutes and Knox dismissed her. Yale grabbed her duffel bag, turned and walked out of the office. As she headed toward the exit, she saw two guards coming toward her with Pam Sutter. Amy's mother looked exhausted. Her shoulders were slumped and her eyes were vacant. When they got close enough, Yale stepped in front of them.

The guards raised their pistols at Yale. The officer quickly put her hands up in protest. "Whoa, wait a minute," she said. "I just want to talk to Mrs. Sutter for a moment." Everyone around them was staring at the scene she was making. "C'mon guys, I'll keep it short." She slowly lowered her hands as she backed away from the guards. They looked at each other and nodded. Yale led Pam to a nearby chair and sat the mom down. The guards stood a few feet away from them with their hands still on their weapons.

Yale lightly placed her right hand on Pam's shoulder. "Mrs. Sutter, I know that this is an extremely difficult time for you and I know that you've been answering all sorts of questions but I need to ask you a few more." She paused to let Pam respond. The woman didn't. She just stared blankly ahead. Yale leaned forward and softly touched Pam's chin to get her attention. "Please look at me, Mrs. Sutter. This is very important."

Pam glared at her. "I don't know what I can tell you that you don't already know," she said. "I had no idea she was going to do this. Our home has been turned upside down by your soldiers. They ransacked Amy's room and took her computer. But they won't tell me what they've found. And they're guarding me like some common criminal."

"I'm sorry for all that," said Yale. "But they're just trying to find any information that could help us bring Amy back. Did she say or do anything unusual in the past few days?"

Pam sighed. "No, nothing. Like I told them already." She turned her head away and clenched her fists. Then she looked back at the officer. "But honestly, I hadn't been paying too much attention to her. I know how horrible that sounds but with my husband gone, I've just . . ." Pam broke down and started to weep. Yale gave her a comforting hug as the guards marched over to them.

"Your time is up, lieutenant," said one of them. Yale backed away as the men eased Pam to her feet. As they marched her toward Knox's office, Pam turned back and pleaded with Yale to bring Amy home. Yale nodded as Pam disappeared into the office and the door closed behind her.

The sun was beginning to rise as Yale walked across the compound toward the launch pad. The morning air was hot and the officer felt the increase in humidity. Her lungs were heavy and a slight dizziness plagued her as she marched forward on tired legs. Yale saw the doughy technician with bad teeth standing beside the *Justice*. The man barked orders to other soldiers as he read from a checklist on a mini-comp. He looked up and saluted when he saw Yale approaching.

"What's the status, corporal?" she asked. Yale dropped her bag at her feet and rubbed her forehead. Her eyes began to ache and she was fiercely hungry. The soldier gave her a quick rundown as two of his underlings finished their final inspection of the craft. "Very good. Am I cleared for takeoff?"

"Yes ma'am," said the soldier. "There are no other ships on radar." He waved his hand and the other soldiers moved away from the ship. Yale watched them leave as she picked up her bag. The corporal escorted her onboard and led her to the bridge. When they got there, Yale saw a flight suit and helmet sitting in the copilot's seat. "Will there be anything else?" asked the soldier, as Yale settled into the pilot's seat. She said no. Then he leaned down and grabbed her bag. "Ok. I'll just drop this off in your quarters on my way out. Good luck, lieutenant." He saluted her with his free hand, then turned and walked off the bridge. A few minutes later, Yale saw him depart the ship.

The lieutenant changed into the flight suit and put on the helmet. Then she turned on the communications system and announced that she was beginning the pre-flight preparations. A voice responded, telling her that she was a go for launch. Yale tested all the instruments on the console in front of her. Everything appeared normal. Then she ignited the engines and the ship began to roll forward. After a few seconds, Yale started the thrusters that pushed the ship upward. She eased the craft into her prearranged flight path and gradually increased her speed. In less than a minute, the *Justice* broke through the planet's atmosphere and plunged into the vacuum of space.

Chapter Five

The *Liberty Bell* cruised through space. Madison entered the bridge and found Amy at the helm, feeding numbers and equations into the ship's navigational computer. Her helmet lay on the floor beside her. The robot sat down in the copilot's chair and placed a mini-comp down on the console in front of it. "I finished my inventory." said Madison. Amy looked up at her friend. "There is no food on board but we do have three atomizers that can replicate edibles and water, just as the blueprints showed. However, we only have five blocks of ramcimite to keep the engines going. That should last us about five days if we conserve it." Amy nodded. "Do you have a flight path?" asked the robot.

The young girl looked at her calculations on the screen in front of her. She made a few adjustments then looked back up at her copilot. "There. I want to go this way," she said, pointing at the screen. Madison leaned over and examined the information. "It's a little out of the way but that should throw off any potential Union pursuers. And we should get there in about four days. Let's hope the ramcimite holds out."

Madison sat back down. "Do you plan to use the Sprint Drive?"

Amy shook her head. "I'd rather not. It never worked in the simulator and every field test was a disaster." Then she shrugged. "I guess we could try it in short bursts in an emergency. What do you think?"

The robot nodded. "The less we use it the better. Even if it doesn't blow us up, it would still be a major drain on our fuel supply." Madison began running a systems diagnostic on the main computer. Amy sat back in her chair and stretched her arms over her head. She yawned as she looked out at the stars whizzing by. "Are you tired, Captain?" asked Madison.

Amy's eyes widened. "Captain? I like the sound of that."

"For all intents and purposes, you are the captain of this ship now," said the robot, as it read the information on the display screen.

"You've earned the title."

"Earned it?" ask Amy. Her copilot nodded. "By starting a fire and stealing a secret military craft? I don't think I'd call that earning it." She watched her pal analyze the data. "What's the verdict?"

Madison pressed a button and the information printed on a piece of paper and slid out of a slot by the robot's right hand. "All systems running normally," it said, handing Amy the sheet. Then the robot pointed to two panels in front of them. "I rerouted all of the controls to these two terminals. The computer will run them unless you do a manual override."

"Excellent job, Madison," said the captain, examining the data on the printout before putting it down on the console in front of her. Then she picked up the photo of her father that she had taped to the flat surface beside the radar screen. Clayton was standing with four members of his graduating class in front of an Academy building. The men had their arms around each other and big smiles on their faces. Amy smiled at the worn image and wondered what he was thinking at that moment.

Madison spoke softly over the low hum of the engines. "I bet your father was an excellent student," it said. Amy replied with a tender yes and kept her eyes on the photo. "He's a very smart man and a good leader. That's why the Union chose him for his mission. If anyone can stay alive through this ordeal, it's him."

"I hope so," said Amy, putting the photo back. Then she stood up and sighed. "I'm hungry. I think I'll atomize a couple of hamburgers. Will you keep an eye on things for awhile?" she asked.

"Aye, aye, captain," said Madison, sliding over to the pilot's chair. Amy turned and walked toward the ladder at the back of the bridge that descended to the lower deck. She climbed down the steps and strolled toward the tiny kitchen area.

The captain strolled along the main corridor that branched off into smaller hallways. The passageway had 12-inch square, eye-level windows on the walls that were four feet apart. The soft carpet under Amy's feet smelled like fresh apples. She passed the hallway that led to the captain's quarters, which, she remembered from the blueprints, housed a single bed and two bureaus. The engine room lay beyond the ship's mess hall, and she could hear the efficient purr of the engines in the distance.

Amy then reached her destination. The ship's mess hall consisted of two small rectangular tables, four chairs, a refrigerator and a sink imbedded into one wall. The atomizer sat in the middle of the table farthest from the wall. The round device was 18 inches high, 12 inches wide and 30 inches deep. Several buttons were located on a gray panel on the front of the machine. Amy tapped the menu button and scrolled through the digital list that appeared on the flat monitor just above the buttons. She found the code for hamburgers and typed it in. Five seconds later, two hot burgers on toasty brown buns appeared on a plate inside the matter chamber. She took them out then atomized a glass of chocolate milk.

Amy sat at the table and ate her meal. After she finished, she put her trash in the disposal unit and started back toward the bridge. However, she stopped after a few steps, and then went back to the table. She scrolled through the menu on the atomizer again until she found what she was looking for. Amy typed in the code and watched the machine work again. This time she pulled out a small rectangular box with a lid on it. She opened the lid and examined the contents. She shook her head in amazement before closing the lid and moving back toward the bridge.

The robot was still in the pilot's seat when Amy sauntered over with the box in her hand. Madison turned around. "What do you have there?" it asked, rising from the chair.

Amy handed her friend the box. Madison opened it and picked up a plastic figurine. "It's a chess set," said Amy. "I thought it could help us pass the time. You do know how to play, right?" she asked.

"Of course," replied the robot. "I'm familiar with more than 1,000 human games. But it has been a while since I played chess." The robot put the piece back in the box and handed the box to Amy. Then it looked around the cramped bridge. "Where shall we play?"

"In the mess hall," said Amy, spinning around on her right foot. "C'mon, I'll race you there." She darted toward the ladder carrying the box under her right arm like a football. When she got to the steps, she turned and saw the robot leisurely walking toward her. "C'mon, slowpoke," she said, scurrying down the ladder. "I'm going to beat you."

Amy dashed toward the mess hall, rushed over to the first table and sat down. She waited with the game in front of her until Madison languidly appeared and walked over to an empty chair. "I prefer to conserve my energy," it said, sitting down. Amy opened the game and placed the board on the table. Madison picked up the white king. "Which color would you like to be?" asked the robot.

"I'll be black," Amy replied, grabbing her own game pieces. They set up the board and she made the first move. "Captains go first," she said. Madison nodded and countered her pawn's maneuver by moving a knight. They both played conservatively during the first game and Amy won by trapping Madison's king with her queen and a rook.

As they set up for the second game, Madison brought up a serious matter. "Captain, what is our plan once we reach Crownaxian space?" asked the robot. Amy kept her eyes on the board and took a deep breath. "We do have a plan, don't we?" asked Madison.

The girl nodded. "Our plan is to break into one of the Crownaxian installations and hack into their computer databases. I'm sure they keep records of their activities, like we do. We'll use that information to track down my dad and his friends and launch a rescue."

"How do we break into one of their buildings?" asked Madison. "And how can we read their data? It won't be in English." Madison picked up its king and lightly tapped the figure against the board.

Amy smiled. "You are good at linguistics," she replied. The robot nodded. "Once we get the data, I'm sure you will be able to decipher it." She cleared her throat. "As far as the breaking in, just leave that to me," she said.

They quietly started the next game. Madison won by taking Amy's king with a knight. "Alright, this one's for the championship of the entire universe," said Amy, as they started their third game. She moved first, and then watched Madison slide up a pawn.

Suddenly, an alarm blared from the bridge! As Amy and Madison scrambled to their feet, something slammed into the ship. The force of the blow knocked Amy to the floor, while Madison crashed into a wall. They struggled to keep their balance as more objects bombarded the *Liberty Bell*. Amy stumbled down the hallway and fought her way up the ladder to the bridge. She finally made her way to the pilot's seat. Madison then dropped into the copilot's chair beside her.

"We're getting hit by meteors!" yelled Amy. She turned on the thrusters and tried to steer through the onslaught of space rock. "What's our shield strength?" she asked.

Madison looked at a display screen. "We're down to 75%." Then another large rock hit the port side of the ship. The collision nearly knocked Amy out of her seat. "Now it's 70%. We've got to get out of here."

"Thanks for the tip," said Amy. "Why didn't the radar pick this up sooner?" she asked. Madison said that not everything onboard was fully functional since the ship wasn't supposed to be in space yet. Amy sighed and pushed the yoke to the left and tried to shoot through a gap between two large rocks. But the gap closed before they could get there, forcing Amy to fire the reverse thrusters.

Another rock slipped through a hole in the shielding and smashed into the ship's left wing. A terminal behind Madison exploded, sending up a shower of sparks that started a fire on the carpet. Madison hustled toward the back of the bridge and pulled a fire extinguisher out of a cupboard. The robot put out the small fire then returned to the copilot's seat. A red light flashed on a monitor. "Our weapons systems are down," said Madison.

Amy snarled. "They'll have to wait." She pushed hard on the yoke as the ship's right wing nearly clipped another meteor. However, the maneuver sent the *Liberty Bell* into a spin. "I can't pull up!" yelled Amy, as she saw that they were heading for a large rock beneath them. "Brace for impact!" She let go of the yoke and grabbed her helmet off of the floor. She slid it on just before the ship crashed into the rock.

The rock was thinner than it looked and shattered like a pane of glass as the *Liberty Bell* broke through it. The craft finally cleared the debris field a few minutes later and although the damage from the last collision was minimal, the ship's engines stopping working. Amy growled and looked over at her shipmate. "Are you alright?" she asked.

"I am fully functional," said Madison. "But our ship took quite a beating. We should assess the damages." The robot ran a ship-wide diagnostic from the terminal in front of it and a report printed out. Madison glanced at it before handing it to Amy.

The captain sighed again as she read the report. "It looks like we've got a lot of work to do," she said. "Let's start on the internal repairs. Getting the engines online is our top priority." The robot agreed and followed Amy to the engineering section of the ship on the lower level.

Madison removed an aluminum panel covering one of the engines and steam shot out of the enclosure. The robot laid the panel down and examined the mass of wires and computer components. Amy leaned in and shook her head. Several components were fused together. "Can we fix this?" she asked.

"I think so, but it might take an hour to do it," said Madison.

"Ok, let's get started." Amy walked over to a supply cabinet and pulled out two repair kits. She gave one to the robot and took the contents out of the other one. Madison did most of the work but Amy was able to help. She followed her friend's directions and they managed to complete the task in less than forty minutes. Then the duo spent the next hour making other repairs inside the ship.

"We should take a break," said Madison, as the robot reattached the panel covering the weapons console. "You need to rest before we begin repairing the outside of the ship." They sat down on the floor and leaned against the console. "Have you ever done a spacewalk?" asked the robot.

"No, but I was on this ride once on Earth that was sorta like the same thing," she replied. Madison gave her a skeptical look. "Really, it was. My parents took me to Space Castle in Virginia one summer during break. There was this ride where you went into this sphere and they sucked all the air and stuff out. Of course you had to wear an oxygen tank or you'd die." Amy closed her eyes for a moment and pictured that vacation in her mind.

When she opened her eyes, she saw Madison studying her face. "You are so lucky," said the robot. Amy just looked at her friend and wondered what the robot meant. "You have all these wonderful memories of your family. All the places you've visited, all the fun times you've had, and all the joy you've brought to each other. I have no such memories."

"Does that make you sad?" asked Amy.

"Sometimes. You see, I only have memories of being a servant. First to Dr. Greenland, then to the Union. But I never had any kind of childhood. I have always been an adult. Until I followed you on this mission, I'd never even broken any rules. And I've never had the chance to be part of a family." Madison folded its hands and rested them on its knees. "To be loved by someone the way your parents love you. That's very special."

"I know," said Amy, barely nodding. She put her hand on the robot's shoulder. "But I've always thought of you as a friend, so I guess that makes you part of my family."

The robot looked at her and smiled. "Thank you, Amy. That means a lot to me. If I could choose a family, I'd definitely choose yours." They remained quiet for a few minutes as Amy reflected on what they said. Then Madison stood up. "I guess we should continue."

Amy rose to her feet. "Yeah, we should. Gather up whatever tools you think we'll need. I'm going to put on a spacesuit. I'll meet you at the bay doors in ten minutes." Madison nodded and went over to the supply cabinet and began sorting through the instruments. Amy took a suit out of another cabinet and went to the captain's quarters to put it on.

The spacesuit was heavier than Amy had anticipated and she had some trouble getting into it. The polythermal material on the inside of the suit was coarse and itchy. The helmet was too big for her, so she had to pull the chinstraps extremely tight to keep it on her head. The straps dug into her skin and made it hard for her to move her mouth. Even the boots were too big. Amy wished the designers had kids in mind when they made the accessories. After struggling with the equipment for several minutes, Amy finally emerged from the captain's quarters. She met up with Madison at the bay doors. The robot had an odd smile on its face. "Not a word," said Amy. "I know how ridiculous I look," she grunted.

The robot tapped the top of Amy's helmet and it wobbled slightly on her head. "That's not supposed to happen," said Madison. "Are you sure your suit is on securely?" Madison scanned the suit with its eyes. "Even the smallest gap can be fatal." The robot spun Amy around and checked the rest of the apparel. The abrupt move nearly knocked the girl off her feet and she had to put her hand on her pal's shoulder to keep her balance.

Madison then checked her airtube before activating the oxygen tank at the back of the helmet. Amy heard the faint humming sound of the tiny motor and she felt the cold oxygen filter out and surround her face. "It's working," she said. "How much air do I have?"

"The tank is full. You have four hours' worth of oxygen." The robot picked up the enclosed toolbox and they entered the decompression chamber on the other side of the bay doors. Madison then attached a tether line to the front of Amy's suit and hooked the other end of the line to a metallic hoop on one of the bay doors. "This will keep you from floating away," it explained. Amy nodded, and then watched her friend connect another tether line to a loop attached to its right leg.

"Let me know when you're ready and I'll start it," said Amy. Madison double-checked the tether lines, and then nodded. "Alright, here goes." Amy flipped a switch and the inner bay doors closed. Then she pressed a button and the chamber began to decompress. Amy tried not to breathe too deeply but the sudden loss of pressure made her nervous and she found herself rapidly inhaling. Her visor began to fog.

"Take it easy," said Madison, laying a hand on her shoulder. Amy closed her eyes and slowed her breathing until she finally relaxed. She then snapped her eyes open and gave her friend a thumbs-up. Madison hooked a small line to the toolbox and attached the other end to its leg loop. "We're ready to go," said the robot.

Amy pressed a combination of buttons and the outer bay doors opened. Madison stepped out first and guided itself along the ship with its hands. Amy carefully followed but she had to fight the urge to vomit as her stomach began to churn from the eerie feeling of weightlessness. She looked up at a nearby star and momentarily lost her balance. The girl quickly grabbed onto the hull and regained her composure. Madison turned around and offered a hand. Amy waved it off and pointed to the damaged panel a few feet away from them. Madison turned back around and continued on, with Amy close behind.

Madison took a small drill out of the toolbox and began loosening the bolts on the first panel. Amy put the bolts in one of her outer pockets and zipped it closed, and then she watched in amazement as Madison's hands quickly repaired the damaged equipment.

The duo crawled across the hull and repaired 18 panels on the port side and 22 panels on the starboard side. The exhaustive work took more than two hours to complete. Although Amy knew all of the ship's specifications, the girl wasn't as adept at electronic repair as her friend, so Madison did most of the labor, while Amy assisted.

After they finished the last repair, Amy decided to have some fun. She rechecked her tether line then pushed herself away from the ship. Her body flew backwards until the line tightened and pulled her back toward the craft like a yo-yo. Amy smiled at the adrenaline rush and she pushed herself away again. Madison saw her and vehemently shook its head. The robot waved its right hand at her and pointed at the hull. The girl laughed it off and continued playing her game. She bounced back and forth two more times before Madison was able to reach her.

The robot tried to get her to sit still by gently grabbing hold of her arm and pulling her toward the hull. However, Amy slipped away from the robot and continued bouncing off the ship. Madison then pointed to the bay doors. Amy knew that her friend was telling her to go back inside the ship, but the girl was having too much fun. She pushed away again and let the line pull her back, laughing as she grabbed a handhold on the hull.

Suddenly a red light flashed on her suit and Amy began to choke! Madison hustled over to her. Amy pointed to her airtube where she saw the crack in the hose. The robot quickly pulled out the broken tube and replaced it with a spare one from the covered toolbox. Madison eased the girl toward the bay doors as she fought to regain her breath. The duo reentered the ship and Madison closed the outer doors behind them. The robot started the recompression sequence. After a few seconds, they were able to open the inner bay doors and walk further inside.

Amy ripped off her helmet and tossed it onto the floor. She continued to struggle for breath while Madison raced to a cabinet. The robot opened a door and took out a medical kit. Madison dug through the kit until it found a ventilator. Amy was bent over with her hands on her hips when her friend returned and put the plastic mask over her face. Madison turned on the unit and kept a hand on the girl's shoulder until Amy was able to breathe freely again. Then the girl stood up and pushed the mask off of her face.

The embarrassed youngster turned away from her pal and sat on the cold, hard floor. "I know what you're going to say, so you can save it," she barked. Madison stayed behind her. "You're right. I shouldn't have been fooling around out there. It was stupid." She kept quiet for a moment before turning around to face the robot. "I'm sorry. I was just trying to have some fun. I didn't realize what could happen."

The robot offered her a hand and pulled her to her feet. "As long as you're ok, that's all that really matters," said Madison. They started to walk toward the bridge. "I should run a diagnostic of the entire ship to make sure we didn't miss anything," said the robot, as they approached the ladder. Amy nodded and let her friend go first. Then she followed her copilot back to their seats. Madison sat down and began its task.

A few minutes later, the report printed out. Madison examined the data before handing the paper to the young girl. "Everything checks out," said Madison. "We can resume course on your command." Amy read the paper then handed back to the robot. "What are your orders, captain?"

Amy checked the radar screen and saw nothing unusual around them. "Fire up the engines," she said, sitting back in her chair. Madison typed in a command and the ship roared to life. "What is our shield strength?" The robot said that they were at full power. "Good. We'll follow our original plan. I hope that we don't run into any more surprises."

The captain hit the accelerator and the *Liberty Bell* flew forward. The yoke remained steady in her hand as Amy steered the ship back on course. She tried to remain calm but her heart raced as she realized how serious her mistake was. She began to wonder if their mission had any chance at all of succeeding with her in charge.

Chapter Six

Forty-eight hours later, Yale sat in the pilot's chair aboard the *Justice* and analyzed data from a long-range probe. The report showed traces of several ion trials in the region. The lieutenant used the ship's database to try to determine which trail belonged to the *Liberty Bell*. The process was much more difficult than Yale had imagined, mostly due to the swift-decaying rate of the ion trials. There were many technical factors to take into account as well, including the size of the ship, the purity of the ramcimite used and the influence of various gravitational forces in the area. Yale had only a basic understanding of the procedure, so, despite the computer's help, the complex calculations became extremely frustrating for her.

Annoyed with her lack of success, Yale decided to take a break after working for more than five hours on the project. The officer checked the radar and saw nothing threatening in the area. Then she ran a diagnostic scan on the entire ship. All systems were running normally. Yale deployed one more probe then headed for the ship's kitchen area.

Yale atomized a chicken sandwich and a tall glass of orange juice. She sat at the tiny table and ran the details of the ion trail scans through her mind as she ate her meal. The food was filling but it lacked an authentic taste to it. Most people grew accustomed to the texture of atomized foods but Yale never did. She had a strong sense of taste and could always tell the difference between real edibles and their artificial counterparts. She often grew depressed after these meals, their fraudulent fulfillment just reminded her how far away from Earth she was, which is why she ate so little and was always considered underweight during her annual physicals.

The officer threw her trash in the designated receptacle and walked back over to the bridge. She sat down in the pilot's chair and reviewed the confusing ion-trail data. Information from the last probe came in and provided new figures for her to analyze. Yale added these figures to the database but they failed to shed any new light on her problem. She was beginning to think that she would never find the *Liberty Bell*.

A loud beeping sound drew her attention to the communications console. Yale pressed a button and heard a distress call come over the loudspeaker. It was so garbled that Yale could not decipher what it said. A chill ran up her spine as she wondered if the *Liberty Bell* was in trouble. However, the sound of a man's voice allayed that fear as Yale adjusted the ship's receiver and the transmission became clear.

Yale listened intently to sounds of the frantic message. "To anyone who can hear me, my name is David Zigler." The anxiety in his voice was so palatable it made Yale quiver. She clenched her fists as the words poured of the speaker. "I'm a Union diplomat from the starship *Harmony*. Crownaxian warships attacked my ship. I've been in this escape pod for several days. I'm nearly out of water, food and power. Please help me!" The message repeated again and again as Yale nervously scanned the area for the pod.

It took a few minutes but Yale finally located the tiny craft. It was nearly 650,000 miles away. The officer set a course for the pod and activated the autopilot. At top speed, it would take the *Justice* about two hours to reach the stranded diplomat. Yale then prepared a brief status report for Gen. Knox, outlining all that had happened thus far. She read it over twice, and then sent it by email to her superior officer using a Union-coded carrier wave.

The waiting was the worst part. Yale busied herself in order to ease her mind. She took a medical kit out of a supply closet and brought it over to the inner bay doors on the lower level of the ship. Then she went back to the kitchen area and atomized some food and water for her passenger, which she stored in a small refrigerator. As she sat on the chair and yawned, she realized that she hadn't slept in over 20 hours. Despite her worry over Zigler's condition, the officer knew that she needed to get some sleep.

Yale dragged herself over to the captain's quarters. The *Justice* was still an hour away from the pod, so Yale set an alarm to go off in 45 minutes. Then she plopped down on the small cot and wrapped her arms around the lumpy pillow. Her eyes were red and dry from reading so much data and it felt good to finally close them. Her breathing gradually deepened and she dozed off in just a few minutes.

A fowl stench filled the air as Yale opened the pod door. Steam from the burned out consoles leapt at her face. Then she gazed in horror at the sight of the two decomposing bodies leaning back against the bloodstained seats. The officer stumbled forward and pulled the smaller body toward her. She screamed when she saw the rotting flesh on the young girl's face. "No, no," she said running her fingers along the brittle brown hair that ran down to the girl's shoulder. "How did you get here? You're not supposed to be here!" She then looked over at Zigler's corpse and tried to figure out how Amy Sutter could possibly be aboard this pod.

Yale spun around when she heard a creaking sound behind her. There stood a six-foot figure with a laser rifle in its hand. The black visor on its helmet obscured the intruder's face. The creature quickly raised its weapon and fired. The concussion knocked Yale onto her back. A burning pain seared through her chest. She tried to speak but the intruder fired again, hitting Yale on the chin and she slammed her head against the floor.

The blaring alarm brought an end to the officer's nightmare. She reached over to the digital clock in the wall and pressed a button. The alarm ceased. Yale sat up and wrapped her arms around her thin frame. She rocked herself back and forth on the cot to calm her frayed nerves. After a while, she was able to stand. She stretched her aching arms over her head and drifted toward the sink on the other side of the room.

Yale turned on the water and splashed her face with the cool liquid. She looked at the mirror above the sink and saw how disheveled she was. A puffy purple circle swelled under her ruddy eyes and lumpy locks of her hair stood up on the left side of her head. She took a deep breath and noticed the pungent smell of her sweaty uniform. The lieutenant craved a hot shower but she knew she didn't have time for one. Instead, she wet her hair and tried to smooth out the strands with her fingers. Then she opened the mirror door and found a sealed toothbrush and an unopened package of toothpaste. She vigorously brushed her teeth and rinsed out her mouth.

Yale returned to the bridge and checked the radar. The pod drifted a few hundred miles since the last reading, so Yale readjusted her ship's heading. The officer did another long-range scan and saw that there were still no other ships in the area. After the *Justice* got a little closer, Yale sent a message to the pod. There was no response. She then scanned the little craft and the computer detected one faint lifesign on board. Yale wondered if she would get to Zigler before it was too late.

The *Justice* finally reached the coordinates and Yale eased the ship next to the drifting pod. She then initiated the laser grapnels that pulled the pod to a stop. Next came the docking clamps that lined up the bay doors of both crafts. After that was secure, Yale took a spacesuit out of a cabinet on the bridge and put it on. Then she hustled down to the inner bay doors.

The decompression sequence went smoothly and Yale was quickly aboard the small pod. Steam from overloaded consoles filled the single room and eerily reminded her of her nightmare. She shook off the bad feeling and moved swiftly to the lone seat in the craft. There she found Zigler's limp body in a chair. His head lay against his right shoulder and Yale could see that he was unconscious, but his spacesuit was intact. She took out a mini-comp and read his vital signs. The man was close to death and Yale knew that the next few minutes would be crucial.

The lieutenant unbuckled Zigler's seatbelt and carefully lifted him up. She slipped her arms under his shoulders and hoisted him onto her back. Then she cautiously stepped toward the exit, squatting close to the floor to avoid bumping his head against the ceiling. The weight of his body bore down on her and she struggled to maintain her balance. Her chest tightened as she labored to breathe. Each step strained her legs and back, and she felt like she was pulling a boulder behind her.

Yale was only a few feet away from the door when her left foot bumped into a fallen storage crate and she crashed to the hard floor. She landed on her side and Zigler's body tumbled down on top of her, pinning her against a console. The man's right arm was lodged against her chin and pressing against the side of her throat. She pushed up several times with all her might but the weight of her spacesuit negated her efforts and she wasn't able to lift him off of her. Panic ran through her as she thought about their limited air supply. Then she forced herself to calm down.

The officer managed to roll onto her back but then she was too exhausted to do anything else. Her heavy breathing made her dizzy and she felt a queasy churning in her stomach. The bile then raced up her throat. She held her breath and tightened her fists as she fought the impulse to vomit. The repulsive feeling soon subsided and Yale looked around her for anything that could help her lift up Zigler's body.

She rolled her aching head around until she spotted a broken pipe to the right of her. Yale stretched her arm out to reach it but she was only able to touch the thin copper tube with the top of her fingers. Slowly she began to drag the pipe toward her with her fingertips. Her eyes burned as sweat dripped down from her forehead. The pain in her temples increased, causing her to clench her teeth together. She let out a scream as she forced the pipe into her outstretched palm.

Once she was able to get her thumb around it, Yale slid the pipe under Zigler's body. She pushed up again, using the tool as a lever. The body rose slightly and Yale tried to slither out but the pipe slipped and his body flopped back down onto her. She let out another scream, this one filled with pure rage. However, her adrenaline began to pump through her and she felt the strength to try again. She grabbed the pipe and thrust it under the heavy body. Pushing with everything she had, Yale managed to lift the man up high enough to pull her legs out. She rolled onto her stomach and dropped the pipe as Zigler's body thumped back down onto the floor.

It took a few minutes for Yale to regain her composure. She slowly drove herself to her hands and knees and she crawled over to the fallen diplomat. Zigler lay face down so Yale gingerly rolled him onto his back. His eyelids shook and his lips trembled slightly. Yale found the mini-comp on the floor by the man's feet and she scooped it up. She used the machine to check his vital signs again. Amazingly, they were no worse than before but he still needed immediate medical attention. Not wanting to repeat her mistake, Yale cleared a path to the door before picking him up again.

Once aboard the *Justice*, the lieutenant eased Zigler to the floor and began the recompression sequence. Then she opened the inner bay doors and grabbed the medical kit before slowly carrying the injured man to the captain's quarters. She carefully placed him onto the cot. After catching her breath, she removed her helmet, opened the medical kit and took out a syringe. She filled the sharp instrument with a clear fluid from a tiny bottle then plunged the needle into his right arm. She wiped the puncture hole with an antiseptic then put a small bandage on the spot.

Yale sat on the edge of the bed for twenty minutes to see if the medicine was helping him. She scanned him again with the mini-comp and saw that his vital signs were improving. Zigler began to breathe easier and his high temperature lowered. He rolled his head a little and mumbled a few incomprehensible words as he slept. Yale realized that there was nothing else she could do for him at the moment, so she covered him with a blanket and headed back to the bridge.

The lieutenant disengaged the laser grapnels and the docking clamps and waited for the pod to drift a few hundred feet away from the *Justice*. When the pod reached that safe distance, Yale fired a missile at the tiny craft and watched it blow up in a fiery explosion. The debris floated toward a nearby planet and burned up in that planet's atmosphere. Normally, a full search of the craft would have been performed first, but Yale knew there wasn't time, and she suspected that Zigler would have kept anything important close to him. She didn't find anything near him when she entered the pod, so she felt safe with her decision. She then input the original set of coordinates into the ship's navigational system and restarted the autopilot. The *Justice* resumed its pursuit course as Yale went back to the captain's quarters to check on Zigler.

The officer pulled up a chair and sat close to the cot. Zigler was still asleep and continued to mumble incoherently from time to time. Then forty minutes later, his eyes popped open and he rolled his head from side to side. When he spotted Yale, he pressed his lips together before speaking. "Where am I?" he asked. His voice was weak but he managed to sit up by himself.

"Take it easy," said Yale, as she leaned over and tried to steady him. "Mr. Zigler, my name is Lt. Yale Brown. I'm stationed at Paldor under the command of Gen. Knox." The man looked at her with clearer eyes and appeared to recognize her. "You're aboard the *Justice*. You're safe now."

"You found my pod?" he asked.

Yale nodded. "Yes, I picked up your distress call and followed it to your location. Once I got you on board, I destroyed the pod to keep the Crownaxians from getting it." The man pulled up the blanket with his trembling hands. "You're still a bit feverish but that shouldn't last much longer. I gave you 20cc's of Boltrimin, so you should feel better soon." The man nodded and lay back down on the cot. Yale guided his head to the pillow. "Can I get you anything?" she asked.

"Some water, please," he replied. Yale smiled and told him she'd be right back. She hustled to the kitchen area and grabbed the pitcher of water she atomized earlier. The officer then took two cups out from a cupboard before heading back to the captain's quarters. Zigler smiled when she approached him. Yale helped him sit up again before she poured his drink. The man eagerly drank the water as Yale removed a recorder from a drawer in a nearby bureau.

"I need to ask you a few questions," she said as she sat back down in the chair. The diplomat nodded. Yale turned on the recorder. "This is Lt. Yale Brown interviewing the honorable David Zigler, diplomat for the Union Defense. Mr. Zigler, please start at the beginning and tell me what happened on the day the *Harmony* was attacked by the Crownaxians." She leaned the recorder toward Zigler and he began recalling the events.

The diplomat said that the *Harmony* reached the rendezvous point on time and the Crownaxian science ship was waiting for them. The *Harmony* tried to contact the ship but got no response. Suddenly, two Crownaxian destroyers emerged from a nearby nebula and fired missiles at the human ship. The *Harmony* fired back but was unable to defend itself. The crew quickly headed for the escape pods as Crownaxian soldiers boarded the ship and fired their laser rifles.

"Do you know how many got away?" asked Yale.

Zigler shook his head. "I saw a few pods launch before mine but everything was happening so fast, it's hard to say." He finished the water in his cup and handed it to Yale. "May I please have some more?" he asked.

"Of course," said Yale, putting down the recorder. She refilled his cup and handed it back to him. Then she restarted the recorder. "Do you remember who was still on board when you left?" she asked.

"No, there was so much confusion. I just don't know."

Yale took a deep breath, dreading her next question. "Did you see any casualties?" she asked, tightening her grip on the recorder.

The man's eyes began to water. "I saw Kalowski go down as he was heading toward engineering. A Crow shot him in the back. Evans was hit in the shoulder by a laser blast as he was defending the bridge. I don't know what happened to him." He turned his head away and wiped his eyes with the back of his hand. "Sutter was hit too, in the chest."

Yale's eyes widened. "Sutter? Clayton Sutter?" she asked.

"Yeah, that's right," said Zigler, his voice cracking. "I was one of the men he was leading toward the back of the ship. Two Crows appeared in the hallway and shot at us. Clayton went down right in front of me. But I got away. I got to a pod while they were still firing at us."

Yale looked down at the floor and tried not to cry. She wondered if Amy's enormous efforts were in vain. Then she lifted her eyes up and continued. "Did you get a good look at the Crownaxian soldiers?" she asked. "Can you describe them?"

Zigler shook his head. "I never saw their faces. They wore helmets with dark visors. The best I can tell you is that they're far taller than we are. I'd guess about 7 feet tall. They appeared to be humanoid, with two arms and legs, and they were expert marksmen. I'd never seen so few missed shots." He took a deep breath. "They were all over us, lieutenant. We never had a chance."

The exhausted man began to shiver. Yale turned off the recorder and compassionately patted Zigler's left shoulder. "Try to get some rest," she said, standing up. "If you think of anything else, we can go over it later. I'm going to the bridge for a while but I'll check on you in a bit."

"Wait, I have a question for you," said Zigler as Yale turned to walk away. She spun back around and he motioned toward her chair. Yale nodded and sat back down with her arms folded across her chest. Zigler leaned forward with a quizzical look on his face. "I don't see anyone else onboard the ship," he said. "What are you doing out here all by yourself?"

Yale lowered her arms and rested them on her legs. "Well, after we learned about the attack on the *Harmony*, Gen. Knox refused to allow any ships into this sector to help you." Zigler's eyes widened.

Yale nodded. "Believe me, it wasn't a popular decision. But I guess he didn't want to risk any more casualties. However, one of your crewmates' relatives decided to take matters into her own hands."

"What do you mean?" asked Zigler.

Yale sighed. "As crazy as it sounds, Clayton Sutter's daughter Amy stole the *Liberty Bell* and flew the ship in this direction." An odd smile crept across Zigler's face. Then he suddenly began to laugh. Yale's face reddened and she knew that she too would be laughing if this weren't her fault.

"Let me get this straight," said the man, as he leaned back against the cot and wiped his eyes again. "A child stole the Union's top secret weapon and got away from our military's best soldiers?" He shook his head in disbelief. "How did she manage to do that?"

"She is a very crafty child," replied Yale. "And since the incident happened while I was on duty, Gen. Knox sent me out here to bring that ship back. Which I have every intention of doing." The officer watched the diplomat's face as all this sunk in. "That said, there's something you need to understand." Zigler's smile faded as Yale paused. "Despite your injuries, I cannot take you back to Paldor until my mission is completed."

The diplomat nodded. "And you're wondering if my unexpected presence onboard will jeopardize your mission." Yale didn't respond. "Don't worry about me, lieutenant. I'll stay out of your way," he said, laying his arms across his chest.

Yale rose and slid the chair against the near wall. "I will do whatever I can to protect you Mr. Zigler, but I'm sure you understand how dangerous this mission is." She turned and faced the man. "Even when I do find the *Liberty Bell*, it won't be easy to convince Amy to turn back. And we will probably encounter some Crows while we're out here." Zigler swallowed hard and nodded. "All we can do is hope for the best."

The lieutenant left without saying another word. She made her way to the bridge and began another long-range scan. There were still no other ships in the area. Yale wondered if she should set a different course but she decided not to. The last thing she wanted to do was second-guess herself. Nor did she want to crisscross the region of space and fall even further behind her prey. She knew where Amy was going. It would be best to keep pursuing her and hope that something would slow the *Liberty Bell* down.

A few hours hour later, Yale decided to file another report with Gen. Knox. She began the report with the details from Zigler's debriefing. She also described his general health and mental condition. Then she noted her ship's position and the routine facts about the *Justice's* performance. The engines were running at peak efficiency and the long-range scanners were compiling useful data about the planets and stars in this region.

She was double-checking the data when a proximity alarm suddenly blared. Yale put the report aside and glared at the radar screen. Her eyes widened and her pulse raced when she saw the ship. The officer flipped a switch and spoke into a microphone on the console in front of her. "Mr. Zigler, if you're up to it, I'd like you to come to the bridge." After a slight pause she heard him say his was on his way.

The man hobbled into the room and stood behind Yale. "What is it, lieutenant?" he asked, peering over her shoulder at the radar screen.

Yale pointed at a glowing shape on the screen and smiled. "I found the *Liberty Bell*," she said. "They're 300,000 miles ahead of us."

Chapter Seven

Amy scrambled to the pilot's chair as the alarm blared. Madison sat down beside her and looked at the radar screen. The captain raised her head and sighed. "It's a Union ship and it's closing fast." She typed a command on the keyboard in front of her. "Two life signs onboard. Both human." A flashing light on the console to her right drew her attention. "We have an incoming message." She took a deep breath and nervously tapped her fingers against the console before pressing a button on the communications board.

"*Liberty Bell*, this is the Union ship *Justice*. Please respond." Amy's eyes widened as she recognized the voice. "*Liberty Bell*, come in."

Amy put on her helmet and tightened the chinstrap. She wrapped her fingers around the yoke and pushed on the accelerator. The *Liberty Bell* darted forward as it gained speed. The girl glanced over at the radar screen and saw the *Justice* fall behind. Then the captain flipped the switch for the microphone. "This is the *Liberty Bell*. If you want me Yale, you're going to have to catch me."

"This isn't a game, Amy," replied Yale. The voice crackled over the loudspeaker. "We're in a dangerous part of space and we need to get back to Paldor before we run into any Crows."

"You're right," replied Amy. "*You* do need to go home." The captain glanced at her copilot. "I'm checking the long-range scanners. We need to find a place to hide." She steered the ship hard to the left and examined the area in front of them. She looked past the onslaught of stars and asteroids until she spotted a tight cluster of small planets on their port side. A fat moon shaded the smallest planet. Amy scanned the celestial body and the readings indicated a large amount of thick gasses along the surface. "Look over there," she said, pointing to the target. "That could work."

"If we see it, can't Yale see it too?" asked Madison, leaning forward to get a better look. "She'll just follow us in."

Amy shook her head. "Not if she can't see us in that soupy

mess." The captain began pressing more buttons and the ship's systems gradually shut down. "We already have enough momentum to get there," she said, as the engines stopped working. "I'll glide us into the planet's atmosphere on minimal lifesupport and we'll wait for her to pass over us."

The *Liberty Bell* slithered toward the planet, then began to shake as the gravitational pull dragged the ship downward. Amy held onto the yoke and steered the craft toward a large landmass below them. Then she quickly restarted the engines to smooth out the descent. Out of the corner of her eye, she saw Madison brace for impact. She snickered at the robot's lack of faith in her and she loosened the strap under her chin.

"Relax," said Amy. "We're not even going to land." She guided the ship toward a gap between two mountain peaks, then she eased the craft to a stop and they hovered over a barren valley below them. The captain checked the radar and saw no sign of her pursuer. "She'll never find us now. All we have to do is wait awhile and then we'll head back out into space."

Suddenly the proximity alarm went off again. Amy stared in disbelief as the *Justice* appeared on the radar screen. "Ah, you were saying," said Madison. Amy shook her head in frustration before she gunned the engine. The *Liberty Bell* dashed forward as Amy restarted all the secondary systems. Madison gave her a concerned look after she powered up the ship's weapons systems. "Why are you doing that?" asked the robot.

"We have to be prepared for anything," she replied. Amy steered the craft upward toward the planet's atmosphere when she saw the *Justice* close in on her ship from above. The two starships nearly collided as Amy deliberately cut off her stalker, passing just a few hundred feet beneath the *Justice* before roaring up in front of it. The maneuver caused the *Justice* to spin out of control toward the planet's surface for a few seconds until Yale straightened out the craft.

"What are you doing?" screamed Yale over the loudspeaker. "Are you trying to kill us all?" Amy turned off the speaker and glared at Madison, who had an uncharacteristically frightened looked on its face. Amy eased her grip on the yoke after the *Liberty Bell* broke free of the planet's gravitational pull. A sea of blackness surrounded them as they moved deeper into space but the *Justice* was right behind them. Amy bit her bottom lip and tried to think of a way to get Yale off of her back.

"Do you want me to prepare the Sprint Drive?" asked Madison. The robot reached for the keyboard in front of it, keeping its hands just above the plastic buttons. Amy considered the idea then shook her head. Madison sat back in its chair. "What is your plan?"

Amy shrugged. "I don't have one yet." She looked at the radar and saw the *Justice* gaining on them. "We can't keep up this cat and mouse game, that's for sure. We need to find a way to stop her long enough for us to get away." She glanced at the controls for the weapons then peered up at her copilot. "We don't have any choice," she said.

Madison quickly stood up. "Wait," said the robot. "Think carefully about what you are doing. Yale is in that ship." The robot paused. "Do you think she would fire at us?" The robot sat back down but kept its eyes on Amy.

"We don't have any choice," repeated the captain. Her face filled with a crimson glow. "I won't let anything or anyone get in the way of this mission." Madison nodded and Amy hoped that the robot realized how difficult this decision was for her.

Amy steered hard to the left and flew in a tight circle until she brought the *Liberty Bell* in behind the *Justice*. Then she took a deep breath and fired two missiles at the *Justice's* main engine. They hit their target and Amy sighed as she watched the dreadful explosions.

The captain slowed down the *Liberty Bell* and flipped the switch for the communications board. "*Justice*, this is the *Liberty Bell*. Yale, I'm sorry I had to do that," said Amy. She scanned the ship and saw that the damage was limited to the engine room. "You shouldn't have more than a day's worth of repairs. I'm sending out a distress beacon. Maybe you'll get lucky and a passing freighter will be able to help you." She nodded toward Madison and the robot launched the probe by typing in the commands on the keyboard in front of it.

The loudspeaker crackled again. "Amy, are you crazy?" screamed Yale. "Not only did you destroy Union property on Paldor and steal a Union starship, but you've added assaulting a Union ship to your list of offenses." Amy looked at Madison and the robot dropped its head. "I am going to bring you in, Amy," said Yale. "You can count on it. I just hope you live long enough to face your charges."

Amy turned off the speaker and sighed. "Not until I bring my father home," she said, softly. Then she patted Madison on the shoulder. "C'mon, we've got a job to do. Try to stay positive." The robot nodded and asked her what her orders were. "Same as before. And let's hope the worst is behind us." She pressed on the accelerator and steered the *Liberty Bell* back onto their original course. The *Justice* soon fell off the radar screen and Amy couldn't help but wonder if she would ever see Paldor again.

Chapter Eight

Steam shot out from a panel when Yale pried it open with a crowbar but the lieutenant ducked away quickly enough to avoid serious burns to her hands and face. She glanced over at Zigler, who stood a few feet away from her with a bandage on his forehead. The gash had stopped bleeding but the swelling had not subsided. The dazed man peered at the tangled mess of wires, coils and cables inside the panel and shook his head. Yale reached into the toolbox by her left foot and took out an equipment scanner. She used it to examine the damage to the apparatus that housed the main power relays to the ship's engines. The readings on the scanner were discouraging but not surprising. Yale turned off the scanner and put it back in the toolbox.

"How bad is it, lieutenant?" asked Zigler.

The officer put her hands on her hips. "Very bad," she said. "Sixteen wires are burned out and five coils have fused together. This is the fourth panel that needs to be fixed and we don't have a lot of spare parts on board. I'll probably have to pull some components from other sections of the ship."

Zigler lowered his eyebrows. "Can't you just atomize whatever parts you need?" he asked, as he inched closer to the open panel.

Yale shook her head. "The atomizer can't duplicate materials this complex. The basic components, maybe, but not the intricate microprocessors in them." She rubbed her eyes with the back of her left hand. "That thing can't even create a decent cheeseburger. I guess I can pull some parts from the communication's console. That's the least important system we have onboard right now." She grabbed the toolbox and started toward the bridge. "C'mon, I'm going to need your help," she said.

"Ah, help with what?" asked Zigler as he hustled up next to her.

"Help with the repairs, of course." Zigler stopped and pressed his lips together. Yale stopped too and titled her head to one side. "Is there a problem, Mr. Zigler?" she asked.

The man's face reddened. "I hate to admit this, lieutenant, but I don't know the first thing about mechanical engineering. That's one reason I became a diplomat. I couldn't pass those courses at the academy."

"I see," replied Yale with a slight smile. "Well, I'll talk you through the hard parts but I can't do all of this alone. I need a second set of hands and, as you pointed out earlier, there isn't anyone else onboard." She reached out her hand and he grudgingly took hold of it. "Trust me, it won't be that bad. Just follow my lead and we'll be fine." She let go of his hand as he began to move again and Yale led the way to the bridge.

The duo spent the next three hours removing nonessential parts from the communication system and installing them in the first two damaged panels for the propulsion drive. The work was exhaustive and tedious, and Yale saw that Zigler needed a break. His hands kept shaking and his breathing was labored. The officer didn't want to burn him out so she told him to meet her in the ship's kitchen area. When she arrived there ten minutes later, she found Zigler fast asleep at the table. His head lay on his arms and his chest slowly rose and fell.

Yale softly shook the man's shoulders to wake him up. "Mr. Zigler, you need to get something to eat," she whispered. He slowly raised his head and looked around as if trying to get his bearings. Yale went over to the small refrigerator and took out the food she had atomized earlier. She brought over a container of chicken and placed it on the table in front of the man. "Eat this," she said. "You'll feel better."

Zigler picked up a thigh and bit into the cold meat. "Hey, that's pretty good," he said, swallowing it. "Thank you lieutenant." She smiled as she carried two glasses of water over and placed them on the table as well. Then she sat down and grabbed a drumstick for herself. She bit into it and felt the familiar disappointment she had with fabricated food. "How much longer do you think the repairs will take?" asked Zigler.

Yale shrugged. "At least another six hours," she said. The man sighed and Yale nodded in agreement. "I hate doing this kind of work too but what choice do we have? We'll just have to muddle through."

The diplomat finished his first piece of chicken and started eating another one. "I guess I should be thankful," he said. "I'm lucky that you were able to find me at all. I don't know how much longer I could have survived in that pod. I'm sorry I can't be more helpful with the repairs."

"You're doing fine," said Yale. "Considering all you've been through, it's pretty amazing that you can function at all." She raised her glass. "Here's to the remarkable spirit of man." She tapped Zigler's glass then took a long drink. For the first time since this mission started, Yale actually felt relaxed. And she was glad to have someone to talk to. "So what else made you want to become a diplomat, Mr. Zigler?" she asked.

The man put down his glass and appeared to ponder the question. "I guess I just wanted to help people," he said. Yale laughed. "I know, sounds kind of corny but it's true. Growing up, I was always the one everyone came to with their problems. For a while I thought I wanted to be a psychiatrist but I didn't want to be stuck in a stuffy office all day. I wanted to travel, especially in space. So I joined the academy and studied politics and communications. I graduated and worked my way up until I was offered a job as a diplomat."

They ate in silence for the rest of their meal. Then Zigler sat back in his chair with his hands behind his head. "What about you lieutenant, why did you choose the military?" he asked. The man smiled warmly at the officer.

Yale blushed as she took another sip of water. She was never comfortable talking about herself. It just wasn't done in her father's household. The lieutenant shrugged as she put the cup down. "Same reason, I guess," she said. "To help people. Our people. To put an end to this crazy war." She thought of her parents and her sisters and wondered how worried they were about her. "I was a financial advisor before the war started. When the economy was still good and people had money to invest. I didn't really think much about people then; they were just clients and a way to make some money. But then Blaros was attacked and suddenly money didn't mean that much to me anymore."

"So you enlisted?" asked Zigler.

"Yeah, just like that," said Yale. "I went through an accelerated academy program for college graduates and found myself assigned to Paldor as a security officer. I've been there ever since."

"Have you seen much action?"

Yale nodded. "I've been in a few skirmishes with the Crows while on patrol duties." She took a deep breath and lowered her eyes for a moment. "I've seen some exceptional soldiers give their lives for the Union. It scares me sometimes. Knowing that it could have been me." Yale's eyes welled up and she wiped them with the back of her left hand. She glanced at Zigler, whose smile was replaced by an awkward grimace. Yale stood up and grabbed her cup. "We should get back to the repairs," she said, putting her cup in the dish disposal unit by the sink. Zigler quietly did the same with the food container and his cup before he followed Yale to the engine room.

They didn't speak much during the next hour. Instead, they focused on the work at hand, which was just as grueling and tedious as it had been before. Yale noticed that Zigler was improving with each task and she made a point of telling him so. He graciously thanked her but said little more. The duo was finishing the repairs on one panel when an alarm suddenly blared on the bridge. Yale dropped her tools and raced to the bridge, with Zigler close behind her. Her face whitened when she looked at the radar screen.

"What is it lieutenant?" asked Zigler, eyeing the screen.

Two large ships were approaching at high speed. Yale immediately recognized their unique shapes and designs. She turned to Zigler and spoke with a palatable urgency. "You need to find a place to hide," she said.

Zigler's eyes widened. "Hide? From what?" he asked. Then he looked back at the radar screen. "They're Crows aren't they?" Yale nodded. "Why don't we use the escape pods?" he asked.

Yale shook her head. "The *Justice* doesn't have escape pods. But they wouldn't help us anyway, the Crows would just fire on them." Yale typed a command into the computer and examined the *Justice's* weapons. "We don't have enough firepower to defend ourselves." Then she typed in another command and looked up at Zigler. "We are going to be boarded."

"How long 'till they get here?" asked Zigler.

"About three minutes," said Yale. She hurried over to a small arms locker at the back of the bridge and opened the cabinet door. Then she took out two laser pistols and a holster. She wrapped the holster around her waist and put the pistols in the holders. The lieutenant then grabbed another pistol and hustled over to Zigler. "Take this," she said, shoving the weapon into his right hand. "You'll need it."

Zigler looked at the weapon and held it gently in his shaking hand. "I've never fired a pistol before," he said. Yale sighed then showed him how to unlock the safety catch and fire the weapon. The man swallowed nervously and wiped sweat from his head with his free hand. His breathing was shallow again and he looked like he might pass out.

Yale put her right hand on his shoulder. "You need to calm down and stay focused, Mr. Zigler," she said. "Go to the back of the ship and find a place to hide. Don't make a sound and don't fire until you absolutely have to. They might leave without finding you."

"Not find me? Won't they scan the ship for lifesigns?" he asked.

Yale nodded. "Yeah, they will. But I sent out a signal to jam their scanners. It's worked before and I think it will work again. You've got to trust me. Hide somewhere and don't come out." She gently pushed him toward the bridge's exit. "Go now!" she yelled.

The officer watched him scamper toward the back of the ship with the pistol in his hand. She said a quick, quiet prayer before pulling a cabinet away from one wall and moving it to the bridge entrance. Then she sent out a distress call on a Union frequency that she hoped the Crows hadn't discovered yet. Finally, she sat in the captain's chair and typed in the commands that loaded the few missiles onboard into their firing tubes. Using the radar to guide her, Yale launched two of them. They hit their targets but both Crownaxian ships were heavily shielded and suffered no damage. Not giving up, Yale continued firing in pairs until there were no more missiles to launch. However, her efforts yielded no positive results.

Suddenly the *Justice* shook violently as several Crownaxian missiles struck the outer hull. The shields held but Yale knew they wouldn't last for very long. More missiles hit, causing consoles around the lieutenant to explode. She ducked under one console and kept her hands over her head. Then the concussions stopped. Yale sat up with her hands close to the holster as she realized that the Crows were getting ready to board the ship. She thought of her family again and tried to steady her quivering jaw.

To Yale's surprise, the communication's light began to flash. The officer instinctively reached over and pressed the button on the board. A gravelly voice came over the loudspeaker. "We've scanned your ship. You have no missiles left. Prepare to be boarded." Yale was surprised to hear the Crownaxian speak English. She checked her pistols again to make sure they were at full power. Then she hid behind the cabinet and waited for the invaders to arrive.

The *Justice* shook again as one of the Crownaxian ships docked with it. A few minutes later, the lieutenant heard footsteps as the soldiers marched through the ship. Laserfire then echoed off of the metallic walls. Yale cringed and hoped that Zigler was able to evade the intruders. Then her heart raced as she heard the troops approaching the bridge. Yale leaned to the right of the cabinet and aimed her pistol at the partially blocked entrance. A dark, helmeted figure appeared at the doorway. It was wearing a light green uniform and holding a laser rifle in its hand. Behind it, several similarly dressed warriors approached. They all held rifles in their hands and they swung them around as they looked for their prey.

Yale fired her weapon and hit the first solider in the chest, knocking him onto his back. His comrades returned fire and forced Yale to hide behind the cabinet. She fired back when she could but she realized that they would eventually get her. After several minutes of exchanged shots, the fighting suddenly ceased. Yale tried to control her breathing as she peeked around the cabinet to see what the Crownaxians were doing. However, the smoke and mist from the wrecked machinery around her made it difficult to see. She covered her mouth with her free hand as she tried not to cough.

One of the soldiers shouted to her. "We've lost one of our brothers. We don't want to lose another. Drop your weapon and we can end this right now. You know you can't escape and we don't want to kill you." Yale wondered if this was just a ploy to draw her out. "We already have the other human. So you have to choose: Fight and die or surrender and live. You have ten seconds to decide."

"How do I know you have him?" she shouted back. She heard them speak to each other in what she assumed was their native language. It sounded to Yale like a bizarre mixture of Russian and French. Some of the words were throaty and gruff, while others were lyrical and smooth. Footsteps echoed again and she heard Zigler's terrified voice as he struggled against his captors.

"Do as he says, lieutenant," pleaded Zigler. "It's our only hope." He started to say something else but his voice was suddenly muffled. Yale heard him struggle and she felt guilty for leaving him out there on his own. She looked around the damaged room for anything that might help her rescue the diplomat, but there was only shorted-out machinery and burned equipment around her. She shook her head and realized that she was beaten.

Yale slowly stepped away from the cabinet with her hands over her head. "You win," she shouted. The soldiers pointed their weapons at her and one of them told her to toss her pistols aside. She carefully removed her weapons and threw them toward the near wall. Two of the soldiers lowered their rifles and darted toward her. She closed her eyes and felt them grab her wrists. They threw her to the ground and one of them put his foot on her back to secure her. She had never felt so humiliated.

The lieutenant lifted her head up and looked at the Crownaxians. They all stood over six-foot tall, with long legs, and broad muscular shoulders. Yale, like most humans, had never seen a Crownaxian that close up and her eyes widened when she saw the aliens' most distinctive feature: a foot-long horn that protruded from their foreheads. It made the bipedal species look like a rhinoceros or its hind legs. She couldn't help staring at the odd appendage and her rude behavior caused one soldier to kick her in her stomach. She screamed out in pain and clutched her midsection.

Two of the aliens grabbed her and pulled her to her feet. She quickly found herself standing face to face with the Crownaxian who appeared to be in charge. This one wore a dark purple uniform that was adorned with medals. The citations were pinned to the upper left-hand corner of his shirt. He was slightly taller than the rest of the squadron, and his teeth weren't as yellow or chipped as the others. "You were wise to surrender, human," he said in a low voice. "However, you will pay for killing a Crownaxian soldier." Then he said something in his native language to his men and two of them grabbed the woman by her arms and dragged her out of the bridge. As she passed through the exit, she saw Zigler on his knees with his arms tied behind his back. There were tears in his eyes and his body was shaking.

The Crownaxians led the prisoners through the ship to the docking area. They were marched aboard the alien's vessel and down three flights of stairs to a dimly lit hallway that smelled like urine. Yale tried to mentally record details about the craft. She focused on the size of the ship, the temperature, and the number of soldiers that she could see onboard. At one point, she peeked back to see how Zigler was doing but one of the soldiers swatted her head and she was forced to turn back around.

The Crownaxians forced their human captives into a dank room no bigger than the captain's quarters on the *Justice*. There were no windows in the dark room but Yale caught a glimpse of two other figures huddled against the far wall. Before she could get a better look at them, the guards exited and slammed the door shut behind them. The room was completely dark. Yale had to blindly feel her way around. She accidentally bumped into Zigler and nearly knocked him over. With one arm wrapped around his waist, Yale waved her free hand in front of her until she located the nearest wall. Then she helped the terrified man sit down.

After she caught her breath, Yale called out to the two strangers on the other side of the room. "Hello? You two over there," she said. "Can you understand me?" They responded with a piercing screech that made Yale put her hands over her ears and cringe. After the noise subsided, the lieutenant decided to forgo any future attempts to communicate with their cellmates. Instead, she huddled close to Zigler and hoped that they would find a way out of this prison.

Chapter Nine

Amy Sutter snapped her head back as her heavy eyelids fluttered open. She rested her head in her hands with her elbows propped up on the console in front of her. The radar screen displayed numerous planets and stars in the space around the *Liberty Bell*, but the long-range scanners detected no ships of any kind in the area. Amy lazily traced the bottom border of the radar screen with her bare finger and looked over at Madison. She felt guilty about firing on Yale and putting Madison in the middle of all of this, but she knew it was for a good cause. However, she couldn't help wondering what would happen to her and Madison when they get home.

The robot sat still in the copilot's chair. An electric cable was attached to Madison's right wrist, with the other end plugged into a terminal located on the near wall just inches above the floor. A sudden beeping sound caused the robot to stand up and unplug the cable from the outlet. Then Madison disconnected the cable from its wrist, wrapped the cord into a tight band and stored the cable in a nearby supply cabinet. "I'm fully charged," said Madison, as it returned to the copilot's chair. "However, you look very tired Amy. Perhaps you should get some sleep."

Amy nodded and pushed herself to her feet. "We've still got a long time until we reach Crownaxia, but wake me up in about six hours," she said, yawning and stretching her arms over her head. "Or sooner if something happens." Madison nodded as the captain dragged herself to the bridge exit. She stumbled along the hallway until she came to the captain's quarters. There she dropped onto the bed and pulled the single cover over her body.

As she slept, Amy dreamt about a picnic that she went on with her parents when they were still living on Earth. Amy was 4 and only concerned about the issues that normally challenged a girl of that age. She was starting a new preschool in the fall, which meant sifting through all the faces in hopes of finding a friend. She wanted to fit in with the few kids who lived in her neighborhood. Amy liked the small town of Cedarbrook, Pa. and she hoped that they could stay there for more than just a year or two. She understood that her father's job required frequent relocation but it grew tiresome having to start from scratch with the other kids.

On this day, the Sutters relaxed on a red blanket under a tall maple tree at Taylor Park. The June sky was clear with a purplish tint to it and a slight breeze kept the day from becoming too hot. Pam had packed sandwiches, chips, pretzels, sodas, plates and napkins into a picnic basket. Amy and her dad were talking about soccer when the girl jumped up and grabbed the ball they brought with them to the park. She kicked it toward the open meadow and raced after it as her dad hustled after her. Amy got to the ball first and played keep-away with Clayton for a few minutes. Then they kicked it back and forth to each other as Pam leaned back against the tree with a cold soda in her hand. Classical music poured out of a tiny radio on the blanket beside the basket.

Without warning the music stopped and was replaced by a harsh male voice. Amy stopped and looked over at her mother. The girl couldn't hear what the man on the radio was saying but the ashen look on her mother's face made it clear that it wasn't good news. Amy and her father darted back to the blanket and asked her what was wrong. Pam just stared forward without answering. She absentmindedly dropped the soda in her hand and it spilled all over her lap. Then she snapped out of her mini-trance and peered up at her husband's face. "There's been an attack," she said, in a shaky voice. "Some alien race attacked the settlement on Blaros. There were three million people there and they're all dead." She dropped her head into her hands and wept as Clayton sunk down beside her. His face whitened as he stared down at the green grass around them.

The little girl dropped to her knees and threw her arms around her father's shoulders. She closed her eyes and cried. She didn't fully understand what her mother had said, but seeing her parents so upset was frightening for her. Clayton pulled her close to him and hugged her tightly. Amy opened her eyes and saw her mother lean toward them and wrap her arms around them both. A moment later, Clayton let go of his family and turned up the volume on the radio. The announcer said that the aliens sent an interstellar message that the

Union military had just released to the public. The aliens called themselves Crownaxians and claimed that the settlers had invaded their sacred territory on Blaros. The Crownaxians threatened future attacks unless the Union removed settlers from three other planets in that sector of space within the next five days.

Amy looked around at the tall trees and the birds flying around them as the news began to make sense to her. She wondered if the aliens would attack Earth someday. Then she ran her fingers through the thick green grass and tried to memorize how it felt. She turned back toward her parents and watched her father cradle her mother in his arms. He kept telling her that everything would be all right but Amy could tell that he didn't believe that. Then the girl shivered when she saw the tears slip away from his eyes. She had never seen her father cry before, not even when they attended her grandfather's funeral the previous winter.

A blaring alarm aboard the *Liberty Bell* snapped Amy out of her sleep. She sat up, shook her head and tried to remember where she was. She regained her senses after a few seconds and leapt to her feet. Then she raced to the bridge to find out what was going on. When she got there, she saw Madison looking at the radar. "A Crownaxian ship is on an intercept course with us," it said. "We'll be in its firing range in about six minutes." The robot paused and waited for the captain's response but Amy's mind was a blank. "What are your orders?" asked Madison.

Amy shook her head and sat down in the captain's chair. She rubbed her eyes and typed in a command on the keyboard in front of her. A series of star charts appeared on a monitor. Amy searched through them until she found one that mapped out this section of space. She scanned the map in with index finger, and then she tapped the monitor. "Let's head for this moon," she said, pointing to the map. "We should be able to get there in less than three minutes. Hopefully we'll be able to find a place to hide this time."

Madison nodded and typed the coordinates into the helm's computer. Amy put on her helmet then hit the accelerator. The *Liberty Bell* blasted forward as the captain followed the path to the moon's location. Her dream was still fresh in her mind and she considered sharing it with her copilot. However, she decided not to. She didn't want the robot to worry about her or think that she was too preoccupied to continue leading this mission.

They reached their destination in just under two minutes. Amy eased the ship into a slow orbit around the moon. There were 11 planets in the system and the captain plotted a contingency course that would take the craft between the two closest planets if need be. Then she slowed the ship to a crawl as they reached the dark side of the moon. Amy shut down all the non-essential systems to conceal the ship. "This didn't work before," said Madison. "Do you think it will this time?"

"Yeah, I think so," replied Amy. "Last time Yale was looking for us. The Crows probably don't even know we're out here. If we sit still, they'll just pass right by us." She forced a smile and hoped that she was right. Amy and Madison then kept a close eye on the radar screen. The Crownaxian ship decreased its speed when it got to the *Liberty Bell*'s previous location. Amy held her breath and wondered if they were looking for her craft. The ship stayed in that section of space for nearly twenty minutes before it continued on its original course. Amy let out a sigh of relief as the Crownaxian craft sped away and disappeared from the *Liberty Bell*'s radar.

Just to be safe, Amy kept the *Liberty Bell* on the dark side of the moon for another half-hour. When she was satisfied that the coast was clear, she turned the non-essential systems back on and removed her helmet. Madison ran a routine scan of the ship and announced that all systems were functioning normally. The captain then steered her ship away from the moon and back out into space. They traveled a few hundred miles when their proximity alarm suddenly blared. Amy looked at the radar and saw four missiles headed straight for the *Liberty Bell*. "Where'd they come from?" she yelled as she steered hard to the port side.

Madison scanned the area around them again. "The ship was hiding behind the largest planet," said the robot. "Radiation scrambled their image." Amy tightened her grip on the yoke and watched the missiles on the radar screen. Her initial maneuver didn't shake them off, so she cut back hard to the starboard side. The first two missiles flew by the ship and continued on toward the planet beneath them. However, the second pair got close enough to lock onto the heat crated by the *Liberty Bell*'s exhaust ports. Amy fired two counter missiles at them and they struck their targets but the force of the explosions pushed the ship into a spin.

The captain struggled with the yoke as Madison fired the ship's reverse thrusters. Together they were able to level out their trajectory but the Crownaxian ship closed in. The enemy craft flew in behind the *Liberty Bell* and fired a volley of laser shots. Amy countered by releasing four proton mines, which emitted a forcefield between them. The mines absorbed most of the artillery and gave Amy time to plot their escape. Before Madison could object, the captain initiated the Sprint Drive and hit the accelerator. The *Liberty Bell* darted forward, slamming Amy and Madison against their seats. The girl's hands shook as she struggled to keep control of the ship.

After a few seconds, Amy cut off the Sprint Drive and the craft jerked forward as the regular engines reengaged. The Crownaxian ship was far behind them and trying to close the gap. The *Liberty Bell* flew between two planets and began to shake again from the competing gravitational forces. "Let's go for the one on the right," said Amy. "Scan the surface for anything big enough to hide the ship." Madison nodded and set about the task.

The planet's misty atmosphere was comprised of green, blue, red and yellow gasses that played havoc on the *Liberty Bell*'s scanners. Madison feverishly typed various commands into the computer to try and compensate for the distortions. Finally, the robot turned toward the captain and nodded. "I've cut through the interference," said the robot. "The sensors detect several structures on the surface. I've found one that looks large enough. I'm inputting the coordinates." The robot typed the location into the navigational system while Amy watched the radar. The enemy ship continued to pursue them so the captain tried one more tactic.

"I have an idea," she said to Madison. "I wish I'd thought if it before." She reinitiated the Sprint Drive for a few seconds and led the Crownaxian ship away from the planetary system. They followed the *Liberty Bell*'s new course. Amy again turned off the Sprint Drive and glided forward before she shut down all the ship's non-essential functions. Using the ship's momentum, she was able to steer the *Liberty Bell* back toward the direction of the planets behind them.

Then Amy deployed a homing beacon that emitted a signal mimicking the *Liberty Bell*'s ion emissions.

The captain and her copilot kept a close watch on the radar screen as the *Liberty Bell* glided back toward the planet they wanted to land on. The Crownaxian ship headed straight for the beacon without detecting the *Liberty Bell*. Amy held her breath as the two ships passed within five miles of each other. The enemy craft maintained its course and speed and Amy waited until it was far enough away before she restarted the *Liberty Bell*'s main engine. Then they flew toward the site that Madison had found.

It was a bumpy ride through the planet's atmosphere as the ship cut through the levels of colorful gasses. Suddenly, something slammed into the ship's right wing. The jolt startled the captain and her copilot. "What was that?" asked Amy. "Is there any damage?"

Madison ran a diagnostic scan of the *Liberty Bell*. The robot shook its head as it read the printout. "No, nothing damaged, captain." Then another object struck the craft on the right side just above the main engine. A few seconds later, the ship passed through to a clearer level of the stratosphere. Amy's eyes widened when she saw what they were colliding with. Madison quickly scanned the debris that whirled around them at high speeds. "They're metal and definitely not natural," said the robot. "They look like fragments of starships but there are no lifesigns aboard any of them."

"How did they get stuck up here?" she asked as she steered around the spinning objects. The robot shrugged. "Well, I don't want to join them. How far away is that structure?" asked Amy.

Madison looked at the monitor in front of it. "About 8,000 feet down," said the robot. "Wait, there's something else." The robot typed more commands before looking over at the captain. "I've detected lifesigns near the structure. Humanoid lifesigns."

"Are they Crownaxians?" asked Amy.

The robot analyzed the data on a printout from the computer. "Yes, they're Crownaxians. There are about 600 of them. I'm also detecting ships, land vehicles and large amounts of weapons." The robot looked at Amy. "Are we still going to land?"

The captain took a deep breath. "That Crownaxian ship must have found the probe by now. If we try to leave, they're sure to catch us. Let's take our chances on the surface." Amy guided the ship to the structure; a long, rectangular building that resembled a Union hangar. She eased the ship into the building and immediately shut down all the systems, except for life support. Amy scanned the building and it appeared to be empty. Then she walked over to a supply cabinet and took out two laser guns and handed one to her copilot.

Chapter Ten

After waiting for an hour, Amy restarted the *Liberty Bell*'s systems and began powering up the main engine. Madison ran another routine diagnostic and told the captain that all systems were functioning normally. "Good, then it's time to get out of here," said Amy. "That Crownaxian ship must have moved on by now. I'm kinda of surprised the troops on the surface didn't detect us. I guess all that radiation must have cloaked our ship." She started to ease the craft toward the exit when a proximity alarm blared. Amy hit the brakes while Madison checked the radar screen.

"There are four land vehicles heading straight for us," said Madison. "I count 16 Crownaxians on board." Amy nodded and revved the engine. She guided the ship out of the building but was cut off by the first two vehicles. The other two then flanked them. The four-wheeled transports looked similar to jeeps used by Union soldiers. Amy shut off the engines and put her hand over her weapon as she watched the Crownaxians hop out of the vehicles.

The troops stood side-by-side in front of the *Liberty Bell*. Some had laser pistols, others had laser rifles, but none of them drew their weapons. One soldier stepped to the front of the group and waved an arm at the fighters, who responded by lining up in a U-formation. The soldiers were dressed in green uniforms but the leader wore purple clothing. He then reached into his coat and took out a small, handheld device. The soldiers were too far away from the ship for Amy to see their faces but she did notice a small horn protruding from each of their foreheads. It was the oddest thing she'd even seen.

The leader spoke into the device and Amy was surprised to hear the message as it came over her ship's loudspeaker. She was even more surprised to hear it in English. "We come in peace," said the voice. "We saw you outrun that cruiser and we are here to offer you any assistance you need. Please join us out here." Then the leader held the device close to his ear.

Amy turned to Madison. "He spoke English," she said. "How is that possible?" The robot shrugged. "And what's with that horn on their heads? They look like rhinoceroses."

"Does that really matter right now?" asked Madison.

"No, I guess not." She turned back and looked at the troops. They remained in their places with their weapons at their sides. "It could be a trap. But then again, they could have stormed the ship if they wanted to. Still, I don't know if we should trust them."

"What are we going to do, Captain?" asked Madison.

Amy turned on the microphone and spoke in her most authoritative voice. "We'll only come out if you drop your weapons," she said. The leader nodded and said something to his troops. They placed their weapons on the ground and took several steps back. Amy patted the robot on its shoulder and grabbed her flight jacket. "Keep your pistol drawn and follow me."

The duo slowly exited the *Liberty Bell*. Amy noticed the Crownaxian leader's tense expression as he kept his eyes on their weapons. Amy stopped at the edge of the ramp and Madison stood next to her. The leader took tentative steps forward until he was a few feet away from the ramp. His eyes widened as he looked the duo over. "You can put those away," he said, nodding toward the pistols. "You won't need them." Amy nodded and slowly lowered her pistol. Madison did the same. "You are a child," the leader said to Amy. "What are you doing this far in our space by yourself?"

Amy didn't answer. Instead she looked at the other troops as they stood as still as statues. She marveled at their discipline. Finally her gaze fell back onto the leader. "My name is Travar," said the Crownaxian. "I command this unit of Faction 12."

Madison glanced at Amy then looked back at Travar. "What is Faction 12?" asked the robot. "And how is it that you speak English?"

Travar smiled. "Come with us. You look like you could use some provisions. I'll explain everything when we get back to our base." He looked up at the sky then back to the duo. "It isn't safe to stay here too long."

"Why not?" asked Amy, as she finally spoke to him.

"The radiation levels on this planet are extremely high," said Travar. "It's not good to stay outside for long periods of time. And you see those clouds over there?" he asked, pointing to the sky over his right shoulder. Amy nodded as she saw silver and black clouds forming in large numbers. "The rain is acidic from the gaseous atmosphere. It's so strong than it can burn through metal. Imagine what that does to the skin." He opened his hand and offered it to them. "Please come with us. You'll be safe. I promise."

"Give us a moment," said Amy. Travar nodded and walked back toward his troops. Amy waited until he was out of earshot. Then she sighed and looked at Madison. "Those clouds do look pretty nasty. And this atmosphere could produce acidic rain. What do you think?"

Madison nodded. "As you said before, they could have easily killed us by now if they wanted to. I guess we can trust them. For now."

Amy nibbled on her bottom lip. "Agreed. But we need to keep our eyes open. This could still be some sort of trap." She holstered her weapon and Madison did the same. "C'mon, let's go."

Amy introduced herself and Madison to Travar, and then she and the robot followed Travar to his jeep. They climbed into the back of the vehicle and sat down on the rawhide seats. Travar sat in the front seat next to the driver. The other troops got back into their vehicles and followed Travar's jeep as it sped toward a wooded area. The bumpy ride lasted more than an hour and Amy used that time to survey the land. Along the way, she made mental notes for getting back to *Liberty Bell*'s location, while she also tried to size up the Crownaxian leader.

The jeep emerged from the woods and arrived at the entrance to a massive cave. The vehicles traveled along an artificial path that descended into a monstrous mountain. Florescent lights flickered overhead as the convoy rumbled along the rough roadway. After trekking for nearly a mile, the caravan pulled into a parking lot inside a makeshift military installation.

The rectangular compound was four miles long and half-a-mile wide. Several small buildings lined both sides of the main road, which ran down the middle of the base. The sounds of marching troops and heavy machinery filled the air as Travar's jeep came to a stop. The leader got out of the jeep and told his visitors to follow him. Amy and Madison fell into step behind Travar and his driver as they walked toward one of the buildings. Amy made more mental notes as she watched the troops around them. They, in turn, could not resist the opportunity to sneak a look at their unexpected guests.

Travar entered the building first, while his driver stood guard outside. Amy stepped into the tiny enclosure with Madison alongside her and she watched the Crownaxian leader sit down in a chair behind a desk. The office was surprisingly similar to human designs. The brown furniture appeared to be made out of wood, but there were no lines in the timber. Various papers and folders were stacked on the tidy desk and two cabinets stood in either corner behind Travar. A small window in the wall behind the desk was partly open. There was only one empty seat in front of them, so Madison graciously offered it to Amy with the wave of a hand. She smiled at her pal and sat down Madison stood beside her with its arms folded across its chest.

Travar glanced over Amy's shoulder and spoke to the robot. "You were surprised that I speak your language," he said. Amy turned around and saw Madison nod. Then she looked back at Travar. The leader shifted his focus to the girl. "I bet there are many things about my people that would surprise you," he said. Travar opened a folder and glanced down at the contents. Then he sadly shook his head and closed the report. "Our emperor, Drelk, has given our people a bad reputation. His desire for conquest has left innumerable worlds in ruins. Many of our own soldiers have died for his greed." He nodded toward the folder in front of him. "This is a casualty report from a raid by his forces on a desert planet not far from here. The names of the dead are written in his blood."

Amy crossed her arms over her chest. "So, you and your soldiers, you're some kinda rebels?" she asked.

Travar nodded. "That's right. We belong to a group called Faction 12. Our mission is to remove him from power and aid those who also seek to unseat him." He sat back in his chair and took a deep breath. "We are the only friends his enemies have."

"What does Faction 12 mean?" asked Madison.

The Crownaxian glanced at the robot then looked back at Amy. "My people's history is a bloody one. Our planet has little natural resources but plenty of hungry mouths to feed. For centuries our ancestors fought over the scarce food and water. Various tribes were formed. Some banded together to form larger factions. Eventually eleven such factions dominated the globe." He closed his eyes for a moment before continuing. "However, those eleven were just as petty and violent as the groups that preceded them. Fierce fighting continued to claim innocent lives. Then about sixty years ago one Crownaxian set out to unite the factions."

"And that would be Drelk?" asked Amy.

"Yes. Drelk," said Travar. "He capitalized on our hunger, our fear, our hopelessness and our rage. He blamed our problems on our neighboring planets. He said that we needed to end our bickering and join together to forge a new Crownaxia. Drelk is very charismatic. He knew what it was we wanted to hear. So we listened and we obeyed." Travar stood up and moved over to the open window. He looked out over the camp as he spoke. "The factions banded together with him as the leader. He had immediate success as he ordered the construction of new homes, schools, libraries, highways, and hospitals. The people cheered the improvements but no one questioned where the resources were coming from. I think most didn't want to know."

"Where did they come from?" asked Madison.

Travar turned around and sat back down in his chair. "Drelk ordered secret raids on Ursisis, the planet closest to our own. The Ursisins are a peaceful race and they were no match for our soldiers. Drelk initially denied the rumors that we had attacked their world. Then he said that we did it to thwart their planned invasion of our planet." Travar shook his head. "How could we believe that anyone would want our planet? But we did. Or at least enough of us did, anyway. So we showed support for the operation and Drelk sent more and more troops until we conquered Ursisis. Amazingly, we did it in less than sixty days." Travar folded his hands together. "We then had a new supply of resources and a subjugated race of slave workers."

"But that wasn't enough for Drelk, was it?" asked Amy.

Travar shook his head. "You're very perceptive for someone so young," he said. Amy smiled and glanced down at her feet for a moment. "No, that wasn't enough. Drelk wanted an empire and he was willing to sacrifice his soldiers' lives to get it. We should have stopped him then but we were happy with his results. It's hard to be angry with your government when you have a nice home and a full belly. I was among the most foolish of my people for I had the ignorance to admire him. So much so, I joined him."

"Joined him?" asked Madison. "How?"

Travar took a deep breath. "I was the military leader for one of the original factions. He asked me to be a part of a governing council he formed to show the people that they had a political voice. But it was all just for show. He never listened to the Council and he used us as scapegoats for any unpopular decisions he made. Still I believed that everything he did was in the best interest of Crownaxia."

"What changed your mind?' asked Amy, strangely riveted by this tale.

Travar shook his head. "No. Enough about me. Tell me what you are doing in this part of space," he said. "Are you lost?"

Amy turned to Madison and the robot nodded its approval. "No, we're not lost," she said, turning back to face Travar. "We're on a rescue mission." The Crownaxian raised his eyebrows. "I'm here to find my father." Amy told him about Clayton's diplomatic mission, his disappearance, her theft of the *Liberty Bell* and her skirmishes with Yale and the Crownaxian cruiser. She watched the rebel leader as he listened intently without interrupting her. Then she sighed and sat back in her chair after she finished.

"That's quite a story," said Travar, as he stood up. "It's hard to believe that you stole the *Liberty Bell* so easily. Maybe you have a career as a spy before you." Amy rose and pushed her chair aside. "Those provisions I promised you, please follow me." Travar led the way out of the office, and Amy walked beside him with Madison behind her.

They strolled across the compound while the soldiers around them continued their normal activities. Amy noticed more stares from the warriors and she did her best not to stare back at them. She smiled as she realized how normal they now looked to her. Travar opened the door to the mess hall and entered the room that was crowded with rowdy soldiers. The makeshift building was lined with rectangular tables made from the same material as the furniture in Travar's office. The chatter in the room ceased as the soldiers all stood up and saluted their commanding officer. He saluted back and said something in his native language. The troops then resumed eating. Travar walked over to the food line. Amy turned to say something to Madison, when she noticed that the robot was not behind her.

Amy saw Madison standing close to one of the tables. She walked over to the robot and saw what her friend was looking at. The soldier on the end of the table was eating from a bowl that contained a mixture of crawling bugs, wiggling worms and fresh, raw meat. Amy turned her head away and tried not to vomit. She wished that she had an atomizer with her. As she regained her composure, she turned back to see Madison inching toward the bowl to get a better look at the contents. However, the soldier growled at the robot, and Madison quickly backed away from the eater. That made the solider and those around him laugh. Amy then took her friend's hand and guided Madison to the food line where Travar was waiting for them.

The rebel leader smiled at his guests and handed Amy a tray. Then he turned to Madison. "Do you require food?" he asked the robot.

"No," said Madison. "I'm mostly self-sufficient."

"Wish I were," said Amy, louder than she meant to. "Oh, sorry," she said to Travar, after she noticed his alarmed expression. She looked at the food containers in front of them and noticed that the selection was limited to what that other soldier was eating. "I'm just a picky eater, I guess."

Travar laughed. "I'm sorry we don't have a more accommodating menu but we weren't expecting guests. Especially not human." He nodded toward her tray. "You're welcome to try our cuisine, if you like," he said.

Amy shook her head. "That's ok, I'll get something from my ship later." She then wiped her dry lips with the back of her right hand. "But do you have any water?" she asked. Then a puzzled look flashed across her face. "Ah, do you guys drink water?"

Travar nodded. "Yes, that's a need we do have in common, as I mentioned before." He opened the lid of a round cooler that sat at the end of the line and he pulled out two bottles filled with water. He handed one to Amy and put the other on his tray. Then he picked up a bowl and filled it with the grub from the food containers. Amy pressed her lips together as she watched him shovel the gross mixture into the bowl. Her stomach churned but she wasn't hungry enough to eat that. Amy put her tray down and followed Travar as he headed toward one of the tables. The soldiers at the table made room for them and continued with their meals.

Amy sat across from Travar and Madison sat down next to her. The rebel leader started eating, so Amy opened her bottle and drank some of the cool water. "So, tell me more about your rescue plan," said Travar.

The girl glanced at the robot then looked at the rebel leader. She cleared her throat before speaking. "Ah, we don't really have a set plan as of yet," she said. She noticed the comical expressions on the soldiers' faces.

"I see," said Travar, swallowing a mouthful of food. "Maybe we can work together." Amy smiled and nodded. "Good. Consider this unit of Faction 12 at your disposal," he said.

"You never did finish your story," said Madison. Travar looked at the robot and asked it what it meant. "About how you joined this group." The other soldiers around them grew quiet and Amy wondered if Madison had struck a nerve. She lightly kicked her pal in the leg and the robot dropped its head in embarrassment.

Travar took a sip of his drink then slowly put it back down on the table. "No, I guess I didn't. Well, like I said, I joined the council and for three years I stood by every decision Drelk made," he said. "I supported him, even when I knew he was making a mistake. But one day he asked me to do something that went too far."

Amy couldn't resist. "What was that?" she asked.

Travar's expression grew serious. "Drelk ordered the execution of a scholar for a crime I knew she didn't commit. He insisted that all of the council members sign the order, to make it easier to justify to the public." Travar took another sip of his water. Then he pushed his half-empty bowl aside before he continued. "I was the only council member who refused to sign it. I knew she was innocent."

"How did you know that for sure?" asked Amy.

"Because my fiancée would never commit an act of treason," he said, through clenched teeth. Amy dropped her eyes and wished she had kept her mouth shut. "Drelk had me arrested and I was sentenced to death for treason as well. However, I was lucky. Some of the guards were friends of mine and they knew that Drelk was wrong, so they helped me escape. But my fiancée's execution could not be stopped."

Amy looked up and saw the moisture in Travar's eyes. She also saw the anger and the sorrow.

"I'm really sorry," she said in a soft voice. "I shouldn't have asked."

Travar shook his head. "It's ok, you didn't know." He drank more water before he pulled the bowl back in front of him and ate more of the food. "Anyway, those guards joined me and we formed Faction 12, the only faction dedicated to Drelk's removal. We are on the top of Drelk's death list so we must hide wherever we can. Our numbers have grown, more so than even he realizes. We even have secret members among his own troops. That's how we receive sensitive information about his military actions. That information has saved us more than once."

Amy kept quiet for a few minutes to allow the leader to finish his meal. The other soldiers began talking and laughing, and the room was soon filled with the noise of their chatter again. After he was done, Travar stood up and dumped his tray into a basin that was filled with other dirty, empty trays. Amy followed close behind him, while Madison stayed at her side. As the trio exited the mess hall, Amy asked a pressing question. "Do you know where Drelk keeps alien prisoners?" she asked Travar.

The rebel leader stopped and smiled. "I was wondering how long it was going to take you to ask me that," he said. "Yes. There are two military prisons on Crownaxia that house such inmates. I have spies at both of them. I'll find out if they know where your father is." Without thinking, Amy stepped forward, wrapped her arms around the rebel leader and thanked him. Other soldiers around them stopped and drew their weapons. "Stand down," Travar said to them. Then he carefully put his hands on Amy's shoulders and gently moved her back. "I appreciate your gratitude but you must be careful how you demonstrate it." Amy looked around and saw the tense soldiers lowering their weapons. Travar laughed. "It's ok. Come with me, I'll show you where you can sleep tonight."

Amy sheepishly followed Travar to an empty tent a hundred yards away from the mess hall. The commander held the door open and allowed his guests to enter first. The rustic dwelling was sixty feet long and fifty feet wide. Inside were two six-foot cots, two small tables with electric lights on top of them, and a stove with an exhaust pipe that ran through the top of the canopy. There were other scattered items on the floor as well, including boxes with medical supplies in them, crates filled with military clothing and a pile of blankets that sat in one corner. "As you can see, we store some extra supplies in this tent but there are cots for you to sleep on," said Travar, pointing to the crude beds. "I'll post a guard outside the door in case you need anything else."

"I can't thank you enough for your help," said Amy. She carefully extended her right hand and Travar knowingly shook it. Then he told her that they would discuss an escape plan for her father in the morning. The leader then wished them a good night before he exited.

Madison and Amy sat down on their cots and looked at each other. "He seems rather helpful," said the robot.

"Yes he does," replied Amy, stretching her arms over her head. Then she leaned closer to her friend and whispered. "Still we need to keep our guard up. I know you just repowered your batteries today so I want you to stay awake and keep watch. Wake me if anything odd happens." The girl lay down on the cot and blinked her eyes.

Madison nodded. "I will captain. You can count on me." The robot rose and picked up a blanket from the corner of the room. Madison carefully placed it over the tired girl. "Get some sleep. I'll watch over you."

Chapter Eleven

The creaky door to the jail cell opened and cast a bright light into the unlit room. Yale scrambled to her feet and tried to see who was entering but the encroaching light enveloped the intruder. Yale's stomach grumbled and her head ached. She tried to determine how long she and Zigler had been in the cell but she had nothing to measure the time with. She looked over and saw that Zigler was laying in a ball on the hard surface. His body was shaking and he didn't appear to react to the sudden light. The rumble of heavy footsteps preceded the sound of something metallic landing in front of the lieutenant. The odd sound repeated three more times before the bright light abruptly disappeared.

A rancid smell soon filled the tiny room. Yale reached out into the darkness until her fingers bumped into something rectangular on the floor. She pulled the object closer to her and the stench intensified. Yale ran her fingers over the flat tray until she detected a bowl on top of it. That's when she realized that they had just been served their first meal. Despite the foul odor, Yale scooped up some of the food and shoved it into her mouth. It tasted like a mixture of rice and worms. She forced herself to eat it before she drank all of the water in the cup that was also on the tray.

Then she stumbled over to Zigler, who was still curled up on the floor. She softly shook him. "Wake up, Mr. Zigler," she said. "You need to eat." In the darkness, she heard the other prisoners devouring their meals. Beside her, Zigler remained still. "Zigler, C'mon. You need to wake up. There's food here and you really need to eat something." She put her hands on his shoulders and eased him into a sitting position. Yale then put his bowl of food into his hands. She felt him scoop up some of it and put it into his mouth. Then she heard him spit it out. "I know how nasty it tastes but you need to get something in your stomach," she said.

"Later," he said, weakly. "I'll eat later." Yale heard him push the tray aside. She also felt his quivering body as he leaned against her.

She put an arm around him and tried to comfort her cellmate. Yale rubbed his back as the man began to cry. "Hey, everything's going to be ok," she said. "I'll find a way out of this place. Trust me. Before long, we'll both be out of here." Soon his shaking subsided and he drifted off to sleep. The lieutenant eased him back down to the floor and let him rest. She then leaned against a near wall and wondered if an escape was even possible. Yale knew that Gen. Knox would not send out a rescue party and that she and Zigler were on their own.

After what seemed like hours, the cell door opened again. Yale sat up and pulled her knees to her chest. The bright light again made it impossible to see who was entering but she heard heavy footsteps coming toward her. "Get up," said a harsh voice. "The magistrate is waiting for you." Yale's eyes finally adapted to the light and she saw two Crownaxian guards standing before her. Both were armed with laser rifles. The one who didn't speak had his aimed at the lieutenant. She kept her eyes on the weapons as she slowly stood up. The one who spoke than raised his rifle as he moved laterally toward Zigler. He kicked the sleeping man in the leg. "Get up," he repeated. "It's time to go."

The guards carefully backed out of the cell with their rifles pointed at the prisoners as Yale helped Zigler to his feet. They entered the hallway and followed the first guard as the second one stayed behind them. The humans were marched down a long corridor toward a pair of tall metal doors. They passed through the doors and into a round room packed with chattering Crownaxians who sat in a crowded balcony. Several gray stone pillars with intricate artwork on them soared toward the towering ceiling.

An older Crownaxian in a black robe sat behind an elevated marble desk. Two armed guards stood on either side of him. Yale saw him glare at her and Zigler as they were led to the center of a purple circle on the floor. The lieutenant glanced at the spectators in the balcony as the angry mob shouted at the prisoners. The guards who escorted the humans backed away from them as a bright blue light shined down on Yale and Zigler. The room abruptly grew quiet. The older Crownaxian banged a gavel on his desk. "Let's begin," he said, nodding toward the humans.

A timid-looking Crownaxian hobbled toward the prisoners. He

was missing his right leg and a metal knob stuck out from his pants where his foot would be. He made a clip-clop sound when he moved and he breathed heavily from the exertion. The handicapped figure looked at the judge and spoke in a frail voice. "Your honor, Flormuk representing the accused. We plead guilty," he said.

A roar of approval showered down from the balcony. The judge banged his gavel again to quiet the crowd. Yale turned toward Flormuk with an exasperated look on her face. "Whoa, wait a minute," she said, grabbing his left arm. "When did you become our lawyer?" Flormuk pulled his arm away and glared at her. Yale then turned toward the judge. "We don't plead guilty to anything!" she shouted. "We've never even seen this guy before!" Just then, two guards grabbed her and threw her to the floor. She landed on her left shoulder and banged her head against the hard surface. Then Yale glanced at Zigler for a moment before she passed out.

Yale woke up in complete darkness. She felt the floor and the walls around her before a putrescent smell made it clear that she was back in the jail cell. She called out Zigler's name but got no response. The only sound she heard was the squealing of the other prisoners. Her mouth was dry, her shoulder hurt and her head still ached. Worse, she felt the fullness of her bladder and despite her best efforts to ignore it, she knew that she had to relieve herself. Swallowing her disgust, the lieutenant crawled toward an empty corner, lowered her pants and urinated. The fowl smell engulfed her and she did her best not to vomit. After she finished, she pulled her pants back up and stumbled to the other side of the room.

Some time passed before the cell door opened again. Yale squinted through the bright light and saw two Crownaxian guards drag Zigler back into the room. His face was bruised. A large cut over his left eye was bleeding and his right eye was swollen shut. The guards dropped him into the middle of the cell then turned around. Yale got a good look at one of the guards. He was shorter than the others she'd seen, and he had a long thin, scar on his right cheek. He also had an odd expression on his face, not one of anger or disgust, but rather one of regret. Yale locked eyes with him, and silently pleaded for help. The guard then exited with his partner and the cell door slammed shut.

Yale felt her way through the darkness until she bumped into

Zigler. She carefully lifted him up and guided him to where she was sitting. She eased him back down to the floor and put her right arm around his shoulder. "What did they want from you?" she asked.

"There were four of them," he said, weakly. "There was a cold room. Lots of light. They kept asking me what our mission was." Zigler then started to cry. "I told them," he said between sobs. Yale held him and said it was ok. "I told them that I was on the *Harmony* when it was attacked. They said that wasn't good enough. They wanted to know what I was doing with you." He took a moment to catch his breath. "I'm sorry Yale. I told them about Amy Sutter and the *Liberty Bell* and your mission to find her. I tried to hold out but they kept hitting me. I begged them to stop but they wouldn't." He began to cry harder and his entire body shook. "Please forgive me. I didn't want to tell them. I didn't."

He collapsed into her arms and muttered incoherently. "Shhh, its ok Zigler," said Yale, holding him like an infant. "You did the right thing. You told them what they wanted to hear. The important thing is that you're still alive. We're both still alive and we will get out of here." She hoped that if she said it enough times, somehow it would come true. Still she realized that it would take a miracle to save them now.

After Zigler fell asleep, Yale lowered him to the floor. Then she stretched out her legs and closed her eyes. She wanted to sleep too but her aching head and grumbling stomach kept her awake. The lieutenant blinked open her tired eyes and looked around in the darkness. She listened to the sound of Zigler's breath and the screeching noise made by their cellmates. Yale then wondered about Amy Sutter. *Was she still alive? Had the Crownaxians captured her? Would any of them make it back to Paldor?* Yale's heart pounded in her chest as the anxiety raced through her, but soon her rapid heartbeat decreased and she passed out from exhaustion.

The jarring sound of the cell door jolted the lieutenant awake. This time she kept her eyes closed and didn't bother to try to see who was coming. It wasn't until she felt a pair of hands on her shoulders that she opened her eyes again. She saw the face of the guard who pulled her to her feet, and his partner, who stayed back with his rifle aimed at her. Without a word they dragged her into the hallway and shut the door behind them. One of them stepped in front of her, while the other pushed a rifle into her back, so Yale began to march forward.

The lieutenant was led in the opposite direction of the courtroom and found herself walking down a quiet, better-lit corridor. She thought about the bruises on Zigler's face and wondered if they were going to interrogate her now. She got her answer when the guard in front of her entered a drafty room and forced her into a metallic chair. A large wooden table sat in the center of the room. Several rectangular, luminescent bulbs hung from the ceiling by metal brackets. Two hulking Crownaxians relaxed in reclining chairs across from her. The guards left and closed the door behind them.

One of the Crownaxians stood up and slowly circled toward her. He stopped directly behind the lieutenant and spoke in a low-growl of a voice. "Your comrade was very helpful, human," he said. Yale kept still and locked eyes with the other interrogator, who simply stared back at her without speaking. The one behind her put his hands on her shoulders. His harsh grip sent a surge of fear through her body but she did her best to hide her discomfort. "I'm sure you will be just as cooperative." He let go of her, sat down on the edge of the table and stared down at her. "My name is Jarstic and this is my associate Mong. Tell me, what is your mission, Lt. Brown?" he asked, crossing his arms over his chest.

Yale remained silent. She then saw him nod his head. He said something to Mong in his native language and Mong replied with a grunt. Then Jarstic leaned closer to Yale's face. The lieutenant cringed at the scent of his bad breath. "Are you tracking one of your ships?" he asked. "One taken by a child?" He laughed for a moment then regained his composure. "How is it that the mighty Union lets a little girl steal their latest secret weapon? Have you no security crews?"

The lieutenant's face reddened at the insult to her authority. She realized that Jarstic was trying to push her buttons, so she took a deep breath and tried to remain calm. Jarstic laughed again, while his partner remained stoic. Then Jarstic's face grew serious. He got off the table, pulled Yale's chair close to him and pushed his face against hers. "Where is your base located?" he asked. "How many troops are stationed there? What are the security codes for the facility?"

Yale looked down at her feet and said nothing. Suddenly, Jarstic stood up and slapped her across the face. Yale fell out of the chair and landed on the floor. Her sore shoulder took the brunt of the fall and she screamed out in pain. "So you can speak," said Jarstic. "Good." He grabbed her by her shoulders and pulled her to her feet. They stood toe to toe and he glared at her. "You will talk, human," he said. "Or you will die."

Chapter Twelve

Amy woke the next morning to the sound of soldiers marching outside her tent. She sat up and stretched her arms over her head as a blanket slipped to her knees. The girl looked over at Madison's cot and found the robot sitting still with something in its hands. Amy rubbed her bleary eyes and focused on the object. When her eyes cleared, she saw that her friend was holding a portable computer that had a ten-inch screen. "What'cha got there?" she asked, as she got up and wrapped the blanket around her.

It was so cold Amy could see her breath. She laid the blanket down on the floor and put on her flight jacket. Then she inched closer to Madison and leaned toward the computer screen to see what the robot was reading. The material was written in Crownaxian and she didn't recognize any of the strange symbols that glowed on the screen. "I didn't know you could read their language," she said.

The robot nodded. "I can now. I found this on the table. There is a dictionary programmed into it. It took a few hours, but I think I've got most of the words figured out." Amy smiled and asked what the text was. "It's a play," said Madison. "In it, the main character gets tormented by her peers because she acts like a boy. Soon she begins to wonder if life would have been easier for her if she had been born a boy." Madison clicked off the machine and laid it on the cot. The robot looked straight ahead for a moment before it spoke again. "There were other stories in the database but I liked that one the best. I read it three times."

Amy smiled at the irony. "We are whom we choose to be," she said.

Madison looked down at the floor and spoke in a soft voice. "My creator didn't find it necessary to give me a gender. I guess he didn't think I needed one. But sometimes I wish he had." The robot shook its head. "Even my name is neutral." Amy tried to think of something comforting to say but they were abruptly interrupted by a knock on the tent door.

100

The captain looked over at the door and saw Travar enter with two guards behind him. "Good morning, my friends," he said, walking over to his guests. "Did you sleep well?"

Amy nodded. "Yeah, I did, but Madison stayed up all night reading." The rebel leader glanced at the robot then back at Amy. The girl picked up the computer and handed it to Travar. "Madison found this." The Crownaxian turned it on and scanned through the data. "It seems like you have some good playwrights among you," said Amy.

Travar turned off the gadget and tossed it to one of his soldiers. "Glad to hear it," he said. "Now if you're brave enough to try some more of our cuisine, I'd like you to join us for breakfast. I promise it won't be as bad as dinner was." He gestured toward the door and the guards opened it. "After you," he said to Amy. The girl and the robot walked past him and exited the tent. Travar and his soldiers followed.

Amy walked beside the rebel leader as they headed for the mess tent. Madison and the guards stayed close behind. "There's one thing that you still haven't explained," said Amy, keeping pace with her host. "How is it that you speak English?" she asked.

The leader laughed. "Still stuck on that, are you?" he asked. Amy shrugged. "Well, I told you before, there's plenty about us that would surprise you. Yes, I speak your language. I also know some French, German and Spanish too." Amy flashed a surprised grin. "My people have a gift for languages. I don't know, something in our temporal lobes, I guess." Then he leaned closer toward her. "Or maybe it's the horn," he joked.

Amy laughed and glanced at Madison behind her. The robot seemed less amused. She then looked back at Travar. "So what did your people do? Study our television signals or something?" she asked.

They reached the mess hall and Travar opened the door. "Not all of our people, just our scientists," he said with a straight face. Amy raised her eyebrows. "Really, they studied transmissions from your planet and others in various sectors of space. Once they deciphered them, they shared the knowledge with the public. We've even seen some of the television shows from as far back as your planet's twentieth century." He waited for her to enter, then he followed behind the girl. "*Family Ties* was my personal favorite," he said. "That show was hilarious. But I never understood the appeal of those reality shows that came later. Why would people want to humiliate themselves in front of the whole world?" he asked.

Amy shook her head and waited for Madison to catch up to her. Then she whispered to her friend. "What's a reality show?" she asked. The robot shrugged. "Must be before my time," she said. The girl then moved in behind Travar as he stood in line for his breakfast.

The grub looked less threatening than it did the night before. Instead of bugs, worms and raw meat, the chow consisted of green vegetables, red fruit, and something resembling oatmeal. Travar scooped a few spoonfuls of the cereal into his bowl, then handed the spoon to Amy. She leaned close to the utensil and sniffed the residue on it. There was a light cinnamon scent to it. Then she scooped two spoonfuls into her bowl while Travar grabbed two water bottles. He handed her one before he filled his tray with two helpings of the fruit. Amy did the same, and then she followed him as he moved toward an empty table in the middle of the tent.

Amy again sat across from Travar, while Madison eased into the seat next to her. The rebel leader ate a few spoonfuls of his cereal before he spoke. "I contacted one of my associates in Drelk's army before I went to bed last night," he said. Travar sipped some water before continuing. "He sent me a message this morning. Your father is being detained at the Nortuck facility on Crownaxia."

The little girl's eyes widened. "He is?" Travar nodded. Amy turned to Madison and saw that the robot was staring at the rebel leader. Then she faced Travar again. "Do you know where that is? Can we get him out?" she asked.

Travar nodded again. "Yes, I believe we can. And we need to do it soon." He glanced at the robot before proceeding. "Your father and his shipmates have been found guilty of espionage. They are scheduled to be executed in two days." Amy sat back in shock. Travar's face turned somber and he remained quiet for a moment. Amy pressed her lips together to hold back her tears. "I have a plan," said Travar. "My advisors and I worked out something we hope will work. But it's dangerous and we're going to need your help."

"What do you need us to do?" asked Madison. The robot put a reassuring arm around Amy's shoulders. The girl took several deep breaths and tried to hold herself together. When she looked up at Travar, she realized the he was waiting for her to regain her composure. Then she nodded at him to show that she was ok.

The rebel leader sipped more water then put the bottle down on the table. "I realize how upsetting this is and I must say that you are acting very courageously for one so small," he said. "You'll need to maintain that courage if our plan is to work. How fast is your ship?" he asked.

Amy exchanged a glance with Madison before she spoke. "I don't know," she said. "It's a new model and we've never pushed it to the limit." She glanced again at Madison and wondered if she should tell Travar what made the *Liberty Bell* so special. The girl ate a spoonful of oatmeal to buy her some time to think. As she swallowed the food, she decided to put her cards on the table. "The *Liberty Bell* has a experimental engine with what we call Sprint Drive propulsion."

Travar tilted his head to one side and pushed his bowl away from him. "And what exactly does this Sprint Drive engine do?" he asked.

"It makes the ship go really fast," said Amy, with a shrug. "That's all I really know about it. I'm not sure how it works. Well, actually it doesn't." She grimaced. "If you use it too long, the engine blows up."

Travar's expression changed to one of shock. "I see how that can be a problem," he said. "How long can you use it before that happens?" He brought his tray closer to him and ate some of the fruit. His eyes focused on Amy as the little girl responded.

Amy shrugged again. "In simulations, the drive lasted only a few minutes. We've used in sparingly on this trip. No more than 45 seconds I think," she said. Then she looked over at Madison. "Does that sound about right?" she asked. The robot nodded. "So, I don't know what the threshold is, but it can't be much more than that."

"Language is not the only thing my people excel at," said Travar. "Perhaps one of my engineers and I could take a look at it." He finished the fruit on his tray and began eating the oatmeal again. Amy wondered if this was what Travar had in mind from the start. She looked down at her food as she finished her breakfast. She realized that showing the engine to a Crownaxian could be considered an act of treason, but if they could find a way to make it work, it might be worth the risk.

"Yeah, I'd like that," she said, after finishing her water. "Any advice you could provide would be greatly appreciated." She turned toward Madison and noticed the surprised look on the robot's face. Then she looked back at the rebel leader. He too had an odd expression on his face. It wasn't one of satisfaction; it looked more like disdain. "Is there something else on your mind, Travar?" she asked.

The Crownaxian nodded. "My source also told me that two other humans were captured yesterday," he said. Amy's eyes widened. "An older man and a young lady. They too have been found guilty of treason and also face execution." He took a breath before continuing. "He said it was the officer who was chasing you and your ship."

Suddenly Amy's face turned pale. She slumped back in her seat as the pieces came together in her mind. Madison leaned closer to her and put both hands on her shoulders. "Yale," whispered Amy. "It's all my fault. If I didn't fire on her ship, she would have never been caught." She turned toward the robot. "You tried to warn me but I didn't listen. It's all my fault."

"You can't blame yourself," said Travar, in a reassuring voice. Amy looked at him and tried not to cry. The leader's expression softened. He folded his hands and rested them on the table. "You did what you had to do. No one can blame you for that. They are in the same facility as your father. We'll get them out too but we'll need to leave soon. It takes more than a day to get there." He paused again but kept his eyes on the young girl. "As I said, we will need your help. You will have to take your ship into battle again. Are you ready to do that?" he asked.

Amy pressed her lips together in defiance of her fear. "Yes. We can do that. When would you like to inspect my ship?" she asked. Amy felt Madison's hands slip off her shoulders as the robot sat back in its seat. She didn't have to see Madison to know that the robot wasn't happy about this.

Travar stood and picked up his tray. "I have a staff meeting in a few minutes," he said. "When it's over, I'll send an escort for you. In the meantime, feel free to browse the camp. But be careful, there are some training exercises going on today." He smiled at his guests. "My soldiers can be a little gruff, so try to stay out of their way." He nodded at them, then dumped his tray in a receptacle before he exited the room with two guards.

Amy swung her left leg over her seat so she could face Madison. The robot looked around before speaking in a quiet voice. "Captain, do you think it's a good idea showing them the Sprint Drive? I know they oppose their leader, and they've been very helpful so far, but they are still Crownaxians. Can we trust them?" Madison looked around again.

"I've thought of all that," said Amy with a sigh. "We are going to have to trust them. Still, it would be a good idea to keep some pistols close by while they visit the ship. Just in case." She rose and grabbed her tray. "C'mon, let's take a walk around the base. I'm curious to see how these guys train." She dumped her tray in the receptacle and headed for the exit. Along the way, she nodded politely at some of the soldiers, but they either ignored her or shot her distrustful looks.

Amy kept Travar's advice in mind as the duo toured the base. They walked along the loose-gravel road that ran through the center of the camp and watched as the Crownaxian rebels went about their business. In one section, a group was taking target practice. Four lines of soldiers stood a hundred feet away from wooden posts and fired laser rifles at the targets while two officers oversaw the drills. In another sector, another group was running through an obstacle course with their rifles slung over their shoulders. Amy was surprised by the similarities in their training techniques. Then she realized that warfare was warfare everywhere in the universe.

Later, the duo came to an area where the soldiers were playing a game on a dirt field. Amy and Madison sat down at the edge of the field and watched the action. Two teams of five players each kicked a round ball and tried to advance it to the opponents' side of the field. There another player stood in front a small, round basket with a mesh net connected to it. The wooden basket was only slightly larger than the ball. It appeared that only the player guarding the basket was allowed to use their hands, the other players were limited to using their feet. "This kinda looks like soccer," said Amy. "But the nets are much smaller."

Madison nodded. "They look like basketball nets."

"What's basketball?" asked Amy, keeping her eyes on the game. The players on one team wore blue vests and the players on the other wore red. The blue team was faster and passed the ball better but the red team's goalie had quick hands and a knack for anticipating the other team's shots.

"In basketball, two teams try to throw a ball into a net, instead of kicking it in," said Madison. "And the nets aren't much bigger than the ball." The robot went into further detail as they watched the match. Amy nodded politely but she was far more intrigued by what they were watching. The players raced around the field, pushing and bumping each other as they fought for the ball. They called out to each other in their native language and Amy asked her pal what it was they were saying. "It doesn't really translate," said the robot. "But I'm guessing that it's something a kid your age shouldn't hear anyway."

A player on the blue team booted the ball out of play and it skittered to a stop just in front of Amy. Instinctively, the girl shot up, grabbed the ball and tossed it back to the players. A player on the blue team nodded politely toward her as she sat down. However, a player on the red team stormed off the field as his teammates tried to stop him. The angry player screamed at them in Crownaxian. Amy turned to Madison. "What's his problem?"

Madison frowned. "From what I can tell, he's not happy that you touched the ball," said the robot. Amy gave him a confused look. "He said that he won't play with a ball that's been contaminated by human trash." The robot put a reassuring hand on her shoulder. "I'm sorry."

Amy acted like it didn't matter but the insult angered her. "I guess hating Drelk doesn't mean they like us," she said, standing up. "C'mon, we should try to find Travar. His meeting must be over by now." Madison rose and walked next to her as they headed back toward their tent. After a few strides, Amy looked back over her shoulder and saw the red team player glaring at them. He snarled at the girl and clenched his fists. Amy shook her head and wondered how many of the rebels felt that way about her.

Chapter Thirteen

Yale blinked her eyes open and looked around. It wasn't a nightmare. She was in the interrogation room with Jarstic and Mong but now she was on the floor and she had no idea how long she had been unconscious. A splitting pain ran through her skull. Her mouth was dry and her shoulder throbbed. The bright light from the ceiling bore into her eyes. An odd stench surrounded her and she nearly vomited when she realized that she smelled her own urine-soaked pants.

The lieutenant peered up at her tormentors and tried to defy their power by crawling back into the chair. She made it halfway into the seat before she slipped and crashed back down onto the hard floor. Jarstic laughed as he rose from edge of the table. The interrogator circled behind her, grabbed her by her shoulders and threw her into the chair. Yale shuddered as she held onto the arms of the chair for support. The lieutenant felt the blood flowing from her nose as it seeped into her mouth. She spit out a mouthful of the salty fluid as Jarstic turned the chair around to face her. "Are you ready to talk now, human?" he asked.

Yale stared blankly forward and remained silent. Jarstic smiled at her. "Tell me where your base is, Lt. Brown," he said. He paused for a moment but Yale didn't answer him. "How many troops are stationed there? What are the security codes for the base?" He clenched his teeth as he stared into her brown eyes. Finally, he nodded and moved away from her. Yale watched as he sat back on the edge of the table.

Jarstic spoke to Mong in their native language. Mong responded with only a nod of his head. Then the monstrous Crownaxian stood up for the first time. Yale's eyes widened at the site of the creature. He stood more than a foot taller than Jarstic. He removed his coat and revealed arms that were at least 35 inches thick. Without a sound, he moved behind Yale and put his massive hands around her neck. "My partner has studied humans for quite some time," said Jarstic. "He tells me that there are limits to how much pain you can endure." Mong tightened his grip on her neck. "Shall we test his theory?" asked Jarstic.

Panicked, Yale kicked her legs up and wrapped them around Mong's neck. Before he could react, the lieutenant pulled him forward and slammed his body against the table. The crash sent both Crownaxians to the floor. Mong lay on his back and clutched his fractured throat. Yale shot to her feet and dashed toward the door but Jarstic grabbed her from behind before she could escape. He had a grip on her shoulders as he spun her around. Yale then kicked him in the groin and let loose a volley of punches to his face and midsection. Jarstic dropped to the floor with a thud. Yale pushed a button on the wall and the doors slid open.

The prisoner dashed into the hallway as the doors closed behind her. She glanced to her left and saw two Crownaxian guards moving toward her. They immediately raised their laser rifles and fired. Yale dove to the floor, rolled to her feet and sprinted down the hallway. She searched frantically for a place to escape as she heard her pursuers closing in. Laser blasts exploded around her as she tried to keep her head low. The guards screamed at her in their native language, while an alarm blared overhead. Yale's heart pounded and her lungs struggled for air. She felt her legs weakening with each step.

The lieutenant turned a corner and saw an elevator at the end of the hall. She mustered up all of her strength as she sprinted toward the exit. The guards continued to fire. One blast struck a cabinet just ahead of her and nearly knocked her off of her feet. She finally reached the elevator doors and smacked the small button on the wall. Luckily, the doors opened immediately, allowing Yale to dive into the car and hit another button as laser blasts bounced off the walls outside the elevator.

The car stopped at the ground floor. Yale carefully stepped out, only to find more guards closing in on her. She raced down a corridor as more laser blasts exploded. The thunder of the guards' footsteps hammered in her head. Her eyes began to blur and she knew her body was giving out. A flash of light ahead of her caught her attention and through squinted eyes she saw an open door. With nowhere else to go, she headed for the opening. She was a few feet away from the door when a Crownaxian guard suddenly stepped through it. In that instant, she realized that it was the short guard who had taken her to her cell. As she tried to pass him, he quickly grabbed the lieutenant around the waist, put one hand over her mouth and dragged her through the doorway. Then he hit a button to close the door as he pushed her up against a wall.

Despite his size, he was remarkably strong and Yale could not break free of his grip in her weakened state. After the guards in the hallway passed the room, the Crownaxian whispered into her ear. "Stay still," he said, holding her tightly. "I'm not going to hurt you." She stopped struggling and he eased his grip on her. "My name is Prestok and I am a member of Faction 12. I'm here to help you."

She backed away from him and spoke in a low voice. "Why should I trust you?" she snapped. "And what is Faction 12?"

He looked at her eyes and sighed. "Your only hope," he said.

Yale frowned at the suggestion. Her mind raced as she glanced around the room and tried to figure out her next move. It was oddly humid in the small quarters. The lieutenant wiped some sweat from her forehead as she leaned against the wall. Her heavy breathing subsided but her body still ached. "Can I sit down?" she asked, pointing to a nearby chair.

"Be my guest," said Prestok. He slowly leaned toward her and offered his arm. Yale cautiously took it and let him lead her to the seat. He pulled the chair away from the table in the center of the room and eased her into it. "You look thirsty. Would you like some water?" he asked.

Yale nodded and leaned against the table. She watched her host hustle to the small kitchen area and remove a glass from a cupboard. He filled it with water from a spout then brought it over to her. Yale shyly took the glass and raised it to her mouth. The cool water felt marvelous on her parched lips. She sloppily slurped it down, spilling some of it on her chin.

Prestok sat down in a chair across from her. Yale winced when she looked at his wrinkled face and the horn protruding from his head. "Don't feel bad," he said. "I have trouble looking at you humans too. You're just so ugly," he said with a smile. Yale smiled back and began to relax. Then she finished her drink and handed him the glass. Prestok rested it on the table. "We need to get you out of here soon. They must be searching the barracks by now and it won't take them long to get to mine." He rose and offered her his hand. She took it and slowly rose to her feet.

The Crownaxian led her to the back of his quarters. There, he picked up a hand-held electronic light and stuffed it into his coat pocket. Then he removed a pair of loose planks in the floor and revealed a homemade tunnel. "Go through there," he said, pointing to the opening. Yale nodded and carefully stepped down into the hole. It was nearly eight-feet deep and it smelled like wet mud and sulfur. Prestok followed her with the planks in his hands, which he then put back into place.

The momentary darkness ceased when Prestok turned on the light. He flashed the beam ahead of them as they walked along the dark burrow that ran underneath the prison. The narrow passageway afforded little room on either side and Yale kept bumping into Prestok. "Sorry," she said, after her elbow caught him in the side. He smiled and told her it was ok. "So, what is this Faction 12?" she asked, as they trudged along the damp, muddy ground. Puddles of water splashed their legs when their feet squished down on the saturated surface.

Prestok sighed before he told her about Drelk's rise to power, the formation of the rebel group, and how his people studied human culture. "There are several battalions located throughout the region," he said. "Many are led by disillusioned officers who want to bring an end to Drelk's tyranny. However, there is much dissent among those leaders as to how this should take place."

"What don't they agree on?" asked Yale, as she struggled to keep her balance on the slippery trail. They came upon a turn that required them to climb over a pair of boulders wedged into the ground. Prestok went first, clutching a handhold on the left rock. He scaled the rock with ease, then turned to offer Yale a hand. The lieutenant grabbed a triangular edge of the same rock with her right hand and tried to hoist herself up. She was halfway over it and reaching for her guide's hand when her left foot slipped and she fell to the ground and landed on her back.

The woman cried out in pain. Prestok hopped off of the rock and moved toward her. Yale held onto his coat with a clenched fist as the

Crownaxian gently lifted her off of the ground and eased her onto a smaller rock. She sat back against the tunnel wall and let go of the coat. "How bad is it?" asked Prestok, as he slid a hand over the back of her shirt.

"I don't know," she replied, running her hands over her thighs. "My legs still work and I can wiggle my toes." She lifted the back of her shirt up a few inches. "Do you see anything wrong?" she asked.

The Crownaxian shook his head. "I don't know much about human physiology but there doesn't appear to be any broken bones in your back. Does your neck hurt?" Yale rubbed her neck with her hand and said no. "Good. But we can't sit here for very long. If they get to my quarters and I'm not there, it will be hard to explain my absence. Do you think you can continue?" he asked.

Yale nodded and hopped to her feet with a grimace. "Yeah, let's go," she said. Prestok took a step toward the boulder but stopped when Yale grabbed his arm. "Maybe I should go first," she said. He looked at her and nodded. Then he helped her climb over the rock before he scaled it again.

They marched along in silence for a few minutes before Yale spoke again. "So what did they disagree on?" she asked. Prestok gave her a quizzical look. "The rebel leaders. You said there was dissent about dethroning Drelk. What was that about?"

The guide glanced at her face before answering. "Some feel that he should be imprisoned. Others want to assassinate him." He pressed his lips together. "I don't know how humans feel about such things but we Crownaxians are taught to treasure life. Before Drelk came along, we didn't even have the death penalty for criminals. The idea of killing someone in cold blood is distasteful to most of us."

"Even if it's to rid yourselves of a tyrant?" asked Yale. Prestok nodded again. "That's quite a dilemma." Yale then felt a cool breeze on her face. She took a deep breath and smelled the fresh air. "We must be getting close. I can feel the air."

"It's just ahead," said Prestok. He tried to hurry her along by putting his arm around her back and increasing his pace. Despite the pain in her back, Yale kept up with him. Then the tunnel became even narrower and they were forced to crawl upward on their hands and knees. Prestok held the flashlight in his mouth to free his hands.

However, gravity worked against the duo as they pulled themselves toward the end of the tunnel. The loose dirt and small rocks they pushed behind them kicked up so much dust that it was hard to breathe. Yale coughed as she struggled to keep going.

The tunnel ended twenty feet from the mouth of a cave. Yale shielded her eyes against the bright daylight, while Prestok turned off his flashlight and put it back in his coat. They stood, wiped the dirt from their clothes and lumbered toward the exit. When they stepped out of the cave, Yale saw a cliff nearly fifty feet in front of them. They cautiously moved to the edge of the cliff that overlooked a raging river below. The water crashed against the shore while squawking birds flew overhead.

Prestok pointed to a boat that was tied to a makeshift dock at the water's edge. "This is how I smuggle prisoners out," he said. "Follow the trial down there and take that boat downstream until you see the edge of the forest. Then get back on land and walk with your back to the water until you see a green house. It may take several hours to find it, but don't get discouraged, it is there. My associates will help you get to a spaceport where we have friends who can get you off this planet." He handed Yale the flashlight then gently laid a hand on her shoulder. "This is as far as I can go. Good luck."

Yale smiled and patted his hand. She started to walk away, and then she suddenly stopped and turned back to face him. "Wait, I can't go yet. Zigler, the man they captured me with, is still in there. I can't leave him here to die. I have to get him out."

"There's no time for that now," said Prestok. "You have to leave." He gently pushed her toward the trail. Yale slipped out of his grip and glared at him. "Look, if we go back now, they'll kill us both," he said. "I'll help your friend escape but first you need to get out of here. It's the only way."

Yale saw the determined look on his face. "Promise me you'll get him out and I'll go," she said. The Crownaxian immediately did. Yale sighed, stuffed the flashlight into her coat pocket and turned toward the trial. She hustled over the thick brush, pushing tree branches out of her face. A few seconds later, the lieutenant heard voices behind her, so she dropped down to her stomach and waited. She tried to quiet her heavy breathing for fear of being detected. The voices continued but didn't sound like they were getting any closer.

Yale lifted her head up and saw two armed guards speaking to Prestok in Crownaxian. They stood a few feet away from him with their rifles aimed at his chest. They didn't look like they believed whatever it was he was telling them. His fists were clenched and he had a terrified look on his face. The guards then began yelling at him and shoving him toward the prison.

Suddenly Prestok took off running in the opposite direction The guards yelled at him again and fired warning shots over his head but the rebel continued to run. Yale watched in horror as one guard took aim and shot Prestok in the back. The blast knocked him off his feet and he rolled toward the edge of the cliff. Prestok grabbed at some branches to keep from going over the edge but his momentum was too strong. He screamed as he fell and Yale closed her eyes when she heard the sickening sound of his body slamming against the rocks below.

Chapter Fourteen

The land vehicles bounced along the road as the caravan headed toward the *Liberty Bell*. Amy and Madison sat in the back of Travar's jeep, which led the two vehicles behind it. Amy was quiet during the trip. The incident with the soccer player weighed heavily on her mind. She hadn't told Travar about what happened and she was debating whether or not she should. Finally, she decided not to.

The convoy stopped and parked in front of the *Liberty Bell*. Amy let out a relieved sigh at the sight of her ship. She didn't know why, but just seeing it again somehow made her feel better. Amy climbed out of the jeep and trotted over to the spaceship. Madison, Travar and the rebel soldiers followed her aboard the craft.

Amy led the troops on a tour of the *Liberty Bell*. They began on the bridge before working their way toward the back of the ship. Three of Travar's soldiers took notes on hand-held computers, much to Amy's chagrin. The robot expressed a similar concern when it cornered the captain as the others left the bridge. "Captain, did you know they were going to be documenting this tour?" asked the robot.

The young girl rested a hand on the robot's right elbow. "No, I didn't and I think we have to make sure those scanners get damaged," she said in a low voice. "Rebels or not, this technology has to stay with us." Amy took her laser pistol out of the pocket of her flight jacket and checked it. It was still fully charged. She then stashed the pistol back inside the pocket before nodding toward Madison. The duo then hurried to catch up to their guests.

Travar and his soldiers were examining panels in the hallway when Amy and Madison approached them. "Is everything ok?" asked Travar. Amy nodded. "We were just looking at the repairs you made after the meteor shower. Very impressive," said the Crownaxian leader. One of his soldiers scanned the previously damaged parts and shook his head. He mumbled something in Crownaxian. Travar laughed. "My engineer likes your work. Where to now?" he asked.

"Right this way," said Amy, taking the lead. She showed them the captain's quarters, the two rooms set aside for the crewmen and the eating area. The soldiers with the scanners took extensive notes, particularly of the atomizer in the ship's mess hall on the lower deck. While his subordinates appeared to be impressed by the tour, Travar seemed anxious, which made Amy wonder again just how wise it was to show him the Sprint Drive.

The rebel leader clapped his hands together and smiled. "So, I see that you're saving the best for last," he said to Amy. "As a former engineer, I'm intrigued by this propulsion system of yours. Shall we have a look at it?"

Amy smiled politely. She did her best not to look at Madison or show her apprehension. "Just trying to be dramatic," she said. "C'mon, it's right down this hallway." She led the way to the engineering section of the ship. When they got there, she pointed to the panels that covered one of the engines and asked Madison to remove them. The robot did, with the help of one of the Crownaxians. Then the soldiers with the scanners moved forward and recorded all the data they could about the drive.

Travar leaned close to the tubes attached to the engine. He ran his hand over them before his fingers touched the outside of the engine. "There's one on each side," said Amy. "But since they're identical, there's no point in opening the other one." She stepped up beside Travar. "Like I told you before, I have no idea how it works. The schematics are stored in the main computer if you'd like to examine them," she said. Out of the corner of her eye, she saw Madison tense up at the suggestion.

"Yes, I think that would be very helpful," said Travar. Amy nodded and asked Madison to retrieve them. The robot accessed a computer terminal nearby and typed in several commands. After a few seconds, pages started printing out from a slot under the terminal. Madison gathered them up and handed them to Travar. The Crownaxian leader shook his head as he read the blueprints. Then he looked over at Amy. "This is truly amazing," he said. "I wonder if the problem lies in the cooling system." He flipped through the pages before he spoke again. "I'd like to take this back to camp to analyze it further, if you don't mind," he said to Amy.

"Be my guest," she replied. "If it is the cooling system, can anything be done to modify it?" she asked. The girl moved closer to Travar and glanced at the blueprints. Then she looked up at him and innocently shrugged her shoulders. "I just don't get any of this technical stuff."

"It is complicated," said Travar. "But I think my engineers and I can find a way to fix the problem." The sound of thunder rumbled over their heads. The leader looked out a nearby window. "We should get back to camp," he said. "We don't want to get caught in that acidic rain." He nodded toward his men, one of whom helped Madison replace the panel over the engine. Then Travar led the way toward the exit.

Both Amy and Madison were quiet on the ride back to the base. The girl tried to figure out a way to get the schematics back and delete the information stored on the Crownaxian scanners. She knew what was at stake if she didn't. She'd be tried for aiding the enemy and handing over the single most important piece of technology to a race led by a tyrant. At the least, she'd be sent to a prison on Earth for the rest of her life.

When they got back to the base, Amy excused herself from the group by telling Travar and his soldiers that she wanted to perform a maintenance check on Madison in their tent. Travar offered to send an engineer to assist her but she told him that it would not be necessary. She saw the suspicious expression on the rebel leader's face and had to think fast. "It's a very simple procedure," she said with an innocent grin. "Besides, their time would be better spent trying to fix the Sprint Drive. We'll probably need that during the rescue."

The rebel leader nodded. "Yes, we probably will. But if you change your mind, feel free to ask for help." Travar removed the blueprints from his pocket and unfolded the sheets of paper. He read them as he and his technicians walked over to his tent. Amy quietly sighed and took Madison by the arm. She noticed a Crownaxian with a star-shaped scar on his face nearby who stared at them as they entered their tent.

"I have an idea," said Amy, as she guided the robot to the middle of the floor. She pretended to check Madison's systems as she spoke in a low voice. "Do you still store extra data disks in your emergency pouch?" she asked. The robot said yes. "Good, turn around." Madison turned its back to the girl. Amy opened a small door on the robot's back. Inside she saw the familiar maze of wires, tubes and fuses. On the right side, there was a slot that held six circular disks. She took one out and stuffed into her coat pocket. Then she shut the door and spun the robot around to face her.

She leaned close to Madison and continued to keep her voice down. "I noticed that the Crownaxian scanners are the same size and shape as ours. I also saw one of the engineers remove a storage disk from one of them when he was scanning the ship." She took a deep breath to calm down. "I want you to write a program on this disk so I can infect their scanners with a virus that will eventually erase all their information about the *Liberty Bell*," she said. Madison gave her a surprised look. "I know it's risky but we need to try this. Can you write one for me?" she asked.

The robot looked around the room for a moment. Then it walked over to Amy's cot and picked up the mini-comp that had the Crownaxian plays stored on it. "With this, I think I can," it said quietly. "But it will take at least an hour. Do we have enough time?"

"We'll stall them if we have to," said Amy. "Get started on that. I'm going to Travar's tent. Hopefully, I'll get a chance to destroy the blueprints before he can copy or store them." She handed the robot the disk. "Good luck with this. I'll be back later for it." She exited the tent and noticed that the scarred soldier was still watching her. Amy kept her eyes forward as she casually strolled across the compound to Travar's tent.

Two soldiers stood guard outside the door. The one on the right side told her to halt. "Travar asked me to stop by when I was finished," she said. "Can you ask him if I can come in?" The soldier who spoke told her to wait where she was. Then he disappeared into the tent, only to return a few seconds later. He said something to his partner in Crownaxian, then he opened the door for the girl. "Thank you," said Amy with a polite smile.

Travar smiled and said hello from behind his desk. Two engineers from the tour stood on either side of him. The blueprints were spread out on the desk. "Done so soon?" asked Travar, pointing to the empty chair across from him. "I guess you didn't need any help."

Amy sat down and smiled. "No, it was pretty easy." She peeked at the documents in front of her. "Had any luck with this yet?" she asked.

The rebel leader leaned toward his desk and pointed at one of the pages. "Yes, we think it is a coolant problem, like I suspected. The fluid your designers chose begins to boil when the engine hits 2,430 degrees. That, of course, allows the engines to overheat. So much so, that they explode with enough force to destroy the ship." He opened a file that laid on the desk beside the blueprints and took out a sheet of paper. "We have a synthetic substance called nentracal that we convert into liquid form to cool the parts in our fission-based power plants. Nentracal can stand up to heat ten times that intense," he said. "This should work for your engines."

"Wow!" said Amy with an even bigger smile. "That sounds great. When can we try it?" she asked, rising from her seat. As she leaned toward the desk, she spotted a flashlight lying near the three scanners on a small table to her right.

Travar rose from his seat. "I'm sending a team back out to your ship this afternoon," he said. "The work shouldn't take very long. All they need to do is drain the old coolant and replace it with the nentracal. Then we can test it." He moved to the front of the desk and delicately rested his right hand on the girl's shoulder. "Amy, although I'm certain that this will work, you need to understand that this is experimental and there is a degree of risk involved. If you're not comfortable flying the ship during the test run, I'll assign one of my pilots to do it," he said.

"I appreciate the offer but I'd prefer to do the test run," she said. "It's my ship and I should be onboard in case anything goes wrong." She looked into his eyes to gauge his reaction but he gave nothing away.

"I'm glad to hear you say that," he responded, lifting his hand from her shoulder. "Every good captain wants to be on the bridge. I know I would. Feel free to relax in your tent if you like. I'll let you know when we're ready for the test." He walked to the door and opened it for her. Amy knew that he was telling her to leave. She glanced again at the scanners on the table before thanking Travar and heading back to her tent.

Amy walked back to her quarters and again spotted the scarred solider hanging around outside the tent. This time she looked right at him, smiled and excitedly waved her left hand. "Good morning," she said to him. The soldier turned and drifted away without responding. Amy causally entered the tent and found Madison working on the mini-comp. She moved close to the robot and kept her voice down. "We have a spy outside," she said, nodding in the direction of the Crownaxian. Madison looked outside and shrugged. "Oh, he's gone now. I scared him off. How's it going?"

The robot shook its head and continued typing in commands on the mini-comp. "Slowly. I'm not great with computers." Amy laughed at the irony. Madison glared at her. "Do you know how to perform surgery?" Amy shook her head no. "Then you know what I mean." Madison kept typing while Amy rose and moved to her cot.

"Travar thinks he's found a way to make the Sprint Drive work," said Amy, sitting on her bed. The robot nodded without looking up. "He's sending a crew over to the ship later to modify our coolant system. Then we're going to test the new design." She paused and glanced outside. The spy had not returned. "I'm going to pilot the *Liberty Bell* during the test."

Madison's head shot up. "Is that wise, Captain?" The robot stood up, moved toward Amy and sat down beside the girl. "What if something goes wrong? You could be killed."

Amy nodded. "I know," she said. "But the *Liberty Bell* is my ship and I should be the one who flies it." She sighed. "It wouldn't be right to put anyone else at risk. That's why I want you to stay on the surface during the test." The robot tilted its head in confusion. "It makes sense, Madison. If anything goes wrong, one of us has to survive to complete our mission. My dad must be rescued." She stood up and paced the floor for a moment before turning around and facing the robot. "Promise me that no matter what, you will continue our mission."

The robot nodded. "You have my word, captain." The serious expression on Madison's face told Amy that she could count on it.

Amy sat back down beside her friend. "Good, now get back to work. We'll need that virus pretty soon. And I need to find a way to plant it." She rose again and slipped her hand into her coat pocket. The laser pistol felt cold in her hand. "I'm going to take a walk," she said. "I need to clear my head. I'll be back shortly," she said. The girl smiled at Madison before heading out of the tent.

The Crownaxian rebels went about their normal routines as Amy strolled through the camp. She smiled at whomever noticed her, though most of the soldiers ignored her. The girl kept a sharp eye out for the scarred spy. It took awhile, but she finally found him talking to two other rebels outside the soccer field. She waved at him again as she moved past the group, which caused the other rebels to glare at the spy. Amy sat down at the edge of the field and watched two teams play soccer. She smiled and pretended to get caught up in the action, while she kept a peripheral watch on the spy.

A half-hour passed before the scarred soldier headed away from the field by himself. Amy stood, yawned and stretched her hands over her head. She realized that Madison probably wasn't finished yet, so she waited just a few seconds before she followed the spy. She stayed far enough behind him to not attract the attention of the other soldiers. Amy watched him enter a small tent and turn on a light. She circled his tent until she found a dark gap between the quarters and a supply shed next to it.

Amy sneaked into the dark gap and crawled on the ground until she found a tiny opening that she could see through. The Crownaxian sat behind a small desk and began typing on a laptop computer. Amy didn't understand the Crownaxian symbols that appeared on the screen and she began to think that this was a waste of time. Then she noticed something peculiar. She saw a detailed map of the rebel's base, a chart of this solar system with a planet marked in red and the schematics for the *Liberty Bell* and the Sprint Drive.

Suddenly, there was a knock on the door of the tent. The soldier's expression changed from determined to fearful. He quickly typed in a command that changed all of the data on the screen into some kind of code. Then he shut off the laptop and stuffed it under his cot as the knocking continued. He said something in Crownaxian as he stumbled over to the door and opened it. Both of the Crownaxians that he had been talking to entered with smiles on their faces. Again, Amy couldn't understand what they were saying but they all left the tent and headed over to the mess hall. Amy climbed out from her hiding place and followed them.

The trio entered the mess hall and grabbed food trays. Amy watched them sit down and eat before she forced herself to walk at a slow pace and circle back toward her own tent. There she found Madison on its cot still typing on the mini-comp. "How's it going?" she softly asked.

"Just about done," replied Madison. "Did you have a good walk?"

Amy sat down beside the robot. "Remember that spy I mentioned before?" she asked. Madison nodded. "Well I followed him around for a while and I spied on him when he went into his tent." She filled Madison in on the rest of the details as the robot concluded its task. "What I don't get," said Amy, "is why he would have all of that info on his computer then code it when his pals showed up." She took a breath. "Unless he wasn't supposed to have it," she said. "That must be it."

Madison popped out the disk, turned off the mini-comp, and then handed the disk to Amy. "All done, Captain." Amy took the disk and hid it under her pillow on her cot. "If your suspicions are correct, then he wasn't spying on us, he was spying on this entire camp," said Madison. "Which means that he's probably working for Drelk. We should tell Travar about this."

Amy smiled. "Not right away," she said. Madison gave her a concerned look. "Think about it. We're inside a mountain. Obviously he can't transmit his info or he would have done so already. We need to delete the info on the scanners and destroy the hard copy without getting caught. Who better to take the fall than this spy?" she asked.

"This all sounds very dangerous," said Madison. "You seem to be putting yourself in lots of jeopardy on this mission, Captain."

"We both knew this mission would be dangerous," stated Amy. "But I think we can pull it all off. We have to. It's the only way to save my dad and protect the Sprint Drive." She saw the stern look on her friend's face. "Alright, I know that they have it because of me but I gave it to Travar so he could fix the Sprint Drive. Once that's done I'll make sure his copies are destroyed. And now we have someone to blame it on."

"Have you figured out a way to get to the scanners?" asked

Madison.

Amy nodded. "We'll wait until most of the soldiers are asleep. Then we break into Travar's office, plant the virus and steal the blueprints."

"You make it sound so easy," said Madison. "It won't be. I'm sure there'll be guards posted in front of his office. How will we get by them?"

Amy laughed and shook her head. "Madison, we stole a spaceship from a Union outpost. Breaking into an office should be easy. All we need is a diversion."

"What are we going to burn this time?" Madison asked sarcastically. Amy glared at her pal. "Sorry, I couldn't resist. What are we going to do?"

"Well, we're defiantly not going to burn anything. A fire in this place would spread like a, well, a wildfire. No. We need something more subtle but just as diverting." She closed her eyes and pictured the camp in her mind, searching every image for an idea. Finally, she opened her eyes and shrugged. "I got nothing. How about you?" she asked.

Madison stood up and paced the tiny tent. Amy watched her pal move back and forth six times before stopping. Then the robot stepped closer to Amy and whispered. "The power generators. If we knock out the lights, you can slip into the office, take the disks, erase them, and then plant them in the spy's tent. When Travar notices that the disks are missing, he'll order every tent searched. His soldiers find them and our spy is caught."

Amy's face beamed. "Very good, Madison. Boy, you're a natural at this cloak and dagger stuff. Admit it, it's pretty cool being bad every once in a while, isn't it?" she asked.

The robot shook its head. "I take no joy in this, Amy," it said. "But I know why we're doing this and I will follow your orders while we're out here. But once we get home, you go back to being the student and I go back to being the teacher." Madison suddenly looked toward the door.

Amy turned around and saw Travar and two other soldiers walking up to their tent. Travar knocked on the door before entering. His soldiers stayed a step behind him. "Good, you're here," said the leader. "My technicians just returned from your ship. Everything is ready for the test flight." He offered his hand and helped Amy off of her cot. "Shall we go?" he asked.

As the girl stood, she felt an inch on her right shin. She scratched it with her left boot before zipping up her flight jacket. "C'mon Madison, let's go." She scratched her shin again but her boot wasn't hitting the spot. Amy then leaned down to use her fingernails. Suddenly, her laser pistol fell out of her pocket and landed at Travar's feet!

She quickly reached out to grab it but Travar got to it first. The rebel leader had a shocked expression as he picked up the weapon. His two aids rushed toward Amy but Travar stopped them with the wave of his hand. "What are you still doing with this?" asked the Crownaxian leader.

Chapter Fifteen

Amy pasted a smile on her face as she stood back up. "Oh, that," she causally said. "I forgot it was in there." She reached for the pistol but Travar kept it away from her. She maintained her smile as she stepped back. "It's standard procedure to carry a weapon when visiting alien worlds. Every Union solider does it." Amy felt her heart pound and she knew she was breathing heavier than usual. Still she worked to keep her composure.

"Is that so?" asked Travar. He turned and handed the weapon to one of his aids. Then he looked back at Amy. "I'd feel much better if we held onto it for you," he said. "Just to make sure it doesn't get lost. We'll give it back to you before we take off tomorrow." He pointed toward the door. "We really should get going," he said.

"No time like the present," said Amy. She glanced at Madison before leading everyone out the door. The robot caught up to her but kept quiet as they all walked toward the waiting jeeps. They again climbed into the back of Travar's vehicle and held on as the jeep rumbled forward. Madison patted Amy's shoulder and smiled at the girl. She smiled back and hoped that they hadn't lost Travar's trust.

The land vehicles parked further away from the *Liberty Bell* than before to allow the ship space to take off. Amy walked stride for stride with Travar as he led the group to the ramp. They climbed inside the vessel and Travar turned toward the engineering section. He stopped in front of the Sprint Drive engines, which were now covered by their panels. "As you can see, everything is ready," said the rebel leader. His stern expression then softened. "Are you sure you want to pilot the test flight?" he asked.

Amy nodded. "Absolutely," she replied. She glanced again at the robot before she continued. "However, I'd like to make one request." Travar leaned in a little closer to her. "I'd like Madison to stay on the surface during the test. Just in case."

Travar straightened up and patted her on the shoulder. "I understand," he said. Then he looked at the robot. "Madison, would you do me the honor of standing beside me during the test?" The robot nodded. "Excellent." He looked back at Amy. "Then I'll leave you to your work. Good luck." The rebel leader breezed past Amy and marched toward the exit.

Madison moved closer to Amy. "I'm sure everything will be fine," it said. "You know more about this ship than just about anyone. But please be careful. If there's any trouble, don't hesitate to switch off the Sprint Drive." Madison smiled at her. "I don't want to spend the rest of my life on this planet with these guys. I'd miss you too much." The robot playfully tasseled her hair before turning around and exiting the ship.

Amy zipped up her flight jacket and put her helmet on before she sat down in the pilot's seat. Then she pressed the button to close the hatch. She was about to start the engines when she decided instead to run a ship-wide diagnostic to make sure everything was functioning correctly. The report that emerged from the slot in the console showed that all systems were operating within acceptable parameters. The girl then took a deep breath and fired up the engines.

The captain eased the *Liberty Bell* forward about 50 feet before she switched on the thrusters. The ship steadily rose toward the sky. When she had enough room, Amy cut the thrusters and pressed on the accelerator. She bit her bottom lip when she spotted her friend standing next to Travar. "I'll be back in a few minutes," she said out loud. Then she focused on the sky in front of her and braced for the uncertain ride.

The *Liberty Bell* darted through the planet's atmosphere as Amy steered the craft with whitened knuckles. Once she broke free of the planet's gravitational pull, she turned on the communications system. "Travar, this is Amy," she said into the microphone. "Come in, please."

"Travar here," said the familiar voice over the loudspeaker. "We're tracking you on our mobile radar. Everything looks good so far."

"Same here, Travar," said Amy. "I'm going to start off slowly." She leaned back in her seat and checked the radar screen. There were no other ships in sight. Amy plotted a course that would only take her a few hundred thousand miles away from the planet. Then she eased the accelerator down until the ship picked up considerable speed. She took a deep breath and let it out slowly before she engaged the Sprint Drive engines.

Amy was pinned back to her seat. She held tightly onto the yoke and tried not to over steer. The Sprint Drive engines whined behind her. Through the window she saw planets, moons and space debris whizzing by the ship. Sweat rolled down from her forehead. She tried to breathe normally to keep from panicking. She looked at a dial on the console in front of her and saw that the engine temperature was holding steady at 2,500 degrees. Amy realized that the normal coolant would have evaporated by now. The fact that the ship was still in one piece made her feel much better.

The captain maintained the ship's course and speed for another fifteen minutes. She wanted to go longer but her arms hurt from holding onto the yoke with so much force. She turned off the Sprint Drive engines and allowed the *Liberty Bell* to coast for awhile. Then she turned the ship around and restarted the Sprint Drive. After another fifteen minutes passed, she again cut off the engines and coasted back toward the planet.

Amy eased the *Liberty Bell* down on the planet's surface and shut off the engines. She looked out the window and saw everyone clapping. The girl pulled off her helmet and tossed it onto the copilot's chair. Then she hit the button for the hatch before hustling off the bridge. Her feet motored across the floor of the ship and she had to catch her breath after she darted down the steps and stopped in front of Madison.

The robot patted her on back. "Well done, Captain. You've just made aviation history. No one has ever run the Sprint Drive for that long." Amy hugged her pal then pulled back as Travar approached. The robot took a step back to get out of the way. The other soldiers gathered around them and yelled out in celebration.

The rebel leader stepped through the crowd and offered a hand to Amy. "That was terrific," he said, shaking her hand. Then he showed her a printout from his radar equipment. "We clocked the ship at 800 drysons. No one had over gone over 500 before." He turned and looked at the ship. "There's not a mark on it. Your *Liberty Bell* is one tough vessel." He looked back at Amy. "Let's head back to camp so you can get some rest."

Two of Travar's soldiers locked up the ship while Amy. Madison and the rebel leader drove back to camp in Travar's jeep. On the way back, Travar told Amy his plan for freeing her father and the other prisoners. After following the squadron to the prison on Crownaxia, Amy needed to fly the *Liberty Bell* close to the facility to draw the responding ships into an ambush by the rebels. The Sprint Drive would keep her just out of range of the guard's missiles and laser fire. Once the guard's ships were neutralized, the *Liberty Bell* would join a smaller group of rebel ships that would stage a ground assault on the compound. Once inside the prison, they must locate and free the captives. However, they would have less than 40 minutes before reinforcements showed up.

"Wouldn't Drelk's military detect our ships when we enter the planet's atmosphere?" asked Amy. She glanced at Madison and noticed the uneasy look on the robot's face. Then she locked eyes with Travar, who was simply smiling.

"You've never been to Crownaxia," he said, shaking his head. "Our atmosphere is cluttered with satellites and other space debris that gets stuck in the mucky gas pockets. To those on the ground, we would look like metallic junk falling from the sky, which happens frequently on my homeworld." He then said something in Crownaxian that made the driver laugh, while Amy rubbed her eyes and wondered if this plan would work.

Travar and two of his aids walked Amy and the robot to their tent after they got back to the base. The rebel leader sat on Madison's cot and explained his escape plan in more detail. Amy nodded politely and pretended to listen as she continued to work out the particulars of her own plan in her mind. However, she couldn't block out Travar's voice, so she deliberately yawned and stretched her arms over her head.

The rebel leader didn't look offended as he stopped talking. "You look like you could use some downtime," he said, rising to his feet. "I sometimes forget that you are a child." He nodded toward his aids. "I'll let you get some rest before dinner. Then later I suggest we all try to get some sleep tonight. We'll need to be well rested in the morning." He patted Amy on the shoulder. "I'll see you later in the mess hall."

Amy watched him leave before she lay down on her cot and pulled the blanket over her tiny frame. Madison lay down on the other cot. When she was sure they were out of earshot, Amy spoke quietly to her friend. "We need to slip out of here unnoticed. Turn the light off then put your pillow in the middle of your blanket." The robot nodded and followed the captain's orders. Amy took the disk out from under her pillow and stuffed it into her coat pocket before rigging her cot.

It was dark enough inside the tent to fool anyone on the outside. After she was sure the decoys were set, Amy crawled along the floor toward one corner of the tent. She could hear Madison crawling behind her. They found an opening at the bottom of the canopy and they slid under the canvas and out the other side. They found themselves in the dark area between the tents. Amy pointed toward the power generators and watched her friend slink off toward that target. Then Amy tiptoed along the back of the tents in the opposite direction as she headed for the Travar's office.

Four minutes later, the camp fell into complete darkness. Alarms rang out and soldiers yelled as they scrambled in the blackness. Amy was just outside the office and she slipped into the enclosure the same way she sneaked out of her tent. Once inside, she listened for anyone who might be in the room. Hearing no one, she moved to her right where she remembered seeing a flashlight behind Travar's desk. She felt around until she found it on a small table. The girl carefully turned it on and pointed the beam at the floor. She used the radiant light to find that scanners that lay on the other side of the table. Realizing that her time was short, Amy quickly loaded her disk into one of the scanners and downloaded the virus. She popped that one out and put the other disks in, erasing them one by one. Afterwards, she put the scanners back, and stuffed her virus disk and another she found on the desk into her coat pocket. Then the girl sneaked out of the office the way she came in.

The rebel soldiers stomped around the camp pointing flashlights in various directions, while Amy moved swiftly toward the spy's tent, making sure she stayed in the dark corners between the quarters. The commotion hit a fever pitch as the rebel officers frantically tried to restore order. Amy could hear the Crownaxians yelling to each other in their native language. She focused on her breathing in order to stay calm. Soon, she stood just a few feet away from her target and peered inside the tent.

The tent was dark. Amy slipped inside and felt her way around the sparse room. She eventually found the computer that was back on the soldier's desk. Amy planted the virus disk and the other disk from Travar's office in a pile of folders beside the computer. Then she quickly ducked out of the tent and hustled back to her own quarters.

Amy tiptoed back into her tent. It was pitch black, so she waved her hands in front of her. "Madison, are you in here?" she quietly asked. There was no answer. She sighed and felt her way to her cot. Then she lay down and slipped under the covers. A few minutes later, she heard the door open, followed by Madison's low voice. "I'm over here," she replied.

The girl heard footsteps coming closer to her. "It's a madhouse out there," said the robot. Amy then heard the squeak of a cot as the robot sat down across from her. "How did you do?" asked Madison.

"Fine," replied Amy. "The package was delivered. Nice job with the lights. Did you have any trouble getting back here?" she asked. The robot said no. "Good. Travar will probably check his office soon, if he isn't already there. It won't take them long to start looking for the saboteur. When he comes here, I'll tell him what I saw that spy doing." She took a deep breath. "It's funny, now I really am tired."

Suddenly, the camp lights flashed back on. Amy cupped her hands over her eyes and peered over at the robot. She watched Madison stand up and move to the tent door. The robot looked out. "Travar and his aids are heading for his office," said Madison. The robot stayed in that spot for nearly ten minutes before speaking again. "They just came out. Travar looks mad. He's yelling at his aids." Madison paused. "Now they're yelling at the other soldiers. It looks like they're starting a search."

"Move away from the door, Madison," said Amy. "You don't want to look suspicious." The robot nodded and moved over to the other cot. Amy rested her head on her pillow and closed her eyes. She was tired, more so than she realized. Amy wrapped her arms around the pillow and pulled the pad close to her chest. She thought about her father and wondered if he was still alive. The girl bit her bottom lip and tried not to think about what he would have gone through in the Crownaxian prison. Instead she concentrated on what she would say to Travar when he showed up.

Amy sat up in her cot when she heard the knock on the tent door. Travar entered with two aids behind him. Amy smiled and rose to greet the rebel leader, whose face was red with anger. "What's wrong?" asked Amy, dropping her smile. She glanced at the Crownaxian aids and pretended to be surprised at Travar's demeanor. "And what happened to the lights?"

Travar nodded at his aids and they began searching the tent. "Someone knocked out the power," said Travar through clenched teeth. "And they deleted the information from the scans we took of your ship." He took a menacing step toward the girl. "They also took another one of our data disks. You wouldn't happen to know anything about that would you?" he asked.

The girl took a confident step toward him and glared at the leader. "No, I wouldn't," she said, in an angry voice. She kept her eyes locked on his. "And I don't appreciate the accusation."

The aids rummaged through the tent, checking the cots, the blankets, the pillows and the floor while Amy kept staring at Travar. The leader stared back until his aids approached him empty-handed. "Search them," ordered Travar. The aids asked Amy and Madison to raise their hands over their heads. Amy continued staring at Travar as one aid gingerly padded her down. She saw the aid shake his head as he moved toward the leader. The other aid did the same after frisking the robot.

Travar's expression softened. "I apologize for the intrusion," he said. "I hope you understand that I had to do this. All of the tents in the camp are being searched, including my own. I need to find out who did this and why." He approached Amy and Madison more carefully this time. "Have either of you seen or heard anything suspicious while you've been here?" Amy shrugged and Madison shook its head. "Well, if you do, please let me know." He turned and headed for the door.

"Now that I think of it," said Amy, causing Travar to stop and turn back around. "I did notice one of your soldiers watching Madison and I earlier today. It was kinda creepy." Travar nodded and asked her to go on. "Twice I saw him standing outside our tent and just staring over here." She put her hands on her hips and continued. "I thought maybe he was keeping tabs on us for you," she said.

Travar pressed his lips together. "I assure you that I did not assign one of my soldiers to spy on you," he said. "I didn't think I needed to, even after your weapon fell out of your coat pocket." The leader paused and Amy knew he was trying to rattle her. She just smiled again. "Could you point this soldier out to me?" asked Travar.

Amy nodded. "Yeah, I think so," she said. The girl slipped her boots on and zipped up her flight jacket. Then she tapped the robot on the shoulder on her way out. "Come with us, Madison," she said. "I could use the company." Travar held the door open and followed Amy and Madison out before pointing to his left and leading the group to the next tent.

The duo accompanied Travar and his aids as they inspected eight tents over the next hour. Each time they entered a tent, Amy shook her head to let Travar know that the soldier occupying the quarters wasn't the one she saw earlier. When they got to the ninth tent, Amy nodded as the sight of the spy. Travar nodded back and told his aids to be especially careful.

The accused solider stood at attention and appeared calm as the inspection continued. Travar circled around him with a grim look on his face. Then one of the aids found the planted disks in the pile of folders where Amy had left them. The spy's face whitened when the aid handed the disks to Travar, while Amy smothered a smile. She forced herself not to glance at Madison, who remained quiet.

Travar examined the disks before handing them to the aid. Then he grabbed the soldier by the shirt collar. "What are you doing with these?" he asked, seething. The soldier began to babble, saying he had no idea what they were or how they got into his tent. Amy studied Travar's face and saw that the rebel leader didn't believe the soldier. "Enough!" shouted Travar, shoving the soldier toward one of his aids. "Lock him up," he said. The aid nodded, put a pair of handcuffs on the soldier, and then led him out of the tent. Travar turned to the other aid. "Check his computer. I want to know everything he has stored on it." The aid nodded and turned on the computer.

The rebel leader moved over to Amy and Madison. "I apologize again," he said, extending a hand to Amy. She smiled and shook it.

"Thank you for pointing him out. My men will interrogate him. We'll find out what he was up to." He pointed toward the door. "I don't know about you, but all this excitement has made me hungry. Would you join me for dinner?"

"I'd love to," replied Amy. "But first I need to stop by my tent." She lowered her voice and pretended to be a bit embarrassed. "I really need to go to the bathroom first," she said. Travar nodded and said he would meet them shortly. Then he headed for the mess hall. Amy waited until he was out of earshot before she whispered to Madison. "That worked out pretty well."

The robot nodded and spoke in a low voice. "It was a little too close for me. I can't wait until we finish this mission and go home."

"We will," said Amy, "And my dad's coming home with us."

Chapter Sixteen

Yale stumbled along a muddy trail in the thick forest. She held the flashlight in her hand and the beam of light cut through the gathering darkness. Her legs ached from the arduous hike and her shoulders were sore from paddling the boat. She tried to put the pain out of her mind as she marched with the water at her back, as Prestok had instructed. A cold wind swirled around her, blowing her hair into her face.

The lieutenant couldn't get the image of Prestok's broken body out of her mind. She wanted to be strong, wanted to act like the soldier she was trained to be, but she couldn't help mourning for the individual who had sacrificed his life to save hers. It was not the first time someone had stuck their neck out for her, but this was the first time they had died doing it. Yale felt guilty and with each step toward the green house, the feeling intensified like a raging hurricane.

The sounds of the forest around her grew louder as the darkness finally enveloped the landscape. She heard strange hoots, hollers and cries from animals she saw only sporadically. The animals managed to scurry away from the beam of light before the woman could get a good look at them. That was fine with her, as long as they didn't attempt to discover how she tasted. From the glimpses she did get, Yale noticed a few animals that looked like they could take a huge bite out of her.

With no idea how far she had walked and no idea how much farther she still had to go, Yale decided to take a short break. She sat down on the wet soil and leaned against a mighty tree. Yale crossed her arms over her chest and curled her frigid fingers into tight fists. She wiggled her legs back and forth to keep them warm. Soon, the lieutenant's eyelids grew too heavy to keep open and her head tilted to one side.

A sharp pain in her calves and piercing shrieks from the ground caused her to leap to her feet and drop the flashlight. Yale instinctively backpedaled and brushed away the creatures that were gnawing at her legs. The beasts bit at her fingers as she desperately fought them off.

The officer shouted out in pain and felt the cold enamel of their teeth cutting into her wounded skin. Yale pounded on the intruders with all of her strength but they just kept coming. Trying not to panic, she felt around the wet ground until she found the flashlight. She quickly turned it on and aimed the beam at the creatures' faces. They squealed even louder but finally scooted away from her and disappeared into a nearby hole.

The lieutenant shined the light on her legs and peeled back her boots to examine the wounds. She was bleeding from several punctures on her calves and shins. With nothing else to use as a bandage, Yale took off her boots, removed her socks and wrapped them around the affected areas. Then she put her boots back on and tightened them to hold the socks in place. The cuts on her hands were less serious, which was fortunate since Yale had no way to bandage them at all.

After another hour of walking on her wounded legs, Yale finally saw the green house. The rectangular, two-story dwelling sat in a meadow some 100 yards from the edge of the forest. Yale stopped and took a deep breath before inching her way to the house. She climbed the three small steps to the porch and cautiously approached the front door. Wishing she had a pistol with her, the officer winced as she knocked on the weathered door.

After a few moments, the door creaked open and light spilled out from inside. Yale clicked off her flashlight and stuffed into her coat pocket as she nodded toward the diminutive Crownaxian, who wore a confused expression on a wrinkled face. They stared at each other in silence before Yale mustered up the energy to speak. "Please don't be alarmed. I'm not here to hurt you," she said, leaning against the doorframe. "Prestok sent me. He said you could help me get off this planet. Is that true?"

The native smiled. "Yes, I think I can help you." The Crownaxian offered a hand and helped Yale enter the home. "My name is Garn," she said, closing the door with her foot. "I'm Prestok's sister." She then guided the wounded woman through a hallway and into what looked like a kitchen. A small, circular table sat in the middle of the room, while a stove and a refrigeration unit were embedded in a near wall. Garn pulled a chair away from the table and helped her guest sit down. "What is your name?" she asked, sitting in a chair across from the human.

"My name is Yale," said the officer. "I was captured by a patrol and sent to your brother's facility. He helped me escape." Yale looked into the woman's yellow eyes and tried to find a way to break the terrible news to her. Then she suddenly winced as the pain in her legs increased. Garn asked her what was wrong. "I was attacked by some kind of hairy creatures," she said, pushing her chair back. Yale took off her boots and peeled away the soiled socks. "They got my legs."

Garn rose and moved over to Yale. "Oh, that looks really bad," she said, examining the wounds. "I have a medical kit upstairs. I'll be right back." Garn hurried out of the room. Yale heard her run up the steps and enter a room before stomping back down the stairwell. She reentered with a black, leather bag in her hands.

The Crownaxian opened the bag and removed a green cloth, several bandages, and a tiny bottle with red liquid in it. Garn poured some of the liquid onto the cloth. "This might hurt a bit," she said, as she pressed the cloth over one of the cuts on Yale's right leg. The human screamed out in pain and held onto the table with both hands. Garn covered the wound with a bandage then applied the liquid to the other abrasions before bandaging them as well. She then closed the bag, placed it on a counter by the stove, and carefully disposed of Yale's socks in a trash receptacle.

"You must be hungry," said Garn, leaning against counter. "Would you like me to make you something to eat?" Yale nodded and thanked her. The hostess then removed a box from the refrigerator. She opened it and showed her guest a brown-shelled egg the size of a grapefruit. "These are the best eggs in the region," she said. Garn then took a cooking pot out of a cabinet and filled it with water. She put two eggs in the pot, set the pot on the stove and turned a dial until a flame appeared.

The hostess then sat back down in her chair. She looked at Yale and smiled. "I'm sorry I don't have any atomized food. I know your species likes things done quickly but I'm afraid my people have yet to perfect the process." Yale's eyes widened. "Oh, don't be so surprised," said Garn. "We know quiet a bit about your culture. I find it so fascinating."

Yale nodded. "Yeah, Prestok told me that your people have studied us. He also told me about Drelk and his ambitions. He told me a great many things." She folded her hands and decided it was time to break the news. "Garn, there's something I need to tell you." She paused, trying to find the right words. "After your brother got me out of the prison, he was approached by two guards." Yale saw the concerned look on Garn's face and wondered if she knew where this was going. Yale continued in a softer voice. "He got into an argument with them and took off running. They shot him." Garn covered her mouth with her right hand. "I'm sorry, but he didn't survive."

Garn sat back in her chair and let out a low sigh. Yale kept quiet to allow the news to sink in. The Crownaxian closed her eyes as her body started to shake. Yale saw tears sliding down her face and she tried not to cry as well. Neither spoke for a few minutes. The silence was eventually broken by the sound of the eggs boiling in the water. Garn silently rose and moved like a zombie over to the stove. She turned off the flame and put the pot on a different burner. Then she suddenly slammed her fists against the counter and yelled something in her native language.

Yale wearily rose to her feet and stumbled over to her hostess. "I can't begin to tell you how sorry I am," she said, placing a hand on Garn's shoulder. "I feel like this is all my fault."

The Crownaxian shook her head and clutched Yale's hand. "No, this is not your fault," she said. "I always knew that this could happen. He put himself in danger many, many times to help the resistance." Garn wiped her eyes with her free hand then let go of Yale. She opened a cabinet door and removed two plates and cups. Yale watched her drain the pot and ease the boiled eggs onto the plates. Then she filled the cups with water from a spout over the sink. Garn carried the steaming plates to the table while Yale brought over the cups.

Both women sat back down across from each other. Garn tapped her egg against the plate, peeled away the shell and took a bite of her food. Yale remained quiet and did the same with her egg. "I was the one who urged him to join," said Garn, after a long silence. Yale nodded reverently. "He always talked about how Drelk was wrong to conquer and enslave other worlds. He said that someone needed to do something to put an end to the bloodshed." Garn took a deep breath and slowly let it out. "I told him about a group that was trying to stop Drelk."

"Faction 12," said Yale, with a nod.

"Yes, Faction 12," replied Garn. "Some of my friends were in it. I was planning to join them and I wanted him to as well. It took him awhile to muster the courage but he finally did. That was five years ago." She finished her egg and drank her water. "He died doing what needed to be done. And now I need to finish what he started." She stood up and put her empty plate and cup into the sink beside the stove. Then she turned back toward Yale, who was finishing her food and water. "You can sleep her tonight. Then tomorrow night I'll take you to some friends who own a spaceship. They'll get you as far into Union space as they can."

Yale stood up and brought her plate and cup over to the sink. "I appreciate that, but I can't leave just yet." Garn tilted her head to one side and asked why not. "I wasn't captured alone," said Yale. "One of my friends is still in the prison and I need to rescue him first."

Garn smiled at her guest. "You humans never make things easy, do you?" she asked. Yale shrugged. "I'd feel the same way if I were in your shoes," said Garn. "I have what you would call a jeep. I'll drop you off close to the prison. Get your friend out and come back here. Then we'll work on getting both of you home." She gingerly slipped her arm across Yale's back. "C'mon, I'll show you to your room."

The lieutenant leaned on her hostess as she hobbled up the steps to the second floor of the house. Garn then led Yale to a room at the end of a well-lit hallway that smelled like daises. The modest room had two bureaus, a desk, two small nightstands with electric lamps on them, and a bed set against a wall underneath a window. Garn flipped a switch to turn on the lights and Yale carefully lay down on the bed, resting her head on a pillow.

"The bathroom is one door down," said Garn. "My room is the next one after it. If you need anything at all, feel free to ask for it." She opened the bottom drawer of one dresser, took out an extra blanket and spread it out over Yale's frame. "You should rest as much as you can tomorrow. You'll need your strength if you are going to rescue your friend."

Yale sat up and nodded. "Thank you for all of your help, Garn," she said tenderly. "I just wish there was something I could do for you."

Garn laughed. "Another odd quality of you humans," she said, moving toward the door. She stopped and looked back at her guest. "You have this great need to repay acts of kindness. I suppose that's a good quality to have." She turned off the lights. "Good night," she said, closing the door behind her.

The lieutenant eased back down to the pillow and sighed. She closed her eyes and tried to fall asleep but she couldn't stop thinking about Prestok's death. The image of his corpse was burned into her memory. She knew that the only thing she could do was rescue Zigler and make it back home safely. How she was going to break Zigler out was still a mystery to her. Even if she could get into the prison undetected, she had no idea how to get out again.

Yale forced herself to remember the layout of the facility. In her mind, she saw each room and hallway that she had been in. She traced the path to the elevator that she used to escape to the first floor but then discounted using the lift again, realizing that they'd have a better chance of getting trapped by the guards who'd be expecting her to try to get out that way. No, after she got Zigler out of his cell, they'd have to use the stairs, but Yale couldn't remember where they were located. She shook her head and realized that this was going to be the most difficult assignment that she had ever had. And the most important.

Chapter Seventeen

The next morning, Yale awoke to the smell of something burning. She quickly tossed aside the blanket and sprinted to the closed door. Yale put her hand on the door and discovered that it was not hot. Still, she opened it carefully, fully expecting to find flames on the other side. When she didn't find any, the lieutenant sighed and slowly moved down the hallway toward Garn's room. The hostess' bedroom door was open and Yale saw that she was not in there. The scent of whatever was burning grew stronger as she neared the stairs, so Yale cautiously descended the staircase.

When she got to the first floor, she found Garn sitting in the middle of the front room surrounded by eight candles. With Garn's back facing her, Yale crept around the Crownaxian until she could see what was happening. She noticed that Garn's eyes were closed. The woman's lips silently opened and closed as if mouthing a prayer. Not wanting to disturb the ceremony, Yale quietly sat down on the floor with her knees close to her chest.

A few minutes past before Garn opened her eyes and smiled at her guest. "Good morning, Yale," she said, standing up. "Did you sleep well?"

"Yes, I did." Yale painfully rose to her feet. "You don't have to stop," she said, nodding toward the circle of candles. "I can get out of your way."

Garn bent down and extinguished a candle with her fingers. "You're not in the way," she said. "I'm finished." She put out the rest of the wicks and gathered up the candles. Yale helped her carry them over to a square table where Garn lined them up in some kind of order. "Would you like something to eat?" asked the hostess as she walked toward the kitchen.

Yale hobbled behind her. "Yes, that would be great," she said. The lieutenant eased herself into the chair she sat in for dinner and she watched Garn remove a square container from the cupboard. "If you don't mind my asking, what were you just doing?"

Garn turned to her and smiled. "I was reciting our seventeen prayers to Lumsue, our creator," she said. "Those of us who still follow our forefathers' teachings do that every morning when we awake and every night before we go to sleep." Garn removed a clean pot from underneath the sink and filled it with water. Then she dumped some grainy contents from a square container into the pot, put the pot on the stove and lit the burner. Turning around, she sat down across from Yale. "I know that may seem primitive with all the technology my people have developed, but I find it comforting to practice our ancient customs."

Yale smiled. "On Earth, we have our own religious customs," she said, thinking back to the Sundays she spent in church. "We pray to God, whom we believe is our creator, but He goes by different names because there are so many religions practiced there. We try to find comfort in our beliefs but our religious differences have led to most of our wars."

Garn nodded. "Yes, I've spent a great deal of time studying your religious history. That is one of the many things I don't understand about your people. Each of your religions teaches you to love one another yet all you seem to do is fight over who's right and who's wrong. Why would your god want you to do that?" she asked.

Yale shook her head. "I don't think He does," she replied. The sound of bubbling water caused her to glance at the pot on the stove. Garn turned around too before getting up and shutting off the burner. Then she removed two bowls and two cups from the cupboard, placed them on the counter and filled the bowls with the food from the pot, and the cups with water from the spout over the sink. Garn then took out two utensils that resembled spoons and put them into the piping hot bowls before bringing them over to the table. She placed one in front of Yale.

The food looked like oatmeal. Yale inhaled the steam from the bowl and felt the grumble in her stomach. She watched Garn bring over the cups before finally sitting down. Garn started eating first, while Yale pushed around the contents of her bowl. "It's very good," said Garn. "I promise. I was the best cook in my family. Go ahead, try it."

Yale quickly shoved some of the food into her mouth and

swallowed it, along with the embarrassment of her rude behavior. To her surprise, it did taste good. "Wow! That's fantastic," she said, gobbling down some more. "What's in here?"

Garn paused to sip some water. "It's a combination of several grains and plant extracts," she said. "We call it acra. It's very nutritious." She slowly ate another spoonful of the acra and appeared to savor the dish. "My mother taught me to make 11 different flavors of acra when I was little."

Yale finished her food and washed it down with the water. Garn asked her if she wanted more. "If you don't mind," said Yale, "I would like another bowl." Garn nodded and rose with Yale's bowl in her hand. "Prestok never got the chance to tell me anything about his personal life," said Yale. "Were you and your brother close?" she asked, in a slightly lower voice.

Garn filled the bowl and handed it to Yale. "Yes, my whole family was close," she said, sitting back down. "My father was killed in an accident when Prestok and I were very young. I think his death made us all appreciate each other more than most family members do. My mother worked long hours to make enough money to feed us, so my brother and I had to take care of each other." A sad expression came over Garn's face and a silence lingered in the room as Yale tried to think of something comforting to say.

Sudden knocking at the front door of the house abruptly interrupted the peaceful quiet in the kitchen. Yale and Garn looked at each other for a moment before Garn wordlessly rose and exited the kitchen. Yale hid behind a wall and peeked around the corner to see who it was. The abrasive knocking continued as Garn glanced back at Yale again before partially opening the front door.

Yale heard Garn and two other voices speaking in Crownaxian. Then the hostess took a step back as two hulking soldiers entered the house with laser rifles slung over their shoulders. Garn pointed to two chairs and the intruders sat down in them. They spoke to her in low tones, each talking for a few seconds before letting the other continue. Garn suddenly brought her hands to her face and leaned forward. She rocked her body back and forth as she began to cry. Yale wondered if they had just told her about Prestok. If so, Garn was putting on a convincing act.

One of the soldiers bent down beside Garn's chair and rested a hand on her shoulder. He then helped her to her feet as he said something else. Yale wished she knew the language so she could understand what was going on. Instead, she watched closely, looking for any sign that she might be in danger. Yale clenched her fist when she saw Garn shaking her head in apparent protest. The other guard stepped toward her with his weapon raised as Garn protested even louder. The first guard took her aside and continued to speak in a soft voice. Garn held onto his arms and kept shaking her head.

Not liking what she saw, Yale crept away from the wall and quickly looked around the room. She noticed a door a few feet to the right of the stove and she hustled over to it. Opening it, she saw a staircase descending into a dark basement. A flashlight sat on the top step. Yale quietly grabbed the flashlight and turned it on before she shut the door. Then she used the light beam to guide her way down to the bottom of the stairs.

The lieutenant flashed the beam around the tiny room. There were three metallic cabinets lined against one wall, a row of neatly stacked boxes along another wall, and two rolled up carpets on the floor against the far wall. Yale heard the heavy footsteps of the Crownaxian soldiers moving around above her and she figured that they were searching the home. She also heard Garn's voice over the commotion but whatever she was saying wasn't keeping the soldiers from hunting for their prey. Yale knew that it wouldn't take them long to find the basement and that she had to find some place to hide. She quietly paced back and forth, desperately trying to come up with an idea.

As she moved in front of the cabinets, Yale noticed a hollow sound coming from one of the floorboards. Curious, she flashed the beam down and saw a small, circular hole in one of the boards. Yale slipped her finger in the hole and pulled up the board, which lifted with no resistance. She flashed the beam into the crevice and saw a little storage area. Inside were a mat, a crumpled pillow and two jugs of water.

The footsteps from upstairs grew louder and Yale knew they were heading for the kitchen. The officer hustled over to the rolled up carpets and lugged one of them back to the hiding spot. She unrolled it and laid it over the floorboard. Then she lifted up a section of the carpet and the floorboard and climbed into the crevice, closing the top of the floorboard over her.

Yale turned off the flashlight and tucked it next to her right foot. She curled up on the mat, closed her eyes and tried not to breathe too deeply. The room was hot, with very little air inside. The lieutenant quickly began to sweat. She did her best not to move as she waited for the intruders to leave. Within minutes, she heard them stomping down the steps to the basement. The vibrations from their footsteps shook the tiny room. Yale heard them talking to each other as they continued their investigation.

Despite her best efforts to stay awake, the lack of air and the heat were more than Yale could stand and she soon passed out. The officer dreamt that she was back on Paldor, fighting off an attack by an armada of Crownaxians. There were numerous explosions around her as she lay in a foxhole with three other Union soldiers. They intermittently returned the enemy fire by sitting up and shooting at the infantry that was advancing by foot. However, her comrades were killed one by one as the laser fire from the Crownaxians increased. Knowing she couldn't retreat, Yale stood up and fired her weapon repeatedly until she felt the hot flash of laser fire as it cut through her chest.

Yale awoke in the darkness and stifled a scream in her throat. She listened intently to sounds above her. However, she didn't hear any more footsteps and she wondered if it was safe to get out of the hole. Despite the pain in her legs and her intense thirst, the lieutenant decided against it. Instead, she choose to wait for Garn to come to her. She knew that her friend would figure out where she was once Garn saw the carpet rolled out over the floorboards. So Yale clenched her fists and waited.

Soon she heard the front door close and shortly after, one set of footsteps heading down the stairs. Yale wrapped her fingers around the flashlight, just in case it was one of the soldiers coming for her. She held her breath and blinked away the sweat in her eyes. The floorboards creaked above her as someone approached and lifted the carpet. Yale tensed like a prowling puma and prepared to strike with the flashlight. The board lifted up and Yale saw the diminutive horn on

Garn's head. The lieutenant sighed and let go of the flashlight.

Garn reached down, grabbed Yale's right hand and pulled her out of the hole. The Crownaxian pushed the floorboard back down with her left foot and smoothed out the carpet. "How did you find that hiding spot?" she asked, as she gently led the human to the stairwell. Yale told her that she heard the hollowness of the floor and reached down to find it. "It's a good thing you did," said Garn. "Those guards searched every inch of this house. I thought they'd find you for sure."

The duo slowly ascended the steps and walked into the kitchen. Yale slumped back down in her chair while Garn cleared the table of their dishes. "They came to tell me about Prestok," said the Crownaxian. "They were about to leave when one of them noticed the dishes. I told them that a friend had stopped by to visit but they didn't believe me." She put the dishes in the sink then sat down in her chair. "I should have cleaned up before I answered the door. I can't believe I left them here."

Yale reached over and patted her friend's right hand. "It's ok, Garn. I don't think I would have known to clear the table either. Besides, they didn't find me, you didn't get into trouble and that's what really matters."

"I guess you're right," said Garn. She sighed then stood up. "They told me that they found his body two miles downstream. They suspect that Prestok helped you escape so they're not going to give him a military funeral. It's up to me now to take care of his burial." Garn drifted past the table and headed for the living room.

Yale pulled herself to her feet and followed her hostess. "I am so sorry about all of this," she said, catching up to Garn. "If I hadn't come along, your brother would still be alive and not dishonored like this. It's all my fault." Yale slammed her hand against the table with the candles on it and made them all shake.

"Oh, no Yale, don't blame yourself," said Garn, looking into the human's eyes. "I told you before, this is not your fault. Prestok died doing what he needed to do. And I don't think he'd even want a fancy military funeral, not with the way he felt about Drelk." Garn rearranged a few of the candles on the table and mustered a smile. "In fact, I think he'd be proud to know that he died aiding the resistance." Garn lifted a silver gadget off of the table and opened it up, revealing a sleek communications device. She pushed some buttons on the tiny keyboard then held the device to her ear.

Yale moved away from her friend to allow her some privacy. The lieutenant sat in a chair and again tried to shake the image of Prestok's body in the water. She heard Garn speak in Crownaxian to whomever she called. After a few minutes, Garn clicked off the device and put it back down on the table. Yale stood up and hobbled over to Garn. "Is there anything I can do to help?" she asked. "Anything at all?"

Garn shook her head. "I'm afraid not. The best thing you can do is go back up to your room and get some rest. Remember, you're leaving tonight and you'll need all of your strength." Garn slipped her arm around Yale's back and guided her to the stairs. "The perimeter around the prison is heavily guarded. I'll have to drop you off about three miles outside the building. Then you're going to have to walk through a dense forest that's laden with traps." They eased their way up the stairs and into the hallway. "I'm sure there'll be patrols combing the woods as well. I have a pistol you can take but you'll still be on your own."

They came to the bedroom door and Garn opened it for her. "I hope you realize how dangerous this will be," she said, turning on the light. "If you go through with this they will probably capture you again or worse. Yale, there's no shame in taking my offer to meet with my friends."

Yale sat on the bed. "Thank you, but no, I'm not leaving without Zigler. I owe it to him to try to rescue him. And yes, I owe it to your brother as well." Garn was about to speak but Yale cut her off with a wave of her right hand. "I know, he chose to help me, but that doesn't change the fact that he sacrificed his life for me. I don't want that sacrifice to be in vain."

Garn nodded then spoke softly. "But if you're killed, won't it be just that?" Garn shrugged, turned off the light and closed the door behind her. Yale lay down on the bed and wondered if Garn were right.

Chapter Eighteen

The *Liberty Bell* followed the squadron of rebel ships as they flew through the empty vacuum of space toward Crownaxia. Ten vessels armed with torpedoes, laser cannons and shock bombs flew in a V formation ahead of the Union ship. The armada was 14 hours into their mission, with more than eight hours to go before they reached their destination. With Madison at the helm, Amy Sutter concluded her inspection of the ship and its weapons. She entered the bridge and sat down in the pilot's chair. "Everything seems to be in order," she said. "How's it going in here?"

"Fine, Captain," said Madison, typing a command on the keyboard. "All the ship's functions have been running normally since we left." The robot then looked up at Amy as she stifled a yawn. "Captain, how much have you slept in the last 24 hours?"

Amy shrugged. "I don't know, four or five hours I guess, just after Travar arrested the spy. But it's alright, I'll have plenty of time to sleep after we rescue my dad." She stood up and stretched her arms over her head. "Send a message to Travar. Tell him we're going to use the autopilot for awhile," she said. "Then follow me."

Madison nodded, then sent the message. A moment later, the robot looked down and read something on a console screen. "Travar wants to know if anything is wrong. He says he's moving one of the ships behind us to watch our back. How should I respond?"

Amy shook her head. "Tell him we're fine. We're just going to spend some time on a training exercise." Madison sent that message, then set the autopilot. "What kind of exercise?" asked the robot, standing up.

"C'mon, I'll show you." Amy led the way out of the bridge and headed down the ladder to the lower deck. She stopped at a supply cabinet and removed two laser pistols and six hover-targets. "I thought we should brush up on our skills before we get there." She tossed a pistol and three targets to her friend, then moved to an empty area in the middle of the bay and turned on her targets.

The nine-inch spheres rose up and floated above Amy's head. The girl flipped a switch on her pistol to make her weapon emit harmless light rays, then she aimed and fired at one of the orbs. She missed. Amy fired again, narrowly missing another one. The targets drifted just below the ceiling and continued to dodge the assault. Amy grunted in frustration and fired her weapon more quickly. She hit two of the marks with her next five shots, but she couldn't nail down the last one. Finally, she turned off her pistol, nodded toward Madison and told the robot to try.

The robot hit all three of its targets with just three shots. The orbs fell harmlessly to the ground as Madison turned off the laser pistol. Amy pouted as she gathered up the orbs and reset them. The spheres rose toward the ceiling and the competition continued. For the next half-hour, Amy and Madison took turns shooting at the targets. Amy's aim gradually improved, while the robot's success rate remained the same. Then the captain ordered a short break.

Amy and Madison sat down on supply crates and leaned back against a near wall. The girl was sweating and breathing heavily, while the robot looked quite comfortable. Amy shook her head. "Don't you ever get tired?" she asked, despite being well aware of the answer. Madison smiled and shook its head. "You're so lucky," said Amy. "I wish I had your stamina."

Madison's smile disappeared. "I wish I had your sense of identity," said the robot, looking down at the floor. "When people see you, they can tell you're a girl. Even your name leaves no doubt. But not mine." The robot looked back at Amy and shrugged.

"I always thought you looked like a boy," said Amy, curling her thin lips into a slight smile. "If I were a robot, I'd chose to be a boy. And that's the great thing about being you, Madison. You can decide which you'd rather be." She lightly punched the robot on the right shoulder. "So, the way I see it, you really are the lucky one."

Madison nodded at the suggestion. "I guess you're right, Captain. I never really thought of it that way. Maybe that's why my creator didn't give me a distinct gender. Maybe he wanted me to choose when the time was right." The robot stood up and smiled. "I would like to be a boy."

Amy laughed and scrambled to her feet. "Ok, Pinocchio, from

this point forward, you are a boy," she said. Amy then gestured with her right arm as if knighting her friend. "And quite a tall boy at that." Then she turned her laser pistol back on. "Well, this girl needs some more practice."

The duo went back to their drill. Amy showed even greater improvement as she managed to hit her targets two out of three times. The intense exercise went on for nearly an hour when the session was suddenly interrupted by an alarm that blared on the bridge. Amy and Madison glanced at each other for a moment, then sprinted to the front of the ship with their weapons still in their hands. They dropped into their seats and rested the pistols on the floor beside them. Amy's face paled as she examined the radar screen. "The fleet has been discovered," she said with a sigh. "Eight enemy ships are approaching at high speed."

Amy looked over at Madison and saw the robot feverishly typing in commands on the keyboard in front of him. "I'm jamming their radio transmissions," he said. "They won't be able to report our position." He glanced at the captain and they both nodded. "We have to go after them."

"Let's see what Travar says," said Amy. She then sent a message to the rebel leader, asking him what he wanted her to do. A few seconds later, a reply appeared on a console screen. Amy sighed. "He wants us to stay back and let his soldiers handle this." Then she pointed to the radar screen. "Eight of the rebel ships are breaking off to intercept." Amy grabbed the yoke. "I'm pulling us back a little bit but I want you to power up our weapons."

The rebel ships fanned out and circled the Crownaxian crafts, boxing them in. Then they fired lasers and missiles at their targets. The enemy ships stayed close together and fired back. Neither side gained an advantage as the intense battle raged on for twenty-five minutes. Despite their position, the rebels took as much damage as they dished out. Amy kept the *Liberty Bell* at a safe distance and managed to avoid the enemy fire. However, some of the rebel crafts were not as lucky. When the battle finally ended, the Crownaxians were wiped out and the rebels lost four ships of their own.

The rebels regrouped 120 miles away from the site of the battle and Travar sent a message to all of the remaining ships. Amy read the order and turned to face Madison. "Travar wants us all to land on that yellow planet," she said, pointing to the radar screen. "Three of the surviving ships have taken on heavy damage and we'll all need to pitch in to make the necessary repairs." She stood up and rested a hand on her friend's shoulder. "Take us down there, Madison. I'm going below to gather up some medical kits. I'm sure we'll need them."

Amy left the bridge and climbed down the ladder to the lower deck. She removed several medical kits from different supply cabinets and inventoried the contents. They had plenty of bandages and medical tape but very little antiseptics or antibiotics. As she felt the ship descend toward the planet, Amy said a quick prayer, asking God to watch over Travar's troops for the rest of the journey. She concluded by asking Him to bless her father and to give him the strength to hold on until she arrived.

The captain returned to the bridge as Madison was leveling out the ship's descent. She put on her helmet and sat down in her chair. The yellow surface of the frigid planet was almost completely covered with ice. Two of the rebel ships in front of them slid several miles before coming to a complete stop, but Madison was skilled enough to smoothly land the *Liberty Bell* on the slick ground with a minimum of slippage. Amy powered down the weapons and shut off the ship's engines.

The yellow ice crackled under their feet as Amy and Madison struggled to keep their balance on their way over to Travar's ship. The rebel leader stood in front of his craft listening to one of his subordinates. Two other rebel soldiers with anxious expressions were on either side of him. Amy stopped a few feet away from them, so as not to interrupt the group. Madison remained at her side. "Can you tell what they're saying?" whispered Amy as she leaned toward the robot.

Madison kept his voice low. "They're talking about the damage to their ships." He listened to more of the soldiers' conversation before continuing. "The officer on the right thinks it will take at least two hours to fix his ship. The other one says he'll need at least that long for his, too." The robot shook his head. "It looks like we're going to be here for awhile."

Amy approached Travar after the group dispersed. She looked him in the eye and spoke in a somber tone. "I'm sorry you lost some of your soldiers, Travar." He started to say something but she cut him off. "No, really I am. I know that they died so we could continue on with this rescue mission and I just wanted to let you know that I appreciate everything your soldiers have done for us." She stopped and rubbed her wet eyes. "I'm probably not making any sense here but I just wanted to say thank you."

Travar nodded. "I understand what you're saying but you need to realize that my troops knew the risks when they decided to join me," he said. "Besides, they died fighting their enemies, whom they would have met at one time or another anyway. My soldiers are born warriors. To die in battle is the highest honor for them." He paused and looked toward the sky for a moment. Then he looked back at Amy. "Come now. There's a lot of work to do and we will need your help."

The rebel leader asked Madison to help the crew of the Frolank, the ship that was in the worst shape. Amy was assigned to aid the medical teams who had set up a treatment tent in the center of the landing site. The girl helped bandage the wounded and run errands for the doctors. She knew she was just doing grunge work but she was happy to help in any way. However, the carnage she saw in the medical tent began to take a toll on her. After more than an hour of witnessing open wounds, severe burns and lost limbs, Amy ducked out of the tent and threw up on the yellow ice.

Embarrassed by her lack of fortitude, Amy tried to cover the vomit with some loose ice from a nearby crater. She kicked the heel of her right boot into the crater, gathered up the ice fragments, and dumped the pieces over the affected area. "There's no need for that," said a voice behind her. Amy spun around and saw one of the rebel soldiers approaching. "Most throw up during their first medical shift," he said, stopping next to her.

It took a moment, but Amy finally recognized the Crownaxian. He was one of the soldiers who had been playing soccer back at the base. "It's true," he said. "The first time I worked in triage, I threw up on a doctor's boot as he was sewing up someone's gut. And you know what? That doctor kept right on working, as if nothing happened. Later on he told me that he did the same thing in medical school." The Crownaxian smiled and offered a hand. "My name is Werlik."

Amy smiled back and shook his hand. "I'm Amy Sutter," she said.

Werlik nodded. "I know who you are. We all do. You're the human whose father we're going to rescue." He let go of her hand and looked down at the mess she created. "Might as well leave it. It's frozen solid now." He nodded toward the tent. "I was just in the tent to check on one of my friends. He's in pretty bad shape. Burns over most of his body. When you feel better, you should get back in there. They're really busy."

Amy nodded. "Oh, yeah, I was just going to do that." She kicked more loose ice over the mess, then absent-mindedly wiped her feet on some clean ice. "Ah, it was nice meeting you," she said, before turning and walking toward the tent. She glanced back at him before she reentered and noticed him glaring at her. Amy made a mental note of his name, then sought out the doctor who was in charge of the unit.

Another hour passed before all of the wounded had been treated. Amy sat down on a stool and rested her weary body. She looked around the tent and observed the soldiers' faces. Those who were awake stared off in various directions but some of them did glance at her. She smiled at them and hoped they knew just how much she appreciated their efforts. Then it occurred to her that the least she could do is thank them personally.

Amy rose and moved to the nearest bed. The soldier had bandages on his right arm, left leg, and forehead. His eyes were open and they widened when the girl stood over him. "Hello," she cautiously said. He didn't answer. "I ah, I just wanted to say thank you," she stammered. The Crownaxian nodded but didn't speak. "I know it isn't much but thank you. You and all the others. I owe you so much." The soldier had a blank look on his face and it finally dawned on Amy that he might be able to understand her. She shrugged. "Anyway, thank you."

The girl went to the next bed and spoke to that soldier. He too didn't seem to understand her but she thanked him anyway. She stopped at each bed and spent a few minutes with each soldier. Although she could tell that most of them didn't know her language, Amy saw from the looks on their faces that they did get what it was she was doing. That alone made her feel much better and she hoped that they too benefited from her short visits.

Amy left the tent and looked around the landing site for Madison. The rebel soldiers hustled past her, darting in various directions as their superiors barked orders at them in their native language. The girl floundered over the icy surface trying to spot her friend when she felt someone bump into her. She turned her head and saw the oily smile on Werlik's face as he put his hands on her shoulders to steady her. "Are you looking for your robot?" he asked. Amy thought she heard some bitterness in his voice. Her stomach tightened as he kept his hands on her.

"Yes, I am," she said, forcing a smile. She put her hands into her coat pocket and wrapped the fingers of her right hand around her laser pistol. "Have you seen him?" she asked.

The Crownaxian let go of her and pointed to a ridge about 150 yards away from the edge of the landing site. "Yes I did. He was heading that way with three soldiers. I think they were searching for a fresh water well. We need all the water we can get." He put his left arm around her shoulders. "Come with me, I'll show you were they were going."

Despite the odd feeling she had about Werlik, she began to follow him toward the ridge in hopes that he might be telling the truth. Then he suddenly pushed her forward and tightened his grip on her left shoulder. Amy squirmed and tried to break free of his grip. "Let go of me!" she shouted. However, her protest was drowned out by the commotion around them. Werlik grabbed both of her arms and held them behind her back with one hand as he pushed her toward the ridge. The Crownaxian led her to a dark corner of the encampment and shoved her to the ground.

Amy pulled her pistol out of her pocket and aimed it at her attacker, but Werlik slapped it out of her hand before she could fire the weapon. Then he grabbed her by the throat and pulled her close to his chest. His putrid breath enveloped her face as she struggled to breathe. "Shut up," he seethed. "Do what I tell you or I'll kill you!" He let go of her throat and dropped her onto the frozen ground. Amy rolled to her knees and coughed.

The Crownaxian then yanked her to her feet by her coat collar. "You will walk with me and not make a sound," he said. Amy had trouble keeping her balance as her lungs burned, her eyes blurred and her head felt numb. Werlik kept one hand on her back as he marched her away from the landing site. Amy tried to call out but her voice was too weak. Twice she fell to her knees as her legs gave out, but Werlik quietly picked her back up and pushed her forward.

They came to the ridge and Amy's eyes widened as she looked over the edge. The drop was at least 100 feet. Panicked, she again struggled to break free of Werlik's grip. He shook her and turned her toward him. "That spy that Travar arrested was my brother," said the abductor. "Thanks to you he'll probably be shot. But he will not die in vain." Werlik tried to push her forward but Amy dropped to her knees, wrapped her arms around his legs and tackled him. The Crownaxian fell on top of her. Amy slipped out of his grip and shot to her feet.

Amy only managed to take a few steps before Werlik grabbed her from behind. She fell forward and flipped him over her back. The Crownaxian rolled back up with a look of fierce determination. He charged the girl, grabbing her by the shoulders. Amy countered by kicking him in the groin. Werlik bent over in pain but recovered while Amy slipped on the ice. He grabbed her by the throat again, lifting her off her feet. She pushed on his hands with all of her might while he increased the pressure on her neck. She slowly began to convulse and her hands slipped off of his.

Suddenly two shots rang out and Amy felt Werlik's fingers slip off of her throat. Then she felt like she was floating as they crashed to the frozen surface of the planet. Werlik's body cushioned her fall but she still landed face first on the ice. A warm, salty fluid poured over her eyes, nose and lips as the girl finally lost consciousness.

Chapter Nineteen

A soft wind washed across Amy's face as she opened her eyes. She sat up and looked around in confusion. Instead of the icy, hard surface of the planet the rebels had landed on, Amy found herself sitting in a warm field of tall, green grass. A cheerful yellow sun shined above her, pasted against a blue sky that was dotted with fluffy, white clouds. Amy shook her head and tried to figure out how she had gotten there.

She pressed her right palm against her face but found no blood on her skin. Her throat felt fine and her head was pain-free. In the distance, she heard the sound of laughter, as if there were a schoolyard full of kids nearby. Amy stood up, pushed the tall blades of grass aside and began walking toward the sound of the children. The laugher grew louder with each step as the girl made her way across the field to a clearing at the bottom of a gigantic hill. Then she suddenly smiled. "I'm dreaming," she said aloud. "That's it. I'm just dreaming. That's why I don't remember getting here." She took a few tentative steps forward. The smooth ground felt good against her toes and only then did she realize that she wasn't wearing anything on her feet. "I wonder what kind of dream this is."

The hill ahead of her looked daunting. Still, she had a compulsion to climb the beast and find the other kids. With a shrug, she started climbing the hill with her hands held low to increase her balance. Her bare feet dug into the soft ground, while her legs strained to keep her moving on the steep slope. The sunlight beat down on the back of her neck and it didn't take long for the sweat to run down her cheeks. Her breathing became labored after only a few minutes. Amy looked up at the top of the hill that appeared to be just as far away as when she started. "How am I not making any progress?" she shouted out.

Suddenly the children's laughter ceased. An unnerving quiet settled over the area. Amy instinctively looked around, wondering what caused the abrupt silence. Then she stood perfectly still and waited for whatever did to show itself. Nothing emerged and soon the children's laughter returned. Amy took a deep breath and continued her climb.

The young girl finally reached the top of the hill. She put her hands on her hips and leaned forward to catch her breath. Then she straightened up and saw a carnival just ahead, complete with rides, games and concession stands. Amy hustled forward until she came to the first stand. A boy in a red-checkered shirt and purple pants sat on a stool reading a magazine with a silly look on his face. "Hello Amy," he said, with a lilt in his voice. "We've been expecting you. What would you like to eat?"

Amy took a cautious step back. "How do you know my name?" she asked. The boy didn't answer. He just looked at her and kept on grinning. Amy glanced around and noticed something peculiar. "Where am I?" she asked, stepping back toward the stand. "And where are all the adults? I don't see any around. Just kids." Again the boy didn't answer. "Look, I know you can talk, so tell me what's going on here!" she yelled.

Another eerie silence fell over the land. Amy looked past the concession stand and saw everyone standing still, staring at her. The boy on the stool shook his head. "We're not supposed to yell here," he said. "Papa doesn't like yelling. You should try not to do that again."

Amy looked back at the boy. "Papa? Who's that? Is he your father?" The girl moved away from the stand and tried to spot the man. "I don't see him. Is he around somewhere?"

The boy nodded. "Oh yes, he's around. But he's busy now. He wouldn't want anyone to disturb him. So just go ahead and join the fun but don't yell. He doesn't like that." He went back to reading his magazine but his silly expression remained. Amy inched forward and peeked at the journal in his hands. There was a pair of kids riding sleds on the cover but there were no words on the page, not even a title.

Amy shrugged and walked toward the other kids, who had gone back to their rides and games. The youngsters ran around and laughed but no one laughed too loudly. Amy then realized that they were all trying to limit how much noise they made. She wondered what they were so afraid of. Amy decided to follow their lead until she figured out what was going on.

One girl moved away from a pack of kids standing near a cotton candy machine and walked over to Amy. "Hi there, I'm Suzie," she said, extending a hand. Amy smiled and shook it, glad that someone was greeting her. "Don't mind Billy in there. He's just trying to look out for us. He's like our big brother." Suzie appeared to be about Amy's age. She held a cone of cotton candy in her left hand. "Do you want some?" she asked, pointing toward the machine. Amy shook her head. "It's ok," said Suzie. "It's free. Everything here is free if you just follow the rules."

"The rules?" asked Amy. Suzie nodded and took a bite of her cotton candy. "Who makes the rules?" Suzie frowned, shaking her head. "Really, I'd like to know," said Amy. "Is it Papa?"

"Of course, silly," replied Suzie. "Don't you know anything?" She turned and started walking back toward the other kids. Amy walked next to her. "Papa tells us what to do so we can move on." The girl started skipping and began to pull ahead of Amy, who had to increase her pace to keep up. Suzie's ponytails bounced playfully against her head as she began to sing a song. She abruptly stopped singing when she got to the candy machine.

Amy pulled up next to her. A boy with sparking white teeth stood next to the machine, handing out the candy to the kids. Suzie finished the cone in her hand and tossed into a trashcan beside the machine. Then she put her hand out and the boy gave her another cone. "What did you mean when you said move on?" asked Amy. The boy offered her a cone, so she took it and politely thanked him.

Suzie took a big bite of her pink cotton candy before she answered. "Papa told us that only good kids get to move on. If it's their time, of course. Sometimes kids show up here before their time." She took another bite and smiled. "I love cotton candy. It's my absolute favorite."

"Suzie, I don't know what you're talking about," said Amy, still chewing on her candy. "Good kids move on where? Before what time?" Amy noticed the snickers she was getting from some of the other kids. She glanced at their faces to see if she could figure out what was so funny.

Suzie had a confounded look on her face. She twirled one of her ponytails with her free hand and munched on her snack. "You do know where you are, don't you?" she asked.

"I guess," said Amy, with a shrug. "I'm in the middle of a really bizarre dream." The other kids stopped what they were doing and began to laugh. Amy's face reddened and she tried her best to remain calm. Suzie shook her head as she turned toward the crowd. They quieted down and the girl looked back at Amy. "I'm not dreaming?" she asked.

"No, you're not dreaming," said Suzie. She rested her left hand on Amy's right shoulder and took a deep breath. "This is always the hard part. What's the last thing you remember?" she asked.

Amy frowned. "A Crownaxian was choking me," she whispered. "And then he let go." She looked down at the ground as her bottom lip vibrated. "I don't know then. I guess I fell." She looked up at Suzie. "Yeah, that's it. I fell on top of him. He let go after I heard the shots. Somebody must have shot him." Her mind then went blank. "That's all I remember."

Suzie stepped forward and gently hugged Amy. "It's ok. You seem to remember more than most." She stepped back and smiled. "There's nothing to worry about now. That's all behind you. I'm sure you'll move on soon, and until then we can have so much fun, you and I. Do you like hopscotch?"

"Forget hopscotch," blurted Amy. "You keep saying move on. Move on to where?" She sighed in frustration, curling her fingers into tight fists. "None of this makes any sense. If I'm not dreaming and I'm not on that frozen planet with Madison any more, than where exactly am I?" She turned away from her new friend for a moment, and looked to the sky as if the answer might lie in the fluffy clouds. "What's going on here?" she asked, looking back at Suzie.

"Tell her where she is Suzie." Amy turned in the direction of the deep voice and saw a man in his late thirties walking toward them. He wore a dark blue suit with a red tie and black shoes. A slight smile ran across his beefy face that was highlighted by a thick, black mustache. Amy thought she recognized him but she couldn't quite remember how.

Suzie darted past her and ran to the man. "Papa," she cried out, throwing her arms around him. He picked her up, gave her a big hug, and then gently put her back down. "Meet my new friend," she said, grabbing the man's hand and pulling him toward Amy.

"Hello, Amy, it's nice to finally meet you," he said with a nod. He let go of Suzie's hand and the girl moved next to Amy. "I'm sure you have some questions, now is the time to ask them," he said.

Amy nodded. "How did you know my name?" she asked.

The man smiled. "I know the names of all the children who come here," he replied, bending slightly toward the girl. He ran the fingers of his right hand over his moustache. "It's my job to watch over them for awhile, so it's important for me to know as much as I can about them."

Amy shook her head. "I don't understand. Who are you? And where are we? I've never seen this place before and I've no idea how I got here." Despite her confusion, the girl felt oddly at peace in this mysterious place. She even began to feel as if this is where she was supposed to be.

"You're not dreaming, Amy," he said, softly. "And you're not on that planet with your robot friend." He paused and smiled. "Well, not all of you, anyway. You see, when you and that Crownaxian fell, you hit your head against the ice. Pretty hard, too." He paused again. "If you close your eyes you can still see it in your mind. Go ahead, close your eyes."

Amy closed her eyes and took a deep breath. Suddenly, she felt like she couldn't breath. A pair of strong hands was around her throat. She fought to pull them off but she couldn't do it. Then came that loud sound and the grip loosened. She saw herself falling toward the ground as if watching it happen on television. She thought she heard Madison yell as her head hit the ice. Then everything went black.

Amy gasped as her eyes snapped open. All of the kids were watching her and so was the man. He had a somber look on his face. Amy shook her head, then took a step toward him. "Am I dead?" she asked, finally putting the pieces together. "Are you God?"

The man shook his head as his lips curled upward. "No, I'm not God. Despite what some people may have thought when I was alive." He nodded toward the other kids. "I'm sort of like a shepherd, if you will. Like I said before, I watch over these kids until it's their time. Then I help them make the transition." He reached out, grabbed a hunk of Amy's cotton candy and tossed it into his mouth. "This stuff is so much better than what we had when I was your age. I really missed it later on when I was in Spain. Great bullfights there but they never had any cotton candy."

Amy handed him her cone. "Here, I don't want any more. You can finish it." He took it from her and thanked her. "So is that why I'm here, to prepare for my transition?" she asked. A feeling of hopelessness rose inside of her as she thought about her friend on the icy planet, her mother at the military installation and her father in the Crownaxian prison. Before the man could answer her, Amy closed her eyes and muttered: "I can't believe I failed. I was so close."

The man chuckled. "You haven't failed. At least not yet." She opened her eyes and looked at his comforting face. "No, this isn't your time. The bell does not toll for you." He finished the cotton candy and tossed the empty cone into a nearby trashcan.

"Then why am I here?" asked Amy, more intrigued and confused than she was before. Out of the corner of her eye, she watched Suzie drift away from them and move toward the other children.

The man crossed his arms over his chest as the expression of his face hardened. "You're here because you made a mistake," he said. "You've made a lot of them lately. This endeavor to save your father is far more dangerous than you realize. I'm not even sure if you're up to it." She started to reply but he cut her off. "Now I understand how you feel. And yes, I'd probably do things the same way if I were in your shoes. But if you're going to continue on this mission, you need to be more careful. Don't take so many chances. It won't do your father any good if you get yourself killed."

Amy suddenly felt lightheaded. She stumbled toward the man and clutched his right arm for support. "It's ok, my dear. You're going back now. Please remember what I said." The dizziness increased as her vision blurred. The sound of the other children diminished and all she could hear was the man's voice. "We all make mistakes. I made a crucial one at the end of my life, which is why I'm here now. You could have a great life ahead of you, but not if you rush forward with no regard for your safety." Amy felt like she was falling as the darkness enveloped her. She lost all sensation in her arms and legs. "Good luck and Godspeed," said the man, as everything around her went completely dark.

Amy's eyes snapped open. Her lungs and throat burned as she tried to suck in as much air as she could. Blurry images swirled around her. She saw faces stretched out in grotesque shapes, while shrill voices bombarded her tender ears. Gradually, the faces took on familiar forms. The Crownaxian doctor was leaning over her and pressing down hard on her chest. She couldn't figure out what he was doing. She tilted her head to the right and saw Madison standing beside her with a worried look on his face.

"Her eyes are open!" shouted the robot. The doctor lifted up his hands and gently leaned over her. He said something in Crownaxian. "Yes, she is breathing on her own," said Madison. The doctor moved back and spoke again in his native language. It was then that Amy realized that she was still lying on the ice. Her head ached and her limbs felt heavy.

"What happened?" she asked, struggling to speak. She blinked her eyes as the dizziness returned. Amy closed her mouth when she felt some bile rising in her throat. She turned her head and pressed her lips tightly together when she coughed, as she fought to avoid vomiting. Then she held her breath until the queasiness passed.

"You need to relax," said Madison. He gently placed his hands on either side of her head. "Lie still. You're very weak." Amy saw two Crownaxians hustling toward her carrying a stretcher. She closed her eyes as she was lifted onto the stretcher and transported to the medical tent. Her body was eased into a bed as the girl spotted the robot standing beside it. She saw him look up for a moment before leaning close to her. "Travar is coming over. Don't try to speak." The robot carefully raised the girl's head and slid another pillow under her neck. Then he eased her head back down. With the extra pillow, she could see for herself who was approaching.

The rebel leader stopped at the foot of her bed. He stared at her for a moment before turning to the doctor. They spoke briefly to each other in Crownaxian, while Amy studied Travar's face. He appeared to be genuinely concerned about her. Then Travar spoke directly to her. "It's remarkable that you're still alive," he said. "Blink your eyes if you can understand me." Amy slowly blinked her eyes twice. "Good. You gave us all quiet a scare. You were without oxygen for nearly six minutes. We though you were going to die." He cautiously sat down on the edge of the bed.

Amy forced herself into a sitting position. "Six minutes?" she said. Travar nodded. Amy glanced over at Madison and he nodded as well. "I was only gone for six minutes," muttered Amy. Madison inched closer and told her not to speak. She shook her head. "That's not possible. I was there for much longer than that. It took me almost a half-hour just to get up to the carnival." Travar frowned as he asked her what she was talking about. Amy shrugged. "It doesn't matter. Are you sure it was only six minutes? It seemed like so much longer than that."

Before Travar could answer, the Crownaxian doctor leaned over her again. He had a thin, round object in his hand. He pressed the object against Amy's right wrist. She felt a slight stabbing pain on her skin. The physician then moved away without speaking. Travar leaned closer to her. "That shot he just gave you should ease your pain and help you recover. You need to be at your peak very soon if our mission is to succeed."

Amy nodded. "Don't worry about me. I'll be fine." She looked around the room and saw that there weren't any other beds nearby. "Where did all the injured soldiers go?" she asked. Surprisingly, the pain in her head ceased and she began to feel normal again.

"They've been moved to their ships," replied Travar. "We have just one more thing to do before we go." He stood up and smiled. "I'll check on you in a little while. Hopefully you'll be ready when I come back." Travar nodded at the robot. "Take good care of her," he said before departing.

The robot sat down next to his friend. "What was it you were saying before about a carnival, Captain?" he asked. Amy sighed, and then she told him about her paranormal experience. Madison had an astonished look on his face but he didn't interrupt her as she went over the details of her ordeal. When she finished, Madison sat still for a moment before speaking. "That's the most incredible thing I've ever heard," he said. "Are you certain you weren't dreaming?"

Amy crossed her arms over her chest. "I don't know. I thought I was at first but it was just so real. I'd never had a dream that vivid before." She closed her eyes and saw everything clearly in her mind.

Then she opened her eyes again. "Well, dream or not, the message was pretty clear. I need to be more careful. But how am I supposed to finish this if I'm worried about my own safety all the time?"

The robot rested a hand on Amy's shoulder. "Maybe you just need to find the middle ground between being reckless and being overly cautious. I know that's easier said than done, but I bet you'll figure it out when the time comes. You're a very smart girl."

Amy smiled. "Thanks Madison." The robot moved his hand as Amy struggled to get comfortable in the bed. Her expression turned serious after she found a cozy spot. "What happened to Werlik?" she asked. "Is he dead?" The robot nodded. "I shouldn't have followed him. I should have known that he was up to something." She punched the bed with her left hand.

Madison shook his head. "Despite what this Papa may have said, you had no way of knowing that Werlik would try to hurt you. How could you?" He paused, as if searching for the right words. "The important thing is that you're ok. That's all that matters now."

Travar returned a few minutes later with the doctor behind him. "The doctor wants to make sure you're ok," said the rebel leader. Amy nodded and asked Madison to help her up. The robot guided the girl to her feet. Amy took a deep breath as the doctor examined her again, this time using a hand-held medical scanner. Then the physician said something in his native language. Travar patted the doctor on the shoulder and turned to face Amy. "He says your scans are normal. But you may need to take it easy for the next few hours." He nodded toward the exit. "Follow me," he said.

Amy put on her coat, then leaned on Madison as they followed the rebel leader to an open field. As they approached the terrain, the girl saw six rows of freshly covered graves. Each was marked with a thin pole that held a covered torch. The light from the flames glowed on the faces of the soldiers standing beside the poles. Travar walked to the front of the third row and bent down on one knee. His soldiers did the same. Out of reverence for the fallen, Amy and Madison knelt as well.

The rebel leader began to speak in his native tongue. It sounded like he was praying. Amy leaned toward Madison and asked him what Travar was saying. "He's asking for his god's guidance," whispered the robot. "And he's pleading for the souls of his soldiers." Amy nodded as Travar resumed his oration. Then Madison spoke softly again. "Now he's starting the seventeen prayers to his lord, Lumsue. It's part of their ancient heritage."

After Travar finished the prayers, he stood up and moved to the first grave. The rebel leader turned a knob on the pole beside it and the flame went out. Then he hugged the soldier before moving to the next pit. Travar repeated this act at each gravesite, until the last flame was extinguished. Then he moved back to the front of the group and said a few more words in Crownaxian. The soldiers bowed their heads for a moment, then gathered their tools and solemnly headed for their ships.

Travar walked over to Amy and Madison. The emotional strain of the ceremony showed on his somber face. "It's time to go," he said. "How do you feel?" He tried to smile but it looked unnatural.

"Much better," said Amy. She slipped her hands into her coat pocket and felt the familiar shape of her laser pistol. "That was very interesting. Thank you for sharing that with us."

"C'mon. I'll walk you to your ship," said Travar. Amy gingerly followed him to the *Liberty Bell* with Madison behind her. They entered the craft and Amy sat in the captain's chair on the bridge. Madison sat next to her in his seat. Travar wished them luck, then left to board his own craft. Amy took a deep breath and started the ship's engines. Then she followed the fleet as they headed back into space.

Chapter Twenty

Garn steered her jeep over the smooth road that cut through a wooded area. Beside her, Yale looked out at the trees whirling by. The lieutenant ran her right thumb over the leather cover of a booklet containing her forged travel papers. The documents stated that Yale and Zigler were the personal property of a Crownaxian named Slin, a respected real estate developer who was really a covert Faction 12 operative. If Yale could get Zigler out and safely make it to the spaceport, Slin would help the humans escape. But that was a mighty big if, considering that the spaceport was 12 miles from the prison. Even if Yale could bust Zigler out, the odds of them getting to Slin without being recaptured were very slim.

The sky grew dark as the jeep came to a stop in front of a huge, metal fence that blocked the road ahead of them. A sign with large Crownaxian letters hung on the fence. Yale guessed that it said something like keep out. The lieutenant zipped up her coat and brushed the back of her hand against the laser pistol that sat in a holster around her waist. She took a deep breath, then smiled at Garn as the driver turned off the jeep's engine. "Thank you for everything you've done," she said.

Garn smiled. "It's my pleasure. Do you have everything you need?" Yale nodded. "Good." She reached toward the human and put her hand on Yale's shoulder. "Be careful. If a patrol finds you, they'll shoot you without hesitation. Move quickly and quietly and only use the pistol if you have to. You don't want to draw any unnecessary attention." She leaned back in her seat. "Good luck, my friend."

Yale stepped out the vehicle. "Take care, Garn," she said. The Crownaxian smiled again and restarted the engine. Yale backed away and watched the jeep speed off into the night. Then she tentatively reached out to touch the fence. It wasn't electrified. With a sigh of relief, the lieutenant climbed up the 30-foot high fence and eased her way down the other side.

Twigs snapped under her feet as the officer marched toward the prison. Small, black insects fluttered around her face, attracted by her sweat. Yale waved her hand in front of her face to shoo them away. She kept an eye out for patrols and those nasty beasts that attacked her on her way to Garn's home. Her legs still hurt from their bites. She tried to put that out of her mind. However, it was far more difficult for her to not think about Prestok, floating face down in the water. Shaking her head, Yale forced herself to concentrate on what she was doing.

After an hour on her tired legs, Yale stopped and leaned against a tree. Remembering what happened the last time she sat down in the woods, Yale remained on her feet. Her lungs hurt as she bent over and tried to catch her breath. A few minutes passed before she decided to push on. Yale stretched her arms over her head for a moment, then continued on her trek.

Suddenly, laserfire crackled behind her. Yale spun around with her pistol in her hand to see where the shot came from. The lieutenant's eyes widened as two Crownaxian guards sprinted toward her. She fired back at them, forcing them to duck for cover behind a pair of trees about 60 feet away from her. The human dove to the ground and rolled toward a fat tree. She peeked around the tree to see exactly where they were and she was met with more laserfire. One of the shots hit her in her right foot. The pain surged through her and she screamed out in agony. Then she felt an odd numbness in her toes. She tried to put weight on the foot but she tumbled to the ground as her leg gave out.

The guards fired again, just missing Yale as she scrambled behind the fat tree. Her hands shook as she tried to spot them again. She saw them move closer toward her with their laser rifles raised. One of them left himself open for an instant, so Yale took aim and fired. She hit him on the right shoulder and he fell to the ground and howled in pain. The other guard turned on an electronic, hand-held device and spoke into it. Yale realized that he had just radioed in their position and probably asked for backup.

Yale spotted a medium-sized rock next to the tree. She picked it up and tossed it to her left. The guard reacted to the sound it made hitting the ground by firing in that direction. Yale shot at him but missed her target by just a few inches. He shot back and just barely missed Yale's head. The lieutenant took aim again when a sudden roar overhead caused them both to look toward the sky.

Yale's jaw dropped when she saw the *Liberty Bell* flying toward the prison. The perplexed guard froze as he looked up at the ship and his rifle slipped out of his grip. Seeing her chance, Yale fired again, and hit him in the chest. The concussion knocked the guard off of his feet. He rolled backward and slammed his head against a tree. Yale then saw the other guard crawling toward her with his weapon raised. She shot him in the head and he collapsed against the ground. With her pistol still in her hand, the officer looked around for other Crownaxian guards. She didn't see any. Yale sighed and slid her pistol back in the holster. She gingerly continued on her way to the prison and wondered what Amy's plan was. Whatever the young girl had in mind, Yale was happy to know that she wasn't the only human trying to get to the penitentiary.

Chapter Twenty One

Amy kept her eye on the radar screen as the *Liberty Bell* cruised toward their destination. The ship's weapons were ready to fire. Madison sat quietly in the copilot's seat. Neither of them had spoken since they separated from the rebel fleet to enter the planet's atmosphere. Amy nervously tapped the yoke with her right thumb. Everything they had planned for was now about to begin.

An alarm blared as three objects appeared on the radar screen. "There they are," said Amy, trying to sound calm. Madison nodded and leaned forward in his chair without speaking. Amy wiped her sweaty hands against her pants before gripping the yoke again. "Remember, don't fire until we have to," she commanded.

The three ships approached at high speed, firing lasers at the *Liberty Bell*. Amy dodged the first few shots but the ship took two blasts on the portside wing. However, the shields held and they only suffered minimal damage. Amy gunned the engines, flew underneath the ships and began to lead them North of the prison. They followed and kept firing. When they began to gain on the *Liberty Bell*, Amy initiated the Sprint Drive.

The ships quickly fell behind. Amy cut the engine after a few seconds and allowed the pursuers to catch up. Then Amy swung the ship around. "Aim for the one in the middle," she ordered. Madison fired the laser cannons and hit both wings on the middle ship, causing the craft to spiral toward the surface. Amy then turned on the Sprint Drive again and flew through the gap between the other two crafts.

The captain let the Sprint Drive run longer this time. Soon they were only a few thousand miles from the prison. Amy turned off the drive and swallowed a lump in her throat as she looked at the facility for the first time. Her eyes began to water. She bit her bottom lip to keep from crying. She knew that she had to keep it together in order for the plan to work, so she forced herself to smile. "Are you ok, Captain?" asked Madison.

She nodded. "Yeah, I'm fine." An alarm blared again and Amy

looked at the radar screen. "Two more ships approaching," she said. "Let's bring them along with us." Amy steered the *Liberty Bell* toward the late arrivers as the ships behind them got closer and closer. "Time to see who's chicken," she said. Amy increased the speed and headed right for two ships. Madison fired the laser cannons again but missed as the Crownaxian ships darted out of the way. Amy smiled and steered toward the planet's atmosphere.

With four ships on their tail, Amy headed for the rendezvous point. The Crownaxian guards repeatedly fired their laser cannons but the captain was able to dodge the salvo. Three more ships from the prison joined the chase. Amy swung the *Liberty Bell* around a medium-sized moon and led her pursuers into the trap. The rebel ships began their assault and easily destroyed half of the Crownaxian platoon.

The *Liberty Bell* joined in the battle as five more Crownaxian ships arrived from the surface. Madison targeted the newcomers and fired missiles at two of the crafts. They exploded in gigantic fireballs of fuel, metal and trinitrotoluene. The clash raged on for ten minutes before the rebels got the upper hand on the prison ships. Then an audio signal came over the loudspeaker on the bridge of the *Liberty Bell*. "Rescue party, depart," said the gruff voice. Amy followed the rebel leader's orders and fell in behind the three lead ships that headed back toward the surface.

When they reached the prison, Amy saw the military vehicles parked outside of the facility. The soldiers in the armored transports immediately fired at the incoming rebel ships. Two of the spaceships shot missiles at the enemy forces, while Amy steered the *Liberty Bell* behind the first rebel craft as it came in for a landing. The bombardment sent the Crownaxian soldiers scrambling for cover. Amy took that chance to line up a shot for Madison, who responded by wiping out three armored jeeps.

Amy then landed the *Liberty Bell* behind the first rebel craft. Drelk's soldiers moved inside the prison and fired laser rifles at the insurgents. The second rebel craft landed next to the *Liberty Bell*, while the final ship stayed in the air to provide continual coverage. Amy adjusted her helmet before grabbing a laser rifle from a supply locker and handing it to Madison. Then she picked up another for herself. "We have about thirty five minutes before more of Drelk's units arrive," said the captain. She took a deep breath and nodded at her friend. "Let's go."

The duo hustled down the ramp to the surface of the planet. They fell in behind a group of rebels dashing toward the prison entrance. The guards fiercely defend the facility with laserfire and shock grenades. The rebel advance slowed as they were forced to drop to the ground and take cover. Amy and Madison ducked down behind a pillar with five other rebels.

The ground battle went on for nearly fifteen minutes before the rebels forced Drelk's soldiers to fall back deeper into the prison. Amy and Madison began to follow the platoon inside when the robot suddenly stopped dead in his tracks. Amy nearly ran into him as she frantically tried to stop. "What are you doing?" she screamed. The robot silently pointed to an area 50 miles away. Amy turned in that direction and saw Lt. Yale Brown limping toward them.

The young girl blinked her eyes a few times to make sure it was really her friend in the distance. Once she knew her eyes weren't fooling her, Amy darted toward Yale. She reached the lieutenant in just a few seconds and threw her arms around the officer. "Oh, Yale! You're alive!" she screamed, hugging her tightly. "I can't believe you're here." Then she pulled back and looked at the woman. "What are you doing here?" she asked, bouncing on the balls of her feet.

Yale put her hands on Amy's shoulders to calm her down. "The same thing you are," she said. "You won't believe this but a Crownaxian guard actually helped me escape. But I came back to get another prisoner out." She paused to catch her breath. Then she nodded toward the rebel soldiers. "Who are they?" she asked.

"They're members of a group called Faction 12," said Amy. She noticed a look of recognition on Yale's face. "Have you heard of them?" Yale nodded but let Amy continue. "Well, Madison and I met them after we got away from a Crownaxian battle cruiser. They're helping us get my dad out. Who are you trying to rescue?"

Yale put her right arm around Amy's shoulder. "Help me toward the prison," she said. Amy nodded and let Yale put most of her weight on the young girl's shoulders. "I picked up a survivor named David Zigler from the *Harmony*," she explained. "He worked with your father. He told me what happened when they were attacked. I planned on taking him back with me to Paldor after I found you but we were captured after you disabled my ship."

Amy suddenly stopped as the guilt rushed through her again. "I am so sorry I did that, Yale. I really am." Yale started to say something but Amy talked over her. "You know I wouldn't have shot at you if I had known that you were going to get captured. I . . .I just didn't think."

The lieutenant nodded her head. "I understand Amy. And if I were in your shoes, I probably would have done the same thing." She patted her friend on the back. "It's time to complete our mission. C'mon, let's get your dad and Zigler out of there."

The duo lumbered toward the front of door of the prison where Madison was waiting for them. "It's good to see you, lieutenant," he said. She nodded and returned the sentiment. "Here, let me help you." The robot gently took her arm and eased her down to the ground. "Captain, you should find a medic," he said to Amy.

"No, I'm fine," said Yale. "We need to get in there and help the rebels." She grabbed Amy's flight jacket as the girl guided her to her feet, but then Madison moved in front of the officer as she tried to pass him. "What are you doing, Madison?" she asked. "Get out of the way!"

"I'm afraid I can't do that Yale," he said. "You're injured and you need to stay here until we can get you medical attention." The robot looked at Amy. "Captain, we need to go. She'll be fine here until we return."

Yale let go of Amy's jacket and glared at the robot. "Madison, I order you to step aside." The robot didn't budge. Yale's faced reddened. "Look, robot, I made it this far and I'm not going to stop now. So move aside or I'll have you dismantled." She started to go around him but he stepped in front of her again and put his hands on her shoulders.

"We don't have time for this, Madison," said Amy. She stepped between them and pushed the robot's hands down. "We need her help to complete this mission. So let her go."

The robot took a step back and turned to let the officer pass him. Amy followed Yale, while Madison fell in behind his captain. As they moved toward the prison, the robot leaned toward Amy and whispered. "This is a bad idea. She isn't strong enough to help."

Amy ignored the comment and stayed close to Yale, who limped her way to the prison entrance. The trio dropped to the ground when they heard an explosion ahead of them. Dust and debris showered over them and made it difficult for the humans to breathe. After a moment, Yale popped back up and waved her hand at her mini-platoon. Laser blasts whizzed off of the walls of the penitentiary and screams, both human and Crownaxian, echoed through the building as they finally entered.

The dim hallway was littered with the bodies of fallen soldiers. Most of them remained motionless as Amy frantically looked in the cells for her father. The trio had to duck behind a support post as the guards fired at them. Yale returned fire and told Amy to stay down. The young girl peeked around the post and saw three rebels positioned just a few feet ahead of them. The rebels were in a shootout with four guards. Two of the guards suddenly fell to the floor and Amy turned to see Yale firing her laser pistol. The two remaining guards retreated. "Nice shooting," said Amy.

"Thanks," said Yale. "C'mon, let's go." The trio followed the three rebels as they advanced through the prison. One of the rebels stopped and shot the lock off of a cell door. Then he kicked the door open and led the sole prisoner out of the small room. Amy stopped to see who the prisoner was and she sighed when she realized that it wasn't her father.

The advance continued as the guards retreated at a faster pace. Amy and her friends soon caught up to other rebels who were freeing prisoners from their cells. Again, Clayton Sutter was not among those inmates. Amy did her best to hide her disappointment. "We need to go this way," said Yale, as she started down a different hallway.

Amy, Madison and two rebels followed the officer as she hobbled along with her pistol clenched in her right hand. They only managed to get a few feet down the hallway when they were met with more laserfire. The group dropped to the floor and took aim at six guards who were entrenched behind some supply cabinets. Yale fired first and hit one of the guards. The rebels fired next and took cut two more guards. The three remaining guards fired back as they began to retreat.

Yale charged forward and aimed at one of the guards. Suddenly, her right leg gave out and she crashed to the floor. Her pistol slid away from her. She frantically reached out for it but it was too far in front of her. One guard smiled and lowered his pistol at the officer. Without thinking, Amy stood up and fired her pistol at the guard. The laser caught him in the chest and he dropped to the floor. Yale recovered her weapon as the last guard took off running. Amy held her breath and looked at the person she had just killed.

Chapter Twenty Two

The young girl didn't move as she kept her gaze on the fallen guard. Madison raced over to Amy and shook her right shoulder. "Are you ok?" asked the robot. Amy didn't answer. She just stared blankly into his eyes. The robot glanced at the dead guard, and then he looked back at his captain. "You had no choice," he said. "He was going to kill Yale. You did the right thing, Captain." Amy remained still. The rebels moved past her and followed Yale along the corridor. "C'mon, we need to keep up," said Madison.

Amy nodded and moved alongside the robot as he hurried to catch up with the others. She took one last glance at the soldier she shot and she felt a stream of bile build up in her throat. Amy held it down by focusing on the search for her father. She and Madison caught up with the rebels as they were freeing more inmates. Yale was resolutely limping toward one particular cell, so Amy decided to follow her, while Madison helped the rebels care for the prisoners.

Yale blasted the lock on the cell door with her laser pistol before kicking the door open. The light spilled over the dark room as the lieutenant headed for the back of the cell. Amy came up behind her and saw a man curled up in a ball on the floor. The man looked like he was sleeping. The light was so dim that Amy couldn't clearly see his face. Yale reached down and gently shook the man's left shoulder. "Mr. Zigler, are you alright?" she asked, breathing heavily.

The man lifted his head and looked at Yale's face. Amy saw the bruises on his pale cheeks. He had trouble keeping his head still and it bobbed from side to side. After a moment, he spoke in a quiet voice. "Who's there?" he asked. "Who are you?"

"Mr. Zigler, it's Yale Brown. I'm here to rescue you." She slipped her hands underneath his armpits and carefully pulled him to his feet. "Get up, sir. We need to get out of here before the Crows return."

"Where are we going?" he asked, wrapping his arms around Yale. The officer guided him toward the cell door and told him that they were going home. Amy stepped toward them and helped Yale carry the injured man out of the cell. When they reached the hallway, Amy saw Madison approaching.

"I'll get him," said the robot. Madison then lifted the man and carried him on his shoulders as he marched toward the exit with the rebels in front of him. Yale slumped against the cell's bars and nearly fell to the floor. Amy held onto her friend's left arm and tried to steady the exhausted woman.

One of the rebel soldiers approached the humans. "Do you need help?" he asked, looking at Yale. The lieutenant shook her head. Then the soldier addressed Amy. "Travar's ship has just landed. He wants me to bring you back to the *Liberty Bell*. Follow me." He turned to exit, then stopped when he realized that the girl wasn't moving. "What's wrong?" he asked.

Amy glanced at Yale, then back to the soldier. "We haven't found my father yet. I'm not leaving without him." The soldier nodded and started marching in the opposite direction. Amy wrapped her right arm around Yale's back and led her friend deeper into the prison. The lieutenant felt heavier than she had before and Amy struggled to keep her balance with the added weight on her back. She was sweating heavily after only a few strides and her legs began to wobble.

Suddenly, the soldier in front of them disappeared in a flash of light that preceded an explosion. The humans were blown backwards and they crashed to the floor as they were bombarded with more dust and debris. Then Amy shook her head as Yale slowly rose and limped forward. Amy forced herself up and followed her friend. They halted a few feet away and Yale bent down and grabbed a small, square object.

"What is that?" asked Amy, helping her friend stand back up. There were shouts and moans from others who were injured in the explosion and from those trying to help the victims.

Yale examined the object for a moment. The charred item had three burned wires attached to it. "It looks like a piece of a mine. The soldier must have tripped it." Then she whipped the object at a near wall and groaned as it shattered into more pieces. "What is wrong with these people?"

Amy kept quiet and stayed close to Yale as the woman tried to hobble forward on her own. The lieutenant stumbled again but Amy caught her before she fell. "I guess Madison was right," said Yale. "I'm just slowing you down." She stood still and took a deep breath. "Go on ahead without me, Amy. I can't keep up."

"No," said the girl. "I can't just leave you here."

Yale raised her hand to quiet her friend. "Yes you can. And you need to. Besides Madison should be back any minute now. He can take me back to the ship." Yale eased her way to the floor and leaned against a wall. "Go on. We don't have much time."

Amy nodded and turned away from Yale. Then she drew her laser pistol and kept it by her side as she moved further into the prison. She met up with more rebel soldiers who were tending to injured and sick inmates. Amy glanced at each inmate's face in hopes of finding her dad. But each time she didn't see him, she felt more afraid that he was already gone.

Amy pushed forward, carefully watching her step. She stayed close to the rebel soldiers as they continued liberating the prisoners. They met occasional laser-fire from die-hard guards but most of the fighting had ceased for the time being. Amy's chest pounded each time the soldiers opened another cell door. She knew that they were almost out of time and that the rebels would soon begin their retreat. The girl tried to remain hopeful.

Amy was helping the rebels clear out a cell when she saw Travar approaching with two soldiers beside him. The leader shouted orders in his native language as his men moved in a flurry around him. Travar's hardened expression dissolved as he neared the girl. "It's time to retreat," he said. "My men tell me that this is the last cell used to house humans."

"No!" cried Amy, backing away from Travar. "He has to be here. He is here, I know he is. We just have to keep looking." Suddenly she found herself pinned against the bars of the cell. She jerked away from the door and stood toe to toe with the rebel leader. "I'm not leaving without him."

Travar sympathetically nodded. "I would say the same thing, if I were in your shoes. But I hope someone would be able to get through to me. There is no reason to continue looking. If your father were still alive, he'd be here in this cellblock. We've searched everywhere and haven't found him." He sighed. "It's time to leave."

The girl sunk to the floor and wrapped her arms around her knees. The air rushed out of her lungs and her entire body felt limp. She didn't try to stop the tears, not that she could anymore. Her wailing echoed off of the walls of the small cell as her arms and shoulders shook. Her father was gone and there was nothing she could do about it.

The metallic hand on her left shoulder snapped her out of her crying fit. She looked up and saw Madison standing alone in front of her. It was oddly quiet, although she could hear some faint commotion in the distance. Madison gently gripped her hands and pulled her to her feet. "Travar told me about your father, Amy," he said. "I'm so sorry for your loss. But we need to get out of here right now. Drelk's reinforcements are just minutes away from here. It's time to head back to the *Liberty Bell*."

Amy rubbed her red eyes. "How can I go back without him? This whole mission was to save him." She balled her hands into tight fists. "Not just some guy, but my dad, Clayton Sutter." She shook her head. "How can he be gone?"

"I don't know what to say," replied Madison. "But we always knew that there was a chance we might not find him. Even if we didn't want to think about it." The robot leaned forward and spoke in a quieter voice. "I really liked your dad, Amy. He was a good man. It may be of little consolation now but he died trying to help end the war. There isn't much more noble that than." He straightened up and spoke louder. "Yale is already aboard the *Liberty Bell*. We have to go, right now. Follow me."

Amy took his hand and absentmindedly followed her friend through the prison hallways. The noise around them increased as they got closer to the exit. The route back was more difficult as the duo navigated through the wreckage from the firefights and explosions. As they were passing an adjacent hallway, something caught Amy's attention. She let go of Madison's hand and curiously stumbled toward an object that was protruding from a row of fallen cabinets. As she came nearer to it, Amy noticed that it was a human foot.

The girl stood absolutely still as the foot rolled to its side. Madison came up behind Amy and asked her what she was doing. "Look at that," she said, pointing to the foot. "That's human and it just moved."

Madison took a closer look, then lifted one of the cabinets off of the floor. Suddenly, a low moan emanated from under the rubble. The robot quickly raised the other cabinets and tossed them aside. There on the floor lay a bloodied man with bruises on his hands, face and legs. A scraggly beard outlined his face and neck. Though he looked much older, there was no doubt that this was Clayton Sutter.

"Daddy!" yelled Amy, as she dropped beside him. "Daddy, are you ok?" She gently lifted his left hand and held in her own. The man moaned again and tried to open his swollen eyes. "Don't move Daddy. We'll get you out of here."

"Stand back, Amy," said the robot. Then he lifted the limp body and eased it over his left shoulder, the same way he picked up Zigler. "I've got him. C'mon, let's go." The robot quickly and carefully darted along the hallway with Amy right behind him. They finally reached the prison exit, where they found Travar ordering his troops to take off.

Amy stopped and stood in front of the rebel leader. "We found him! We found him!" she shouted. Travar looked at Madison and seemed to understand what the girl was saying.

Travar smiled at the girl. "I'm really happy for you," he said. "Now get to your ship right now!" He pointed to the sky and Amy looked up and saw space cruisers racing toward them. "They're Drelk's troops. We're out of time!" shouted the rebel leader.

Madison sprinted toward the *Liberty Bell* and Amy raced behind him. They entered the ship and turned toward the back of the craft. The surviving members of the *Harmony*'s crew were aboard, along with Yale, who was supervising the effort to get everyone settled. Some lay on cots, while others milled near the ship's side windows. Zigler sat on the floor with his arms wrapped around his legs. Madison laid Clayton on a cot as Yale hobbled over to them. "Oh, thank God you found him," she said. "How is he?"

"He's pretty banged up, lieutenant," said Madison. "Please look after him. Amy and I need to get the ship off the ground." Yale nodded and opened a nearby medical kit. Amy froze in her place as she watched her friend examine her father. "Captain, we need you on the bridge," said Madison, as he took the girl by the hand.

Amy let go of his hand and led the way to the front of the ship. She hopped into the pilot's seat and began the launch procedures. Madison took his seat beside her and typed in commands on a keyboard. A paper slid out of a slot on the console in front of him. He read the paper and nodded. "All systems running normally, captain," he said.

"Good, let's go." With the engines engaged, Amy guided the ship off of the ground. Suddenly, a missile slammed into the back of the craft. The *Liberty Bell* shook and Amy nearly lost her grip on the yoke. "Return fire," said Amy. "Aim for their weapons."

The *Liberty Bell* swung around to face the attackers. Madison fired the laser cannons and struck the ship closest to them. That craft took a direct hit on its missile launcher and it exploded in a massive fireball. The wreckage rained down on the prison below, scattering soldiers from both sides of the battle. Amy guided the ship behind the rebel crafts and tried to make a run for it. However, Drelk's troops cut off the armada and forced the group to split up.

With sweat pouring down her forehead, Amy zeroed in on one of the ships and fired a missile at it. Madison provided laserfire as the projectile stuck its target. That ship exploded, forcing the two beside it to veer off. The *Liberty Bell* was only a few miles above the ground and Amy glanced down to see what was happening below them. She saw Travar running for his ship and dodging the enemy laserfire. The rebel leader was just feet away from his craft when one laser shot hit him in the back.

Amy watched in horror as he dropped to the ground. Two soldiers from his ship raced toward him but he waved them off with his right hand. They returned to the their craft. Travar valiantly stood up, but was hit again in the back. He then flopped to the ground with his arms spread out. Amy knew right away that he was dead.

Chapter Twenty Three

The *Liberty Bell* and the rebel ships battled Drelk's troops for another forty minutes before they were able to blast their way through the enemy's defensive formation. After the rebel armada cleared the planet's atmosphere, Amy's ship received an audio message from the lead craft. "*Liberty Bell*, this is Enik." The firm voice crackled through the loudspeaker, distorted by radiation from a nearby moon. "I have assumed control of the fleet. Fall in behind us and we will guide you as far as we can go."

Amy spoke into her microphone. "Will do, Enik." She paused and took a deep breath. "I'm sorry about Travar. He was a brave leader. I owe my father's life to him and the rest of you. Thank you for all you've done." She glanced over at Madison, who nodded in agreement. Then she steered the ship behind the others.

"He died with honor," replied Enik. "That is all any Crownaxian can ask for. And his death will not be in vain." There was short moment of silence before he continued. "Hopefully what we've done today will be a first step toward peace for both of our peoples."

"I hope so," replied Amy. Then she turned toward Madison. "Take over for a while, I want to check on my dad." The robot nodded again and typed a command into the computer. The navigational controls then shifted to his console. "Call me if anything happens." She patted him on the shoulder before moving toward the back of the ship.

Most of the passengers were sitting in the dining area and devouring plates of steak, chicken, and other dishes. Yale was sitting in a chair next to Clayton's cot and carefully feeding him soup. The diplomat struggled to get the food down as his body shook. Amy kneeled down next to the cot across from Yale. "How is he?" she asked.

Yale looked over at her friend. "He's weak but his condition has stabilized. I think he'll be fine once we get him home." She tried to give him more but he turned his head away, so Yale put the bowl of soup down on a nearby counter. "Most of the diplomats are suffering from exhaustion. It doesn't look like they had much to eat in prison." She shrugged. "And some of them are pretty beat up."

"Are they all here?" asked Amy, surveying the room.

"No," replied Yale. "Kalowski and Evans were killed in the attack on the *Harmony*. I don't know what happened to their bodies." Yale shook her head slightly. "I'm sending a report to Gen. Knox. He should get in within a few hours." The lieutenant glanced at Clayton before she stood up. "You probably want to spend some time with your dad," she said. "I'll go see how everyone is doing before I start my report." She quietly stumbled away as Amy rested a hand on her dad's right wrist.

Clayton's eyes blinking slowly as he stared at his daughter. "Amy?" he asked, softly. "Is that you?" He pressed his lips together as if trying to form more words but nothing came out of his mouth.

"It's me, Daddy," said Amy, gently holding his wrist. "Don't try to talk too much. Just rest. We'll be home in a few days. Do you want anything?" He shook his head. Then he tried to lie down on the cot. Amy put her hands on his shoulders and guided him down. After he closed his eyes, Amy gingerly kissed him on the forehead.

Amy rose as Yale limped back toward her. "Everyone is as comfortable as they can be," said Yale. Then she lowered her voice. "I need to ask you something. Do we have enough fuel to get back to Paldor?" She leaned against a near wall and shifted the weight off of her bad leg.

"I think we do," said Amy, "but I'll check with Madison to be sure." Then she nodded toward the dining area. "The atomizer should give us enough food for the trip. Have you eaten anything yet?"

"I'm not hungry," said Yale. "Get something for yourself, if you like, but report to me when you're done. We need to discuss our strategy for getting home safely." She started to turn away, but she stopped when she noticed the frown on Amy's face. "Is something wrong?"

"Yes," snapped Amy. "When did you take over?" She folded her arms across her chest and glared at her friend. The room quieted as the diplomats glanced over at the pair.

Yale leaned in close and spoke quietly again. "Amy, I'm the

only Union officer on board the ship. Under the circumstances, it's my responsibility to take over." Amy didn't respond. Instead she kept her eyes on the lieutenant's face. "Look, you did an amazing job finding and rescuing these people but you are not really a captain. This isn't even your ship."

Amy nodded. "No, it isn't. And yes, I stole it. But I wouldn't have had to if the great Union military had just done their job and mounted their own rescue." She didn't care now that she was making a scene. "If it wasn't for me, they would still be in that Crownaxian prison. So don't think I'm suddenly going to start taking orders from you, lieutenant."

"You don't have a choice," said Yale. Her voice was low but firm and her eyes never blinked. "Don't make me confine you to your quarters."

"Would that be the captain's quarters?" asked Amy, "Because that is where I'll be sleeping tonight." She turned and marched out of the dining area without waiting for a response.

Amy stomped onto the bridge and sighed as sat in the pilot's seat. Madison looked up from the maps that were displayed on the console in front of him and asked her what was wrong. "Oh, not much, just a minor mutiny," she said. The robot kept quiet. "It's Yale. She thinks she's in charge now, just because she's a Union officer. If it weren't for us, she and the rest of them would be dead by now."

Madison eased back in his chair. "I hate to disagree with you, but she is right, Amy." The girl glared at the robot. "Yes, you've been in charge since the beginning, but we were under unusual circumstances. Now that we've completed our mission, I think it's time to return to normal and let her take charge." The robot let that sink in before he continued. "The rebels have moved off and headed for their base. Enik sent his regards and again congratulated us on our mission." Then he motioned toward the star maps. "I've plotted a few routes that we can take to get back to Paldor. You should take a look at them."

"Why should I?" she asked, rising to her feet. "Apparently I'm not in charge anymore." She turned and headed for the exit. "Let Yale decide," she said, as she stormed off of the bridge. Despite her dramatic exit, she soon realized that she didn't have any place to go.

Yale was still in the dining area, along with all of the others who witnessed their argument. Amy stood still for a moment before deciding to go to the captain's quarters.

The girl entered the small room and sat down on the bed. She could hear the diplomats nearby as they consoled each other and traded stories of their ordeal. For the first time since the trip began, Amy felt completely alone. Yale's betrayal was bad enough, but Madison's dissent nearly broke her heart. *He's my best friend,* she thought. *How can he abandon me like this, after all we've been through?* She lay back on the bed and closed her eyes. *Well, at least my dad is ok.*

Soon she was asleep. She dreamt that she was sitting behind an oak table in a large courtroom. A judge in a black robe sat behind an elevated desk with a gavel in his left hand. A man whose face she didn't recognize sat next to the girl. When she asked him what was going on, he curtly told her to be quiet. Amy looked back at the judge and noticed that Yale was seated in a witness stand and recounting the events of the rescue mission. Yale was describing how Amy had fired on her ship and caused her to be captured. Then she told the judge that Amy refused to relinquish control of the *Liberty Bell* after the diplomats were rescued. All the while, the judge nodded his head and ran a thumb along the handle of the gavel.

The judge dismissed Yale after she finished her testimony. Then he turned toward Amy with a stern expression. "Young lady, you've displayed reckless behavior time and again during this mission. It's amazing that you were able to come home in one piece. I have no choice but to find you guilty of the charge of treason." A wave of gasps and mumbling swept through the spectators seated behind Amy. "It is the ruling of this court that you spend not less than 50 years at Darkplace Correctional Facility on Mars. Court dismissed." The judge banged his gavel, then stood up and exited.

Amy turned to her lawyer, whose face she finally recognized. "I told you that you were taking too many chances," said Papa. "This time I can't help you." The man packed up his briefcase and stood up. He looked at her once more, with a sad expression on his face, then turned and left the courtroom. Amy stood up and tried to follow him, but a Union soldier grabbed her by the arm and dragged her in the opposite direction.

The girl suddenly sat up and rubbed her dry eyes. It took a moment for her to realize that she was still in the captain's quarters aboard the *Liberty Bell*. Then she sighed and decided to try and make peace with her friends. Even if she didn't agree with them. She rose and stretched her arms over her head. She had just reached the door when an alarm suddenly blared.

Amy instinctively raced to the bridge. There she found Yale in the pilot's seat and Madison at his usual post. "What's going on?" she asked. Yale glanced at her with an angry expression before she typed a command on the keyboard in front of her. Amy leaned forward and peeked at the robot's console as he powered up the ship's weapons. The girl saw two large objects approaching at high speed.

"They haven't detected us yet," reported the robot. He finished typing and looked at Yale. "What do you want us to do?" he asked.

Amy watched the officer scan the radar screen. "We need to find a place to hide," said Yale. Several images flashed across the screen. Amy noticed a nebula nearby and suggested that they go there. "No, there's a moon a few hundred miles away. We'll head there and hide on its dark side until the Crownaxian cruisers pass by." She began typing in the coordinates for the tiny moon.

"I wouldn't do that," said Amy. "It's too far away. They'll see us before we get there. Head for the nebula, it's much closer."

Yale turned and glared at the girl. "Amy! Sit down and be quiet or get off of the bridge!" she said. The lieutenant finished typing as the young girl sat behind the robot. Yale fired the engines and guided the *Liberty Bell* to the small moon. She then initiated the Sprint Drive until they were a few miles away from their target. Then she cut the Sprint Drive and resumed their course using the standard engines.

After the *Liberty Bell* reached the moon's dark side, Yale shut off all of the ship's systems except life support. Then the craft drifted just above the planetoid's atmosphere. Everyone on the bridge remained quiet as they watched the radar screen. Amy said a silent prayer as she kept her eyes glued on the purple dots that flashed on the monitor. The cruisers maintained their previous course and speed and were soon well beyond the moon. Amy sighed with relief and Yale said that they would hold their position for a half-hour to make sure the cruisers didn't come back.

No one spoke on the bridge as they waited for the half-hour to pass. Amy sat with her arms across her chest and bit her bottom lip. Yale and Madison never turned around to look at the girl, and that made her even angrier. Finally, the time came to move on and Yale ordered the robot to follow a course that she had set. The robot nodded, and typed in the coordinates, while the lieutenant rose and departed the bridge.

Amy rose and slid into the familiar pilot's seat as the *Liberty Bell* broke orbit and headed along the new course. "Ok, so her plan worked," said Amy. "But it was riskier than mine. We could have reached that nebula in half the time." She looked at Madison and waited for a response.

Madison typed a command on the keyboard and then pointed to the radar screen. "Look for yourself," he said. Amy leaned over and studied the monitor. The nebula was gone! "The gasses were dissipating at a high rate," said the robot. "Had we flown into it, the cruisers would have found us for sure. Yale knew the nebula wouldn't hold, that's why she aimed for the moon." The robot sat back in his chair. "I think you owe Yale an apology. And it's time to let her take over."

"Fine," said Amy, rising out of the pilot's seat. "If there are any problems, let her know." Amy slinked off of the bridge and headed for the dining area. There she found Yale sitting with Zigler at a table with other diplomats. Zigler had a cup of coffee in front of him, while Yale sat with her hands folded. Amy leaned over and whispered to the lieutenant. "I'm sorry," she said. "You were right. About everything. The ship is yours." Amy then turned and started to leave the dining area.

"Wait," said Yale, rising to her feet. Amy stopped and waited for what would come. "I do need a first officer to assist me for the rest of the trip." She extended her hand. "How about it?" she asked.

Amy smiled and shook her friend's hand. "Sounds good, Captain," she said. "What would you like me to do first?"

"Get something to eat. Then spend some time with your dad. I'll call you when I need you," said Yale. Amy nodded and moved toward the atomizer. She suddenly had a craving for a cheeseburger.

Chapter Twenty Four

The *Liberty Bell* darted through space as the crew tried to avoid any more complications on their way home. Amy and Yale took turns flying the craft and they used the Sprint Drive more freely as Yale grew confident with the propulsion system. That cut the travel time in half. Amy spent most of her down time sitting with her father, who grew stronger each day.

The ship was four hours away from Paldor when Yale decided to debrief Clayton about his internment. Knowing Amy would want to sit in on the session, Yale ordered Madison to man the controls during the interview. Clayton was sitting with Zigler and other diplomats in the dining area when Yale and Amy approached him. "Mr. Sutter, would you please join us in the captain's quarters?" asked Yale. "We need to go over a few things."

Clayton nodded and rose from his seat. He then followed the ladies to the quarters and sat down on the bed. Amy sat next to him, while Yale sat in the only chair in the room. Yale pulled the chair close to the bed. "As you probably know, I've already debriefed everyone else and I've sent my findings to Gen. Knox. I wanted to give you more time since you suffered the most severe injuries. How are you feeling now?" she asked. Yale then turned on a hand-held device to record the conversation and she leaned it toward the man.

"Better, I guess," he said. "But my ribs still hurt. I think a few of them are broken. And I still have a ringing in my ears." Amy put her hand on her dad's hand and gently squeezed it. "I think I'll live."

"I'm sure you will," said Yale. "I know this is difficult, but start from the attack on the *Harmony*, and tell me what happened to you."

Clayton glanced at Amy before looking back at Yale. "Lieutenant, some of this is pretty brutal. I don't think Amy should be here for this."

Amy gently squeezed his hand again. "Don't worry about me," she said. "I have a fairly good idea what you are going to say. Just tell us what happened." She let go of his hand and nodded.

Clayton sighed and spoke slowly. He recalled the initial attack, and then detailed his transport to the prison. His voice lowered as he discussed the interrogations by the Crownaxians at the prison. Twice a day, every day he was there. The guards dragged him to a room and questioned him for hours. They wanted to know the locations of various Union military sites and the security codes for the facilities. He tried to convince them that he didn't have that information but they didn't believe him. He confessed to Yale that the routine nearly broke his spirit.

The debriefing was entering its second hour when Clayton began discussing his last day at the prison. That day had started like the others but his first interrogation was longer than usual. "That's why I wasn't in my cell when the rebels arrived," he said. "They were still questioning me when the fighting broke out. One of the Crows left to find out what was going on, while the other sat across from me with his pistol aimed at my chest." Clayton took a deep breath and then continued. "Then there was gunfire outside the door and he went to investigate. After he left, I managed to cut my hand restraints with a laserdriver that I found in a toolbox. I slipped out the door and saw him on the ground. He was dead."

"Then what happened?" asked Yale.

Clayton shrugged. "I don't really know. The last thing I remember is a bright flash of light and a loud sound. I guess it was an explosion."

Yale nodded. "There were land mines all over the prison," she said. "The guards must have activated them after the rebels arrived. Is there anything else you can add?" she asked.

"No," said Clayton. "Next thing I knew, I was aboard this ship." He glanced at Amy. "I guess we have this little thief here to thank for that." Amy rolled her eyes and smiled. "And you too, lieutenant."

Yale turned off the hand-held recorder. "Thank you for your time, Mr. Sutter," she said. "You should probably get some rest now. You can stay here if you want; it's the quietist place on the ship." She stood and slid her chair back against the wall. "I'll be on the bridge," she said, heading out of the captain's quarters.

Amy leaned over and gave her dad a hug. Then she too stood up. "Yale's right, you should stay here and rest. I'm going to see how things are going up front." She started to leave but then she suddenly stopped. "I know that Yale is the captain now, but it is hard not being in charge."

"The best leaders know when to let someone else take over," said Clayton. Amy nodded. "I don't know if I've told you this yet, but I am proud of how you managed to pull off this rescue. That showed a lot of courage." Amy's face reddened. Clayton smiled. "But don't get any more crazy ideas like this again. Your life is too valuable to risk it."

"And so is yours," she said. "I'll check in on you later." Amy turned and walked slowly toward the bridge. As she moved, she ran her fingers along the cold panels of the ship's interior. She knew that they would be home soon and that she would probably never be on board the *Liberty Bell* again. So she decided to take one long, last look at the ship that she had stolen and brought back in one piece, with survivors on board that the Union seemed to have given up on.

Two Union fighter crafts approached the *Liberty Bell* as Yale sat in the pilot's chair and guided the ship toward Paldor. Madison was at his post in the copilot's seat, while Amy sat in the chair behind him. The young girl smiled as she gazed at the place that had become her second home. For the first time in her life, she was actually glad to see the small, hot planet. But in the back of her mind, she still longed to return to Earth.

After Yale identified herself and her ship to the fighter crafts, they led the way toward the surface of the planet. The ships then landed at the Pioneer Settlement's military base, where a platoon of Union soldiers, some on foot, some sitting in land vehicles, assembled to meet the vessels. The *Liberty Bell* came to a stop 100 yards in front of the hangar where the experimental spaceship had been stored. Amy looked out the front window and noticed that the supply shed had been rebuilt.

The Union soldiers quickly surrounded the *Liberty Bell* and stood with their weapons drawn. "I think I should go out first," said Yale. She turned and looked at Amy. "Amy, you and Madison see to it that the diplomats are ready to depart, but don't exit the ship until I tell you to." Amy nodded and followed Yale and Madison as they left the bridge. Yale moved toward the ship's main hatch, while Amy and the robot headed for the back of the *Liberty Bell*.

The diplomats were milling around in the dining area when Amy and Madison approached them. The weary passengers looked frightened. Zigler was standing next to Clayton, and he stepped in front of Amy with a genuine sense of urgency. "What's going on out there?" asked Zigler. "Why are they pointing their weapons at us?"

"Please calm down," said Amy. She looked past him and glanced at her father. He too looked scared. "Everyone, please listen. There's no need to be afraid," said Amy. "Yale is outside right now and I'm sure she will straighten this whole thing out." The diplomats muttered amongst themselves. Amy turned to Madison, who nodded at her. Then she looked back the others. "We'll be getting off the ship in no time."

The girl peered out the nearest window and saw Yale moving toward another lieutenant, a confident man named Luke Jefferson. The officers saluted each other before they exchanged a few words. Amy wished that she could hear that conversation. Lt. Jefferson nodded as Yale continued to talk to him. Then Yale turned toward the *Liberty Bell* and waved her right hand.

"Ok, everyone. It's time to go," said Amy. She turned and pointed to the copilot. "Please follow Madison to the main hatch, and he will lead you out. I'll be right behind you." The passengers muttered again as they formed a line behind the robot. Madison took the lead and marched the diplomats to the exit. Amy waited until everyone passed her before she followed the procession. As she moved along, she saw her dad stop and wait for her.

Clayton stepped into the line behind the last of his colleagues and he put his right arm around his daughter's shoulder. "You are going to be in a lot of trouble," he said softly. They walked side by side for a moment before he continued. "I'm not sure how the Union will handle this. Nothing like this has ever happened before." He stopped and looked into her eyes. "No matter what happens, just remember that I love you, and that I'll stand by you."

She leaned forward and hugged him. "Thanks Dad," she said. "I love you too." She pulled back and smiled. "All that matters is that you're home, safe and sound." She gently took his right hand. "C'mon, let's go." They continued on as the row of people in front of them slowed down. Amy peeked ahead and saw Madison stop at the exit and look back at her. She nodded with a smile. Then the robot departed the ship.

It didn't take long to get everyone off of the *Liberty Bell*. Lt. Jackson greeted the diplomats while anxious family members gathered behind the troops. Amy sighed and let go of her father's hand when she finally set foot on the hot, dry ground. Suddenly, two Union soldiers grabbed Amy's arms and shoved her toward the ground. The stunned girl looked up and saw them place metal cuffs on her wrists. Then they pulled her to her feet.

"What the Hell is going on here?" asked Clayton. Amy watched him take a step toward her, but two other soldiers blocked his path. Clayton tried to push past them, but they easily subdued the man. He finally relented and glared at Yale Brown, who appeared to be just as surprised.

"I'm sorry," said Lt. Jefferson. "Gen. Knox's orders." He took a deep breath and waved his hand at the arresting officers. The men pushed Amy toward him. "Amy Sutter, you are under arrest for arson, theft of Union property, and firing on Union soldiers." Then he nodded. "Take her away."

Amy glanced at her father as the men dragged her toward Knox's office. Then she closed her eyes and wondered what would happen to her. She didn't open them again until she felt a pair of hands shove her into a seat a few minutes later. When her eyes cleared, she saw Knox standing in front of his desk with a stern look on his face.

"Remove the cuffs," said the gruff man. One of the soldiers eased her forward in her chair and followed the general's orders. Amy peered over her shoulder. She saw her parents standing with Yale and Madison just outside the office door. "Don't worry, you'll speak to them soon," said Knox. He sat down on his desk. "I have to maintain discipline on this base. I can't have people taking justice into their own hands. That's why I have to make an example of you, Amy Sutter," he said.

The general glared at the girl as he opened a desk drawer and pulled out a folder. He opened it and leaned forward to read the top document. "Despite her reckless behavior and poor judgment, Amy Sutter has shown great courage and resourcefulness during this mission," read the general. "I have no doubt that her actions saved the lives of the diplomats and it is my recommendation that the Union Council show leniency when deciding her punishment." He put the document aside and leaned back in his chair. "That was one of Lt. Brown's reports."

Amy nodded with a slight smile on her face. She took a deep breath and stood up. "General, I'm sorry that my actions put Yale in jeopardy, but I don't regret what I did. I really didn't have any choice. I couldn't just let my dad die." She sat back down and rested her hands on her lap as she maintained eye contact with Gen. Knox.

"I appreciate your honesty," he said. "And I do understand why you did this. Fortunately for you, so does the Council." He then picked up a second document and held it close to his face as he read it. "Having taken into account all of the facts and the mitigating circumstances, it is the decision of the Council that Amy Sutter be placed on probation for a term of two years." Gen. Knox dropped the document on his desk and frowned at the girl. "I received this order about an hour before you landed. It looks like the Council agrees with Lt. Brown."

Amy smiled and glanced back at her parents again. Then she turned toward the general. His expression didn't change. "Sorry, sir," she said. "I guess you won't be making an example of me after all."

"On the contrary," said the general. "I will, the first time you step out of line. Two years is a long time for someone like you to keep out of trouble." He rose and lowered his voice. "I'm sure I'll be seeing you in here again before long." He then nodded to the guards, who opened the door and stood aside. Amy sighed before she turned and left the office.

Epilogue

The party in the Sutters' apartment was in full swing. The place was crammed with diplomats, civilians and military personnel who laughed and shook hands as they celebrated the return of the *Liberty Bell*. Mrs. Cranberry offered the guests various snacks from the round tray in her hand. A "Welcome Home" banner hung over the kitchen entrance where Amy stood with Madison and Yale. "It looks like the whole settlement is here," said Yale, sipping a drink.

"It's good to be home," said Amy. She smiled when she spotted her parents talking to a group of her father's colleagues. A sergeant approached Amy and shook her hand as he congratulated her. Amy thanked him before turning back to her friends. "I'm going to hang out in my room for a bit. I'll catch you later."

"Are you alright?" asked Madison.

"Sure, I'm fine. I just want to get away from the crowd for a minute." She slowly made her way through the mass of revelers and slipped inside her room, closing the door behind her. With a sigh of relief, Amy leaned on her desk and looked out the window. She stared at the stars and wondered how Travar's troops were holding up. Amy swallowed hard as she thought about her friend's death. A part of her felt guilty for celebrating at all.

A sudden knock on the door made her snap her head around. Her smile returned as she watched her father enter the room with an apple-sized rock in his hand. "Hiding out?" he asked, closing the door behind him. She shrugged. "I don't blame you. I was never comfortable in the spotlight." He leaned toward her and kissed her cheek. Then he handed her the rock. "I believe I owe you one of these," he said. Amy held the Morleanne space rock in her hand and smiled as she thanked him. "How do the stars look tonight?" he asked.

Amy turned back toward the window and put the rock on the windowsill. "Beautiful as ever." Clayton stood next to her and also looked out at the stars. "From here, it all looks so peaceful," said Amy. "But it isn't. Is it?"

"No, I suppose not. Not as long as we keep fighting with the Crownaxians." He sighed and pressed his palms against the top of the desk. "At least we know that we're not alone now. Thanks to you, we've learned that we have allies in our struggle. Let's hope they can help us."

"They're doing all they can, Dad."

Clayton nodded. "I'm sure they are. And one day we'll all be able to celebrate the end of this war."

They stood quietly, while behind them, the sound of the party seeped into the room. Amy tried to imagine life with no war. She glanced at her dad's face and saw his hopeful expression. It helped her believe that peace was possible.

About the Author

Steven Donahue was a copywriter for TV Guide magazine for 14 years. His first novel, *Amanda Rio*, was published in 2004. It has received critical acclaim from reviewers for Amazon.com and thebestreviews.com. Steven currently resides in Bucks County, PA with his wife, Dawn. His novel *The Manila Strangler* (Rainstorm Press) will also be published in 2013.

www.ingramcontent.com/pod-product-compliance
Lightning Source LLC
Chambersburg PA
CBHW070019260626
47159CB00005B/1878